'Lady Anne. What brings you out here?'

'I was worried you were not enjoying yourself,' she replied gently. The dim light did not soften the stern lines of his face, any more than it did the carven outline of his mount; both males were too distinctive. No one would call Jack Hamilton handsome, she decided, but nor would any pass him in a crowd without seeing him.

He was arrested by both her tone and her words and felt a faint stirring of interest. Was there a different girl with him now from the lord of the manor's daughter who had been the life and soul of the party inside, distributing her favours with arrogance and assurance?

He said drily, 'Have you not enough strings to your bow this night, but must pursue a renegade out into the cold night?'

Laura Cassidy followed careers in both publishing and advertising before becoming a freelance writer, when her first son was born. She has since had numerous short stories and articles published, as well as four novels. She began writing for Legacy of Love after discovering sixteenth-century romantic poetry, and very much enjoys the research involved in writing in the historical genre. She lives with her husband, who is a creative consultant, and their two teenaged sons, near London.

THE FROZEN HEART

Laura Cassidy

All rights reserved including the right of reproduction in whole or in part in any form. This edition is published by arrangement with Harlequin Enterprises B.V. The text of this publication or any part thereof may not be reproduced or transmitted in any form or by any means, electronic or mechanical, including photocopying, recording, storage in an information retrieval system, or otherwise, without the written permission of the publisher.

This book is sold subject to the condition that it shall not, by way of trade or otherwise, be lent, resold, hired out or otherwise circulated without the prior consent of the publisher in any form of binding or cover other than that in which it is published and without a similar condition including this condition being imposed on the subsequent purchaser.

MILLS & BOON, the Rose Device and PROUD OF YOUR are trademarks of the publisher.

Harlequin Mills & Boon Limited,
Eton House 18-24 Paradise Road, Richmond, Surrey TW9 1SR

© Laura Cassidy 1995

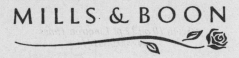

MILLS & BOON

*MILLS & BOON, the Rose Device and LEGACY OF LOVE
are trademarks of the publisher.
Harlequin Mills & Boon Limited,
Eton House, 18–24 Paradise Road, Richmond, Surrey TW9 1SR*

© Laura Cassidy 1995

ISBN 0 263 79487 3

*Set in 10 on 12 pt Linotron Times
04-9602-84144*

*Typeset in Great Britain by CentraCet, Cambridge
Cover illustration by Cecil Vieweg
Printed in Great Britain by
BPC Paperbacks Ltd*

CHAPTER ONE

ANNE LATIMAR was late rising on the day of her brother George's wedding. She was often guilty of lying late abed because she was someone who enjoyed all her waking moments, and enjoyment—when it involved dancing and playing until all hours of the night—was tiring.

But she had vowed to make an especial effort on this day to be early in the hall to help her mother with the wedding breakfast, so, with a swift glance at her new and beautiful gown, made for the ceremony and now laid on her dressing chest, she scrambled into a plain dress and, only pausing to splash a little tepid water on her face, ran down the stairs, her rich black hair flying.

Her mother, Bess, who was of course already hard at work, looked up and smiled.

'Good morning, sweetheart. Your hair is a disgrace.' She added the last remark out of duty, because secretly she thought her daughter looked prettier than any other woman could on waking. It would be a great asset all her life, Bess thought, for so few ladies were clear-eyed and smooth-skinned after sleep.

But then Anne's looks were of the kind which needed little enhancement with cosmetics, or careful hairdressing: she was blessed with an unblemished pale skin, large and lovely dark blue, black-fringed eyes, and abundant curly black hair. Her form, too, was perfect—slender and long-legged, but with an undeniably feminine shape.

Anne embraced her mother fondly, and warded off another reprimand by saying quickly, 'I know I have left my stays off, Mother, and have not dressed my hair, but I was so anxious to come quickly to help you, and there will be time enough to don the usual armour later. Now, what shall I do?'

Bess laughed. 'If there were anything left to do at this late hour I would be worried indeed. In two short hours Her Majesty will be in the chapel and 'tis probably more important not to keep her waiting than the bride.'

Anne looked disappointed. She glanced around the hall. It was high summer and the gardens had been stripped to deck the sizeable chamber with flowers which provided splashes of colour to lighten the dark-panelled room and whose scent mingled with the good savoury smells coming from the kitchens.

The long oak table was laid with silver and glass and snowy napery; the light streaming through the glittering square of leaded windows made its special focus the centrepiece of white rosebuds, their glossy leaves reflecting candlelight from the hall sconces.

The polished boards underfoot in the hall were shadowed here and there by the coloured stained glass which threw a pattern of violet and rose and amber onto the old floor, not distinct enough to show that these panes depicted a white dove with pink eyes resting on a golden sword-hilt set with amethysts, which were the Latimar arms. Anne noticed that, at a right angle to the main table, another had been positioned to accommodate the royal guest and her intimates.

The Latimar manor, Maiden Court, was relatively modest in size, considering it housed an earl and his lady and their three children, but Harry Latimar, its master, had an aversion to changing anything about his home. Although many gentlemen these days were enlarging and extending their houses—building a wing on either side to produce the fashionable E shape so flattering to the new Queen—Harry refused such innovation and was content with his mellow old house, set so beautifully between park and woodland and fertile farm acres.

Maiden Court had stood four-square to the wind since its first owner, a wild Norman nobleman, who had dug its first sod and had relished the battle to wrest its acres from the forest, had laid aside his battle dress and founded his family, and that was good enough for Harry. Besides, Latimars had upheld the English throne for countless generations and needed no outward show of allegiance.

'So, there is nothing I may help with?' Anne enquired. 'Where is Hal?'

Hal, or Henry, so named for the present Queen's royal father, was the baby of the family. Eighteen years divided the twins, Anne and George, from the latest member, but already the small tyrant was making his sturdy presence felt.

A baby so late in life, Bess felt, was delightful but presented its own problems. Anne and George were so *civilised* now—Hal was not and caused her heartburn from the time he rose in the morning until he was thankfully laid in his cot at twilight. 'Twas the energy of the young, she thought.

'Walter has taken him out to the stables,' she said, sighing. 'Thank the Lord for that, for he was driving me to distraction.' Bess crinkled her smooth brow. 'I think, really, he has not yet got over losing Judith.'

'Well, he hasn't lost her, has he? None of us has.'

Anne's tone was brisk and her mother glanced quickly at her.

Anne had not come to terms with the fact that her brother—who could have paid court to any great lady in the land, so eligible and accomplished was he—had chosen to wed his little brother's nursemaid, Judith Springfield, who had come from a poor farm in the west to care for Hal and had so enchanted his older brother. Various scenes at Maiden Court had taken place and been resolved, but Anne had never really accepted the match.

'What are you thinking, love?' Bess asked now.

'Me? Oh. . .nothing.' Anne knew her mother's liberal views—confronted with two young people in love, Bess Latimar had been quite overwhelmed—and respected them, but when *she* chose to tread down the aisle *her* mate would be her equal, in both breeding and wealth! He would, Anne had determined long ago, be as near as possible a duplicate of her father. . .

She said, 'If you are sure there is nothing I can do, I might as well go and change. Where is my father. . .and George?'

'George is in his room with his gentlemen attendants—they are a lively bunch, and I hope they have no mischief in mind before George is safely to the altar. Your father has gone over to Apple Tree Farm.'

Anne smiled. 'I'll go up and make sure George's friends are sober and suitable for the coming ceremony.' She flew up the stairs and her mother, despite knowing that she ought to be doing one hundred and one different things in the kitchens, stared wistfully after her.

The announcement of George Latimar's wedding had caused quite a stir in the neighbourhood, and not only because of his choice of bride. That had been disturbing enough in this close-knit community of country squires. But many of those squires' ladies had been unable to resist a barbed comment or two about the one Latimar twin being settled, but the other—and a girl at that, no longer particularly young—being still unwed, or even betrothed.

Their husbands tended to blame Harry and Bess for this state of affairs—so privileged a family, with strong links to the royal throne, should have seen to *that* a long time ago, and had the girl contracted in her cradle: so the gentlemen thought. But their matrons blamed Anne—so much prettier and livelier than their own daughters, but curiously scornful of those daughters' brothers—and their male friends—or any other young man for that matter. God knew she had not lacked attention!

Bess had very much liked some of the suitors who had applied for her sweet girl's hand, although she had put no pressure on Anne to accept any of them, knowing that, although both twins resembled their father in looks, Anne was more like Harry Latimar in personality and therefore could not be coerced.

But she sometimes wondered if she had failed her in some way. All her friends' daughters were married now, most with several babes, and apparently were happy wives. It seemed a shame that Anne, the most beautiful, the most sought after, was still unwed or even promised.

Bess sighed over this old sorrow but, hearing sounds of strife from her kitchens, recollected herself and trod purposefully towards the disturbance.

Anne tapped lightly on her brother's door and received the laughing instruction to enter. She put her

head round first to be sure that everyone in the
chamber was decent, then threw open the door and
went in. George was at the window, a glass of wine in
his hand; the others were reclining on various pieces of
furniture but rose immediately.

George said, 'Welcome, sister! Have you come to
ensure that we are all present and correct for the
coming ordeal?'

'I have.' Anne did not need to look at George to be
sure that he had not taken too much liquor, for he was
abstemious even when faced with the kind of occasion
he must shortly endure in the little stone church within
the grounds of Maiden Court. But the others— She
looked disapprovingly at four flushed faces, at four
rather unsteady young men, then marched to the table
and picked up the wine jug: it was almost empty. 'So!
You are celebrating before the event has even taken
place!'

The four males looked suitably shamefaced.

'No more until after the chapel,' Anne declared. 'We
have grand company to witness the service, you know.'

All four young men had the identical thought: No
one can deliver a rebuke like Anne Latimar! She may
frown and scold, but how adorable she looks whilst
doing so! If only she would take my suit seriously.

They all set down their glasses.

'Now downstairs with you all while I have a little
word with my brother.' They left the room instantly
and Anne joined George on the window-seat. They
were astonishingly alike, both black-haired, both white-
skinned and with a shared grace of movement. 'Are
you happy this day, my brother?' she asked.

'You know I am. Are you?'

'Of course. You are getting what you want, aren't

you? That makes me very happy.' Anne leaned against him and he put an arm around her.

'Good. At least—good for me. But what about you? There will be those attending my wedding feast today who feel that this whole affair is entirely the wrong way around—that *you* should be the one to be wed—in fact, should have been the one several years ago.'

Anne shrugged. 'But we don't care for what others may think, do we? When it happens for me, it happens.'

'But it won't happen while you gain yourself a reputation for turning away all offers, sweeting. Do you realise that a moment ago the only man in this room who had not proposed to you was myself?'

Anne twisted one of the diamond buttons on his doublet. 'I know, but. . .'

'But you are too fussy. Why? What are you looking for? What are you waiting for?'

'I don't know, but think you are a fine one to preach. You once said to me—about Judith—"She is the one. The one I have been waiting for all my life." Why can't I have that too?'

George removed his button from her destructive fingers. He loved his sister—she was very different from him, but he loved her. He had spoken the truth earlier—every one of his friends, and many other men too, had sued for her hand and had nothing to show for it but rejection.

He knew the reason for this: Anne wanted someone to match the most significant person in her life—her father. Harry Latimar, handsome and charming, and still capable, in middle age, of enchanting any female within twenty miles, had made an early and lasting impression on his daughter.

But George so wanted the kind of happiness he had

found himself for his beloved sister, and he did not think she would find it with a man like their father.

Both Harry and Anne projected light images of themselves which masked sensitive and complex souls. In any gathering they attracted others with their charm and wit, and frequently were surprised that more serious men and women discounted them, failing to recognise that they possessed more kindness and compassion than they showed. George had no need to be concerned about his father: Harry had long ago been rescued from this world of his own creation by a loving and knowing wife.

But Anne... What Anne thought she wanted and what she actually needed were two different things, and George despaired of her ever meeting a man who would know that.

'Anyway...' Anne leaned away from his embrace and looked out of the window at the dazzling day '...this is your day, George. If we are talking, we should talk about you.' She pushed the window further open. 'There's a rider in the yard. If he is a guest, he is unsuitably early.'

George looked down and exclaimed, 'Why, 'tis Jack Hamilton! I did not think for a moment he would come.'

'Who is he?' Anne leaned out of the window to view the arrival. She saw that he dismounted like a young man, but his hair was that of an elderly man—silvergrey. His horse, too, was unusual—not a riding horse but a courser, the swift, strong stallion breed favoured as a war-horse in the tournament lists, or in the more serious business of battle.

'He used to be squire to Father, before Richard de Vere, if you will remember him. Jack served Father for three years, then was knighted upon his recommendation, and so left his patronage. They have remained friends, however.'

'I think I have heard the name, but have never met him. Why should he not come today? I would have thought it an honour to be included in any assembly graced by Her Majesty's presence.'

'You have met him, actually, and here at Maiden Court. But not since you were about three years old. He commands one of the English garrisons in the north, and has done so for fifteen years. As to his not accepting Father's invitation...' George searched his memory. 'He lost his wife in some terrible accident ten years ago, and out of respect for her memory never accepts social engagements.'

'Really?' Anne watched the silver-haired man turn his mount over to a groom and proceed into the house. 'How peculiar...'

George glanced at the hourglass. It was half-done, and he must now make ready. 'I must get along with my dressing, Anne; I would not disgrace Judith for anything.'

Anne was to be one of Judith's handmaidens. She and three others would follow the bride-to-be on foot from the house to the chapel, carrying flowers and the bride cake. George would follow later with his male supporters, also on foot. The lanes would be lined with villagers from the estate who would throw flowers in the path of the bride and groom and cheer them to their union.

Because Judith's aunt and uncle would bring her from Squirrels, one of the farms on the estate, for her to begin her journey, George would stay strictly in his room until she had left so as to avoid the bad luck which might result if he set eyes upon her before the appointed moment in the church. But all this was to come.

Anne was just finishing her toilette when her mother tapped and entered.

'Yes, you look very lovely, my darling,' Bess said, helping to thread the pearls through her daughter's hair, which was left traditionally loose as befitted a virgin handmaiden. 'Now, I have a favour to ask—I must dress now, your father is unaccountably absent, George is confined to his room, which leaves poor Jack Hamilton on his own in the hall. Do you run down and entertain him until your father comes back.'

'Oh, Mother, what am I to say to him? I don't know him at all and George has said to me that he is rather strange.'

'Strange? What can you mean? And since when were you uncertain what to say to a new acquaintance? He is a very sweet boy and was your father's squire for three years and Harry always says he was the very best of a bad bunch, although rather unruly and mischievous...

'Oh, dear, how can I be expected to cope with all this, when I receive no atom of support from—?' Bess looked distractedly out of the window to see if her husband was in evidence. Really, it was too bad of him to choose this morning to disappear!

'Oh, very well,' Anne said ungraciously. She did not like seeing her usually composed mother under pressure. Besides, she could not explain why she had a reluctance to entertain the stranger, except that, although she disliked very much the thought of a loved one dying, she still thought it horrible to dwell upon it to the extent that Lord Hamilton apparently had.

She assured Bess that she would be the perfect hostess and opened the door to speed her on her way to get ready for the wedding of her son.

Peeping over the gallery, she could see the visitor standing at the window, arms folded, staring moodily out at the radiant morning. When she came down the stairs he turned to watch her cross the floor. She curtsied.

'Good day, sir. I am Anne Latimar; welcome to Maiden Court.'

He bowed formally, but made no move to take her hand and salute her. As she had raised it to accommodate him, she used it to gesture towards a settle. 'Please sit down. May I offer you some refreshment?'

'Thank you, but your mother has already provided it.' A flagon of wine and two glasses were set on a small table already laden with a vast silver bowl of red and white striped roses. Anne crossed to it.

'Then I will pour.'

'I never take liquor,' Jack Hamilton said shortly.

'Oh? I believe I will take one myself.' She drank very little, preferring weak ale or buttermilk, which perhaps explained her enviable complexion. She poured a glass, carried it to a chair and seated herself. Jack dropped onto the settle opposite. 'You have not visited us here for some years, my brother tells me. I think I would have been about three years old.'

'Indeed.'

'Perhaps myself at three was enough to put you off for all that time?' she asked, giving him her lovely smile.

'I am rarely at liberty to leave my estate in the north,' he replied, without returning her smile.

'Where is that? Near the border?'

'*On* the border. Northumberland.'

The stilted question-and-answer exchange was not conducive to pleasant conversation, thought Anne. She wondered what her charming, articulate father had found to talk about with Jack Hamilton during the years of his squireship.

'You were my father's squire some years ago?' she asked, finishing her wine and rising to replace her empty glass on the tray. He rose instantly too, and stood waiting until she was reseated.

'I was.'

'And have come to George's wedding today?'

'No, lady. Your parents were gracious enough to invite me, but I declined. Today I found myself in the vicinity of Maiden Court on my way to the capital, and thought I must call in to offer my respects to the Earl. I had, in truth, forgotten that this was the date of the ceremony, therefore will renew my acquaintance with your father, then impose myself no further on this special day.'

Really, thought Anne, he had a very short way of speaking. As if each word was dragged from him at the point of a dagger. She looked at him curiously. If he had been her father's squire some fifteen years ago, he must be in his middle thirties now and certainly looked no older in spite of the thick silver hair.

His face was strongly modelled and smoothly tanned, with widely spaced grey eyes, startlingly light in his dark face. He was well above average height, with broad shoulders, a slim waist and very long and shapely legs. His costume was severely plain: no lace or silk relieved the fine dark cloth. He wore no fashionable ruff and no jewellery save a circle of gold in one pierced earlobe and a broad gold ring on one finger.

He bore her scrutiny without discomfort and what she fancied was total indifference. With relief, she saw a shadow pass the window and looked out to see her father ride by on his wild black horse. A few minutes later, Harry Latimar entered the hall. Jack Hamilton sprang up and the stern contours of his face softened into a smile.

'Harry!'

'My dear Jack! What a delightful surprise—I had no idea you were expected this day.' The two men embraced.

'I was not expected, sir. I happened to be in the neighbourhood and thought I must look in to see you and Bess—I apologise for appearing at such an inopportune time.'

'Apologise? Inopportune?' Harry laughed, holding the other man at arm's length and looking at him critically. 'Both words are an insult between us. But, my boy, you are thin; have you suffered some illness recently?'

'No illness, Harry, unless the Scots may be so described. There has been bitter fighting on the border this spring, and myself bearing some of the responsibility for keeping the unruly chieftains from spilling over into our fair country.'

'Yes, indeed,' Harry said soberly. 'I have heard this, of course. But 'tis quelled now, I have also heard.'

'Indeed. Naturally, I would not be so far from my post if 'twere not so. No... Her Majesty has commanded me to her court to report on her defences in that region personally, so on my way to Greenwich I have called here.'

'Harry? Is that you?' Bess's voice floated down from

above. 'Come you up immediately and change. We are
sorely behind time now.'

Harry grimaced. 'I am guilty of truancy, Jack. One
of my tenants summoned me on a matter of some
urgency. I was able to arrange the matter, then we
drank to the success of the outcome, and one thing led
to another. . .'

Jack grinned. 'You never could resist any convivial
gathering, Harry. Best go up now and placate your
sweet wife.'

'I suppose I must. But you will stay for the festivities,
Jack? Come, I will not allow any other course.'

'If you insist. But, you know—'

'I know, my friend, but on this occasion you would
be granting a favour to an old friend. I need all the
support I can get; say you will.'

'Very well. There is somewhere I may change my
clothes and find a costume more fitting to the
occasion?'

'Of course. Anne will show you where.' Harry drew
Anne to her feet and put his arm about her. 'I will
leave you in her capable hands; is she not a jewel—my
precious daughter?'

'Indeed,' Jack agreed politely, his tone implying,
Anne thought, that he considered her no jewel at all.

'Then excuse me.' Harry released Anne and took the
stairs two at a time. Jack turned to Anne.

'I hesitate to impose upon you further, lady.'

'It is no imposition,' Anne said with elaborate courtesy. She had never in her life been so ignored by any
man with normal eyesight.

She led the way up to one of the guest chambers
which her mother had fashioned out of the maze of
small bedrooms. She looked into it to be sure that it

had whatever a visitor might require. She said, 'I had no notion you were so intimate with my father. He has never mentioned your name to me.'

'No?' Jack enquired coolly. 'But then, Harry has a legion of friends and 'twould take a lifetime to mention them all to you, lady.'

'As you say,' agreed Anne frostily. She was unused also to anyone taking her up on her sharp tongue, and besting her. She stood back to allow him to enter the room and closed the door noisily behind him.

Meeting one of the servants in the passageway, she said, 'Please take hot water to the guest room; we have a visitor,' then, figuratively turning her back on Jack Hamilton, hurried down the stairs to await her sister-in-law's arrival.

CHAPTER TWO

GEORGE LATIMAR and Judith Springfield were married
just after noon that day. The old chapel had seen many
such unions, but perhaps none so happy.

The bride and bridegroom were well matched both
in looks and in intellect. The bride was not the equal of
her new husband in breeding, or status, but what had
lovers ever cared for such conventions?

Both were young and healthy and handsome and
madly in love: not one of the congregation that hot
August day had any fault to find with the arrangement
they witnessed. Not George's parents, Harry and Bess,
who had eventually sanctioned the unusual marriage,
not their sovereign, Elizabeth Tudor, who had indeed
interested herself in the two young lovers, not her best
beloved favourite, Robert Dudley, who stood best man
to the young groom, not any of the aristocratic ladies
and gentlemen who had come to view the nuptials.

These last had a tolerant indulgence to the Latimars,
known for their bizarre attitude to what should, or
should not, be done in noble circles.

Anne had attended Judith up the lane to the chapel,
carefully arranged her long train and put the bridal
bouquet—of myrtle and roses and honeysuckle—into
her trembling hands, kissed her dutifully and sent her
away up the narrow aisle to the sound of the creaking
Prussian organ played by an ancient man provided by
the Queen's court musicians.

I approve of it all, she told herself sternly, watching

Judith gain her bridegroom's side and noting his glance of absolute adoration. I am happy for George, but I want something different for *me*. I want a different kind of love. Someone who has my background, some-one—someone like—

She tiptoed quietly up the aisle and slipped into the pew next to her mother and father. Her glance slid sideways to her father, sitting quite relaxed, one hand entwined in his wife's.

Darling Father! thought Anne. How absolutely beautiful he looks in his wedding white; how absolutely right he is in every way. She returned her eyes to the altar, listened for a while to the ceremony, then looked around the church. How many friends had come to support George this day! Not only his grand friends, but Latimar tenants and representatives from all the villages; the little church was brimming over with goodwill.

As she looked across the aisle Jack Hamilton turned his head and their eyes met. She half smiled in recognition of the fact that he was a guest in her home, and an old friend of her family, but received no acknowledgement.

Jack was recalling with the utmost pain his own wedding day twelve years before. Marie Claire, he mourned, why did you leave me? We had just such a day as this—the sun laid its bright warmth on us as it will upon this boy and girl, we were as much in love, and as ideally suited, but you left me! Knowing I only lived to love and serve you, you left me. Why? I was well enough before I found you; now I am lost forever without you.

Pictures of his dead wife rose to blot out the quiet church. Marie Claire upon their wedding day, a little

shy and tremulous, her fair face flushed with joy. Marie
Claire taking courage in both hands to confront the
men under his command at Ravensglass when she
became mistress; what an ordeal that all-male assembly
had been for her, with her modest and retiring personality. Marie Claire running in the snow that first freezing winter, his dogs at her heels. Marie Claire as he had
seen her after her tragic accident, laid out on cold
marble, her childlike face as serene in death as in life.

Surely she was only sleeping, he had thought, going
fearfully to her side. But no, her lifted hand had been
as chill as her new bed—the hand that had been so
warm and caressing in life.

He closed his eyes, his heart twisting in pain, and
opened them to find Anne Latimar's eyes on him.

How much he disliked her kind of woman! So spoiled
and obviously believing that no male could resist her.
He remembered that empty conversation he had had
with her in the manor hall earlier; she had met him
only minutes, but immediately had come the flirtatious
glances, the feminine tricks of fluttering lashes and
provocative gestures.

He faced the altar again without returning her smile.
Nothing of her mother there, he thought. Dear Bess,
she grew lovelier with each passing year. No, Anne's
bold looks were entirely her father's. But in a man
'twas more acceptable to be so designed.

God, it had been good to see Harry again after so
long; they had met so rarely in the decade following
Marie Claire's funeral.

Jack had not expected Latimar to make the long trip
north, but he had... Jack shifted his position slightly
on the hard wooden bench and thought about Harry.
He had been damned good to him always, both as

master and later as friend. No other friend had said anything of comfort to him that day of his love's interment, when he had been half-demented with pain and anger.

He had, in fact, scorned all others' words: Tragic, yes, tragic, they had all agreed. But life goes on, my boy, my friend, my comrade. And the words unspoken in the air: What was one woman more or less in the scheme of things?

But Harry had understood. 'I imagine you feel your own life to be over,' he had said thoughtfully. 'I know I would so do. In a place far away across three oceans,' he had added, 'a widow leaps upon her dead husband's funeral pyre. What a pity we are so civilised here in the west...'

It had not been, perhaps, quite the thing to say, but Harry had said it just the same, and Jack had gained solace from the knowledge that at least one other human being in the universe could conceive of what he was feeling.

Harry had come again, two years later, to Ravensglass, a grim fortress in a wind-swept landscape, and now no more than a living tomb for its commander. They had had a different sort of conversation on that occasion. 'How much are you drinking these days, Jack?' Harry had asked.

'Too much,' had been the reply. 'Indeed, I cannot now function without a great deal.'

Harry had looked out over the stark countryside. Rain was falling, of course, for cold rain always fell in a Northumberland spring. 'Can you do your duty in such condition?' Harry had asked, with one of his deliberate straight looks. 'If the Scots should come armed over the border, could you do your duty?'

Jack had blustered a little. It had been so quiet for a long time —

'She wouldn't like it, my boy,' Harry had then said. 'Marie Claire had no time for a man who could not perform his duty. In fact, if I had had the writing of her epitaph, I would have carved the words "Love and Duty, in equal measure".'

Jack had been angry that day, but Latimar had remained imperturbable. When he had ridden away, Jack had thought on what he had said and from that day had eschewed all strong liquor.

It had not been easy; his dependency — so insidious over a twenty-four month — had been great, and with sobriety had come the knowledge that he should never again take a drink, but he had done it. And with the return of consciousness he had exchanged numb and dumb misery for hot and agonising grief — a condition with him every waking moment — then, now, and presumably for ever —

'Sir, the ceremony is ended; we go now to Maiden Court to toast the newly-weds.' Jack's neighbour on the hard bench was nudging him and rising.

The wedding breakfast was a great success. The food was tasty and plentiful, the wine the best to be had. There had been no distinction in the minds of Maiden Court's master and mistress as to which guests were most honoured — the tables had been laid to accommodate thirty, but everyone was welcome.

Noble and rustic rubbed shoulders alike once the Queen and her immediate party had been seated. Those who could not find a place at the tables stood with wine or ale in one hand, a plate of food in the other, and no one troubled to question it.

Elizabeth Tudor, naturally, was the centre of attention. Bess had known this would be so when she had arranged the special dais overlooking the hall. Throughout the meal it was possible for anyone to approach her to offer compliments, and how she relished all such, whether from landed country squire or rough villager!

George and Judith, seated at either side of her, were indulgent to this, for they might have been the reason for the celebration, but their sovereign was the Queen of England and so entitled to the lion's share of attention.

With the completion of the meal, the tables were cleared and set aside and all the guests prepared to dance to the music supplied by the village orchestra.

'I think it is all going very well,' Bess said breathlessly as Harry swung her into the dance.

'Of course it is! Why not? And even if our estimable cook had burned all the meats and our old Walter dropped all the wine brought from the cellars it would still be well, for the two it is in honour of are so happy. Only look at them.'

Bess looked towards her son and his new wife. George and Judith danced as if sleepwalking, expressions of rapture on their faces. 'Mmm, it is *nice*, is it not?'

'Nice! What an inadequate word.' Harry smiled down at his wife, then said, 'Do you think we are a little long in the tooth for this activity? I do, so let us sit out awhile.' They left the floor and sank into chairs by the hearth.

'Much better,' Bess said gratefully. 'I find I like to look on at others enjoying themselves these days. Now, who is that with Anne?'

Harry found his daughter in the mêlée. 'That is Tom Monterey. Very well bred, but not overendowed with brains. He came to me a year ago and asked for Anne's hand... Poor lad, he has it badly.'

'Mmm. The Montereys are *very* grand, are they not? You know the Earl well, don't you?'

'I do; John Monterey is part of my ill-begotten youth, although we did not move in the exact same circles.'

'She will meet him again at court, I think?' Bess asked. She did not immediately recall Tom, for there had been so many young men coming and going once George had made friends at court and invited them home to meet his family: his sister.

'Certainly. She will meet most of the young men from that coterie at court.' Harry's gaze was distracted now by a lone figure in one corner of the room. 'I am not sure that Jack Hamilton is enjoying himself.'

Bess looked too. 'Ah, no, but then that is Jack's way since Marie Claire's death. I truly believe he was so badly hit by it, nothing will ever rouse him again. At least,' she amended, 'in that area, for earlier I heard the Queen complimenting him largely upon his prowess in the military field. It seems he is greatly appreciated for his defence of the northern border.'

'I am sure,' Harry said slowly. 'That is his chosen career and I am glad he excels, but he is young yet and I much dislike the thought that he must spend his whole life mourning his dead wife. He used to be such a joyous lad.

'Actually, he was a sore trial to me whilst in my care—so lively and merry and always in trouble. He was quite the most mischievous boy I have ever known.'

'Oh, well...' Bess was pleasantly warm and comfortable, with the difficult day going so well. 'It takes some that way—they lose their most beloved and are never the same again.'

'So it would have been—would still be—for me,' Harry said ardently. 'And for you too.'

'Indeed,' agreed Bess. 'But why think of that on this day, with George so safely set?'

'I do think of it. I think of Jack, and worry about him.'

Bess reached out a fond hand. 'Dear Harry! And there are those who used to call you callous. Now see— Anne has left her partner and is trying to encourage him to join in the fun.'

Jack Hamilton had found himself a chair where he could watch the dancing but not have to be involved. He much resented Anne Latimar coming, with her inbred sense of hospitality, to include him. He rose when she approached, but gave her a forbidding look which she ignored.

'Lord Jack, do come and be a part of the proceedings.' She took his hand to pull him into the fray.

'I do not dance, lady,' he said repressively.

'You do not dance, you do not drink!' Anne laughed up at him. 'One wonders what you do for entertainment, sir!'

'Entertainment value varies according to the participant,' he said harshly. 'Perhaps your own standards are set quite low in that respect.'

Anne looked at him challengingly. 'It must be gratifying to feel oneself so much *better* than everyone else!'

'Not better,' he returned, grimly steering her through the throng. 'Just different. And I have a good reason for not dancing: I swore never to dance again when my wife died.' Now why had he said that? He had never paraded his grief for others to see, never spoke of it, in fact.

Anne faltered in her perfect execution of a step. 'Oh. . .I am sorry; I had no idea. . . Then I will release you from your obligation at once.'

'Thank you.' He bowed and left her. For a moment she could not believe he had done so. For a gentleman to leave a lady in the middle of a dance, however informal the occasion, was a discourtesy not within her experience. Jostled on both sides, she found herself blushing—another practically unknown experience for the self-assured Anne.

George, who had seen what had happened from further up the line, rescued her and took her away to the refreshment table. 'How dare he?' Anne exclaimed angrily. 'What a boor that man is!'

'What did you say to him to cause him to act so?' George asked curiously.

'Nothing! We were speaking of his dead wife, and suddenly—'

'Really? He spoke of Marie Claire? How unusual. I have heard he never speaks her name in company.'

'What happened to her?' Anne asked, trying to calm herself.

'You don't know the story?' George helped them both to wine. 'I can tell you what I know of the tragedy. Jack was sent to the French court fourteen years ago. Whilst there he met a French lady who was Marie Claire. They fell in love, but her father would have none of the young Englishman—he was a stranger, very young, and Protestant to boot.

'Somehow they found someone to marry them and came back to England to be met with even more hostility from Jack's family, firstly on the grounds of her being Catholic, then because Marie Claire had been cast off by her father and had no dowry.

'She must have had a very miserable time at Ravensglass until both the older Hamiltons died in a summer plague and Jack inherited all, including the responsibility for defending that particular part of England.'

'But what happened to her?' Anne asked impatiently.

'Oh... There is a small village some way from the castle and Marie Claire was in the habit of going there to visit what she thought of as her tenants. It is a very small community, but they raise a few animals to supply meat to Ravensglass. On this day a bull had been brought to service the cows and apparently the beast ran mad and Marie Claire was unfortunate enough to be in his path.'

George paused. 'This is a dismal story, and on my wedding day too.'

'It is,' Anne agreed, her eyes wide. 'But go on.'

'There is little more to tell. The poor lady was killed, and horribly, and Jack came home from patrol the next day to find himself a widower.'

'How terrible!'

'Terrible indeed, and the more so because they had lately been transported with joy in the knowledge that an heir was to be born to them. Jack had then the double grief. Father told me that when he went north to attend the funeral he scarcely recognised his young friend for his hair had turned grey almost overnight.'

'Oh, George!' Anne's eyes filled with tears. The whole of her warm nature was shaken by the story.

And she had taunted him because he would not dance!
She set down her glass. 'I am so sorry for him.'

'Yes, well. . .'

'I would like to help him in some way.'

'Now, Anne,' George said warningly, knowing his
sister's impulsiveness. 'Better to leave it alone. Others
have tried to help—well-meaning friends have, over
the years, tried to interest him in finding happiness with
another lady, but to no avail. He is deeply unhappy
and those in that state are better left in peace, unhap-
piness being such a contagious disease.'

'Why, brother, I have never thought you cynical!'

'I don't think I am, but I trust Father's opinion of a
man he knows very well. Jack Hamilton is fatally
wounded by his experience, and such men are unpredictable to say the least. Also, your paths will not cross
again, for Jack is presumably bound for the wilds of
Northumberland and you for Greenwich.'

'Not so. I heard him tell Father this very day that he
is going to Greenwich too, and from there to his home
in the company of Her Majesty, who wishes to inspect
her northern defences.'

'What are you two in such deep conference about?'
Bess appeared at their side.

'Nothing, Mother,' George said placidly. 'Only
gossip.'

'Well, no more of that while Elizabeth is looking
around for a likely partner in the dance. Do you go and
invite her, George. Really, I think Robert Dudley
might be a little more tactful and stop pursuing all the
pretty girls here and look after her.'

'I will take care of it,' George said placatingly.

'And I must go to the kitchens to be sure there will

be ample food for the rest of the night. I believe this will not be a party that will come to a swift conclusion.'

Anne had plans of her own. Her mind was full of distressing images. How romantic was Jack's story! Blighted in his youth, she thought, for she was a devotee of the sentimental poetry of the age, repelling all efforts to make him take another to fill his wife's cherished place. He had sworn he would never make merry again when she died, and his hair had turned grey as an outward show of his grief!

She forgot for the moment her distaste at his pre-occupation with morbid death and felt a surge of compassion and sympathy for him.

With Anne, to think was to act and she asked one of Walter's sons, who was bearing around a tray of wine, 'Wat, have you seen one of our guests? Lord Jack Hamilton?'

'He has gone out to the stables, I believe, Lady Anne. His horse is not the usual, but a war-horse, and is causing trouble.'

The stables at Maiden Court were near the house. Not near enough to cause their smells to invade the house, but just beyond the gardens. Anne followed the light of the lanterns which Walter, as head groom, always lit at twilight, and opened the door of the one stall where she could see activity.

Jack was within its warm interior. 'Stay back!' he shouted peremptorily. Anne flattened her back against the stout wooden wall, watching appreciatively as Jack soothed and gentled the great grey beast.

As she had seen from George's window, Hamilton's mount was a courser, an exalted breed chosen for its excellence of speed and endurance. He was, in fact, the

alternative to the heavy destrier only favoured now for
tournaments by a master clad in full armour. This likely
stallion, tossing its head and showing its mettle tonight,
would carry his rider into battle whether fought in
traditional close style or in more open country.

'Now, sir,' Jack said softly, running his hand over the
quivering flank, 'do you be still and not shame me with
your wild ways.' The animal shuffled his iron-shod
hooves in the straw and lowered his handsome head to
nuzzle his master.

'So, Valiant,' Jack murmured, 'no more tantrums, if
you please, but peace until dawnlight.' He flung a
blanket over the great horse, reached up to lower the
flame in the lantern and turned to Anne.

'Lady Anne. What brings you out here?'

'I was worried you were not enjoying yourself,' she
replied gently. The dim light did not soften the stern
lines of his face, any more than it did the carven outline
of his mount; both males were too distinctive. No one
would call Jack Hamilton handsome, she decided, but
nor would any pass him in a crowd without seeing him.

He was arrested by both her tone and her words and
felt a faint stirring of interest. Was there a different girl
with him now from the lord of the manor's daughter
who had been the life and soul of the party inside,
distributing her favours with arrogance and assurance?

But no, even though her words were softly spoken
they were conveyed with the same tricks of her kind—
luxuriant lowered eyelashes, tremulous mouth—and he
had had his fill of such manoeuvres.

He said drily, 'Have you not enough strings to your
bow this night, but must pursue a renegade out into the
cold night?'

She swallowed. 'I pursued—came here out of kindness, sir. Have you not enough pain in your life without turning away all offers of friendship?'

'Is that what you offer? Friendship? A true friend recognises a desire to be left in peace, lady.'

'But you are not *at* peace, are you? You are tormented, and—'

'Enough!' Jack said roughly. 'If I have failed to do my duty on this happy day then please forgive me, but do not lecture me. I was persuaded to the celebration, and have tried to play my part, apparently badly.'

He turned and slammed shut the stall door. The great creature within heard his master's angry voice and moved uneasily. Jack soothed him once again.

'You speak more kindly to that animal than to me,' Anne remarked. Her generous gesture had been thrown back in her face—very well—but she had no liking for being lectured either.

'That animal knows when to desist bothering others.'

'You are extremely rude, sir,' she said deliberately, 'to your good friend's daughter.'

'I find myself forgetting that fact,' Jack said. 'For you are not at all like him.'

A deadly insult! Not like her beloved father, who was the very essence of everything she admired? Anne turned away and hurried back to the light and warmth of the house. Once inside she she pulled the door shut behind her, an expression of outrage on her face. George, just inside the door, gave her a glance.

'I told you,' he said mildly, 'to let well alone, sister. Jack Hamilton is too unpredictable an animal to be stalked with the weapons at your disposal.'

Anne gave him back his glance with thunder added. 'If it pleases you, George, then I will admit you are right. It will be a cold day in hell before I go a-hunting

the likes of Hamilton again—unless with a sharp sword
and hungry dogs!'

Anne left Maiden Court for her spell in the English
court in the service of her sovereign six weeks later. At
the last moment there had been a hitch in the Latimar
plans. Bess had fallen ill with a sore throat and aching
limbs. Having ascertained that it was not the dreaded
sweating sickness, Harry relaxed, but obviously she
could not make the trip with Anne to Greenwich.

When Bess was on the road to recovery, Anne said
one night to her father,

'Mother is going to be well soon—could we not go
on the date as planned, and she join us later?'

'I think I would like to persuade her not to go at all
this year,' Harry said consideringly. 'I will take you,
naturally, see you safely established, then come home.'

'But you don't want to leave her, do you? Even for
so short a time as a week.' It was no secret to Anne
that her parents were not like those of her friends; an
hour out of each other's company was wasted for them,
and with Bess still frail, although no longer sick, she
knew her father was reluctant to let her out of his sight.

'I believe I know my duty to you, my daughter,'
Harry smiled. 'Come—your mother would be the first
to say, "Go, take Anne to court and present her
properly."'

'I know, but. . .' Anne, who had tried to take her
mother's place as a good housewife in the past weeks,
rose and rearranged one of the ornaments on the wide
hearth-shelf, checking first that it was free of dust '. . .I
believe *I* would be happier if you stayed here at Maiden
Court. Walter is quite capable of taking me the few
short miles to Greenwich.'

Harry frowned. 'So my daughter is to arrive at the greatest court in the world, to serve as waiting lady to the greatest queen in the world, in the care of a *stableman*?'

'Oh, Father,' Anne laughed. 'You know you would trust old Walter with your life—and mine.'

'Certainly I would,' Harry agreed. 'But you must understand that where you are going appearances are everything. Believe me, I know.'

A week later Harry came to the supper-table looking pleased. He said to Anne, 'I have solved it all, sweetheart. Jack Hamilton is coming here in two days' time and will take you to Greenwich to take up your duties.' He reached for the wine flagon and waited for appreciation of his efforts. Instead Anne looked horrified.

'Jack Hamilton? Why should he come for me?'

'Because I asked him to do so,' Harry said. 'It came to me quite suddenly after our conversation that of course he is the ideal person. He is known to Bess and myself—indeed he was a large part of our lives fifteen years ago. He has risen considerably in status since then, and is certainly valued highly by Elizabeth. And you have met him, have you not, at George's wedding a month ago?'

'Met him and disliked him!' Anne returned.

'Disliked him?' Harry put down his glass. 'For what reason?'

'For the reason that he is very difficult to get along with,' Anne replied briskly. 'And don't tell me what a sweet boy he was fifteen years ago for those days are long gone.'

Harry raised his eyebrows. 'Perhaps you are right. Dear me, they say it is a sign of old age when one can only remember others in their youth.'

Anne got up to kiss him. 'Nonsense, you will never be old, Father. But can we think again about Jack Hamilton coming for me?'

'I am afraid not. Since he and I communicated he has left Greenwich for Windsor and will be I know not where until he comes for you at the week's end as we arranged.'

'I don't want to go with him,' Anne said stubbornly. 'You must advise him when he arrives.'

'I couldn't possibly do that; it would be the greatest insult. Besides, why should I? You will spend but a day in his company, not the rest of your life.'

Anne shuddered. 'And thank God for that! But I do think you might have consulted me.'

Harry looked astonished. Possibly some of the men he'd spent his youth with, caroused and gambled with, now felt him to be almost too settled with Bess. But that was his choice, not hers. Certainly he was not so tame a cat that he must ask his womenfolk before arranging so simple a thing as a day's journey.

What had come over Anne, his sweet and docile daughter? he wondered. He had never seen that combative look in her eyes before; always in the past she had been more than ready to fall in with his plans— why, in this moment she had the look of her mother and brother. . .

Besides, he had been quite frank: appearances did count when one joined the ranks she was bound for at Greenwich. She knew little of the society she would shortly be a part of, and a maid's life could be made miserable without pretty clothes, ready money, and the correct escort on all occasions. The first two had been very satisfactorily arranged; the last he had now settled and had had enough of the whole subject. He rose.

'I don't wish to discuss it any more, darling. Please allow me to know best.' He softened his words with a smile, then knew a moment's doubt. Was there some special feeling here? Had Anne some particular reason for not wishing to be with Jack? Harry did not think he was only remembering the boy's interesting personality. Jack was, despite his current dour ways, still extremely attractive.

But not for Anne! Maybe an experienced woman would be able to untangle the muddle that Marie Claire's death had made of a potentially happy and gifted man, but not a young girl.

But no, looking into his daughter's clear eyes he saw nothing but aggravation for not getting her own way. He patted her shoulder.

'Just wait until you get to Greenwich, Anne. There will be fun and plenty to entertain you. Remember how fortunate you are to wait upon a lady who is foremost in England, but who has chosen *you* to attend her above a hundred others.'

An affectionate smile crossed Anne's face. 'I think maybe she chose *you*, Father, as the Tudors have a habit of doing.'

'Hmm.' Harry turned to go up the stairs. Anne, he thought, was very pretty, very gay and pleasure-loving. But underneath her charming ways was sound common sense, and he was glad of it. For a large portion of common sense was, in Harry Latimar's opinion, worth more than all the other attributes his lovely daughter possessed. She would need it in its full measure where she was going.

CHAPTER THREE

THE day Anne left for Greenwich dawned bright and hot. For the second year running St Martin's summer stalked England and for once she awoke early and knelt on her window-seat to watch the sun rising over Maiden Court's acres.

Lovely, lovely place, she thought regretfully, letting her eyes rove over the graceful scene still veiled in drifting mist. She would miss it very much. But today marked a turning point in her life. She had been born here, had grown up here—she and her twin brother, George.

George had hauled her to her feet for her first steps, remarked upon her first word, put her on her first pony, led her out in her first dance. He had also jeered at her on occasion, comforted her when she was in distress, and had finally left her to pursue another life she could have no real part in. At the time of his marriage, in the excitement of the wedding, she had not really thought about what it would mean to *her*.

The Latimar twins were now divided by that most natural thing—the marriage of one of the parts, and Anne envied her brother, she could not deny that. Envied him for casting off a thing outgrown and acquiring another which better fitted. Today she would do the same.

Her trunks, all packed, were standing in the hall. In her dark blue riding costume she came to the breakfast table and saw that both her parents were there for this, her last meal in her home for some time.

Her mother smiled a little wanly. Her illness had taken something from her—one recovered more slowly from sickness when older, Bess had thought when dressing, with many pauses to rest, earlier. But see Anne off in style she would.

Little Hal was at the table too, tied into his chair and fully aware that something unusual was in the wind today. He rocked back and forth and shouted and waved his horn spoon when his sister entered and planted a kiss on his rosy face. The meal was taken with much laughter and frequent last-minute reminders from Bess.

'And do you remember, darling, that Elizabeth is right in *everything*. No matter if you think her moon-touched over some situation, she is always *right*. And stay away from Robert Dudley,' she added as an afterthought.

'Oh, Mother! That old man. Why, I wouldn't give him a second glance.'

'Old?' Harry drew his lips down in mock dismay. 'He is many years more youthful than myself. Perhaps that is something else you should explain to her, Bess. No prideful man likes to be described in such terms.'

'We are not speaking of you, but of gentlemen who might prove a difficulty for Anne,' Bess told him severely. 'And Robert has a reputation in that area.'

Harry shrugged. 'He is also a friend of ours, of George's in particular. Dudley won't make himself a nuisance to Anne, you may be sure.'

'Yah, yah!' shouted Hal, feeling he had had no attention at all in the last half-hour. His sister turned on the bench to put her face close to his.

'When I come back a grand lady, will you remember me, Hal?'

Hal stopped shouting and examined the bright face before him. He was a very forward child physically, had taken his first tottering steps long before was usual, but the gift of speech had so far eluded him. Perhaps, as the third child in a very voluble family, he had never felt a great need to express himself verbally. However, now he said, 'Pretty!'

Anne turned a delighted face to her parents. 'There! On my last day here he speaks! And so fine a compliment. Thank you, little brother.'

A peremptory knocking on the door interrupted this pleasant exchange. Harry said, 'That will be Jack. I will answer.' He rose and opened the door and welcomed the visitor in. 'A mug of ale, Jack? And some food—it will be a lengthy day.'

Jack Hamilton came into the hall with his peculiarly wary step. As if he expected an armed enemy to jump up from behind one of the settles, thought Anne. And that swiftly assessing glance towards all the closed doors, as if he wondered what peril lay hidden behind them! She inclined her head without smiling as he greeted her. Bess patted the bench beside her, with her warm glance.

'Sit you down, Jack. A lovely day, is it not?'

Jack seated himself, first stripping off his riding gloves. They, thought Anne, spoke a great deal of their owner, for they were plain hard-wearing leather, much cut about and clumsily patched. Very different from her father's soft doeskin pair, perfumed and embroidered as a gentleman's should be. She crumbled her bread on the pewter place.

'You are not nervous, are you, Lady Anne?' Jack

enquired, his eyes on her. 'I am sure all will be well at Greenwich.'

'Of course it will be,' Anne answered crossly. 'And I have never been nervous in my life.'

'How fortunate for you,' Jack returned mildly. 'The rest of us greatly envy such self-assurance.'

Bess glanced sideways at her husband. Over the years, whenever she had seen Jack, she had tried to draw him out, to try gently to mend his hurt and get him to speak of the phantoms he obviously kept locked away in his heart. She had failed miserably: Jack did not talk of Marie Claire; in fact, he did not speak at all except in necessary and trivial terms.

But now he seemed to be coming out of his shell with combative force! Had Anne induced this state? Like her husband, she sincerely hoped not, for she felt Hamilton to be an unknown quantity now and there was no worse creature for a fond mother with an innocent daughter to confront. . .

Harry reseated himself and Margery hastened in with hot food. Jack applied himself to the heaped plate with enthusiasm.

'Our little lad has just spoken his first word,' Bess told him.

Jack raised his grey eyes. 'Is it so? Then I pity him, for he will never again be able to take refuge in silence.'

'He made a sweet compliment to me,' Anne said icily. 'So he is off on the right road, so to speak.'

'The road to disaster,' Jack murmured, cutting his meat as if it were a Scottish rebel.

'Why so?' demanded Anne. 'Just because you are above such niceties, it does not mean they are not welcome to the rest of us.'

'Anne, Anne,' Harry said pacifically. 'There is no need, I think, to go to war about an infant's prattle.'

''Tis the principle, Father,' Anne declared, her eyes bright with anger. 'Jack apparently believes that all words spoken with kindness are wasted. I do not agree.'

'That is not what I believe,' Jack countered, his eyes no longer light but cloudy and dark. 'I merely question the value of useless words to anyone who inhabits the real world.'

'And that is where you live, is it?' Anne asked furiously. 'We may not have your understanding of that world, Jack, but we do our poor best to visit it occasionally.'

'Then what a pity it is you do not speak the language!'

Dark blue eyes met grey ones over the table and clashed. Neither of the owners quite knew why they had engaged in this manner.

On the road to Maiden Court Jack had not been eager to honour the promise he had made to his old master. Harry had asked him to convey his daughter to Greenwich, and Jack had felt compelled to do so. But he had left Maiden Court with the Queen, having gained a very poor impression of Anne Latimar.

Why, then, he had asked himself, puzzled, did he keep thinking of her? Why, at Greenwich, had her face come between himself and Elizabeth as he was dutifully giving his report on the northern defences? Why, when he'd surveyed the dancing courtiers each evening, had he found his mind drifting away to seek out another face, another graceful body?

Jack could not account for such a strange state of affairs. When he had dismounted in the Maiden Court stables a few minutes since, he had hastened to the door with a feeling of expectation and, on entering, had immediately sought her face amongst those at the table. Jack did not comprehend his feelings, and so greatly resented them.

Anne had actually been dreading his arrival. He was like no one she had ever encountered before in her life — graceless and lacking in all the flattering skills which she considered her right. But she too had been unable to get the new acquaintance out of her head.

Upon Jack's last remark Bess uttered a cry and bit her lip. Immediately he turned to her in concern. 'Please forgive me. I have heard you were not so well lately — I should be shot for adding to your troubles.'

'And I will undertake that task,' Anne muttered. 'Father has the latest model of firearm in his room.'

There was a small silence, then Harry said easily, 'It is growing late. Bess, I think we must say farewell to Anne and let her be on her way.'

Bess dried her eyes resolutely and untied her little son. With Hal in her arms she came out to the stable-yard to watch Anne mount her elegant mare. Jack swung into the saddle of his restless grey and the two paused to receive the last farewells as Walter led out a third animal with Anne's trunks strapped to its back.

Harry took his daughter's hand. 'Farewell, Anne, and do you give my best respects to Her Majesty and tell her I will offer my renewed allegiance very soon.'

Bess held up her baby son for a last kiss. 'Remember all I have said to you, Anne. And enjoy yourself! That first, my darling.'

'I will, Mother,' Anne said, swallowing hard. Around the yard the stable grooms watched her, caps in hand, and the house servants had all come out to wave her away. Fat Mary, the cook, dabbed her handkerchief to her eyes. Walter—so bent now that he could scarcely remain upright—remembered the day he had physically restrained his headstrong young miss from mounting a full-grown horse when it had been her heart's desire.

At the gate beyond the archway a little group of villagers had gathered, their own memories of the sweet little mistress of Maiden Court in their minds. Anne had been a part of the estate for so many years, with her gay, laughing ways, her tears and joys and brief storms. They loved her, for she was very lovable, and now she was going away.

Dear people, thought Anne. How will I fare without their kind attention? She leaned down to kiss her mother and Hal, saved her last kiss for her father, then touched her heels to Jenny's flanks and trotted away.

'God speed, my boy,' Harry said to Jack. 'Think you that I have entrusted my daughter to your best care.'

'I know that, sir,' Jack said quietly. He touched the tips of his fingers to his forehead, then followed Anne out of the yard.

Bess and Harry looked after them.

'Oh, dear,' Bess said. 'I hope all will be well with them.'

'"Them?"' Harry queried. 'There is no *them*, sweetheart. He but delivers her to her place of employment, then their liaison is ended.'

Bess lowered Hal to the ground, where he took off immediately with unsteady but determined steps. 'You think so? I have not seen Jack so lively for a long time, and Anne—she is normally so charming to any male.'

'So what do you read into all that?' Harry asked, laughing. 'They obviously dislike each other!'

Bess said nothing more, but she remembered the abrasive exchanges she used to have with Harry, when they were newly met, and had not wished to admit a mutual — and serious — attraction.

Elizabeth Tudor was lying in her closely curtained bed, resting. She had her gown off, her stays loosened and her eyes closed, but she was not sleeping.

Beyond the thick drapes she could hear her waiting ladies murmuring to each other — gossiping, thought Elizabeth moodily. What else did her women do, apart from enjoy themselves? Oh, a little gentle embroidery, lute-playing and singing. But mostly they chattered amongst themselves about their clothes, their hair, their skin, and their would-be lovers. All at her expense.

She sighed, because, of course, a great queen must have her retinue of ladies and gentlemen, and that queen must pay the bill. Elizabeth turned restlessly and the talk paused for a moment in the chamber as the women waited to see if she would part the curtains and demand this or that. She lay quite still and the well-bred whispering began again.

Now why did she feel so discontented? All was well within her government and her country. She had made a superb beginning to her reign, she thought, and would go on to even greater things. Formidably intelligent, swift to learn, well educated and polished in all the necessary accomplishments for a monarch, she knew she also had another virtue, which could not be taught or learned. She could choose men both able and loyal to serve her.

In that respect she was very different from another queen — her cousin, Mary Stuart, just over the turbulent border, back from France to sit upon the throne of her native kingdom and already proving a poor tool. Elizabeth's face darkened on the minutely worked lace pillow. Mary might be granted little praises for her statesmanship, but stories of her beauty and charm were legion.

Mary had come back to a trouble land. The Scottish lords in government were arrogant and violent; they ruled over a country divided since her father's death by a savage civil war and had not relished a mere girl from a frivolous and light-hearted court taking her rightful place as their queen.

She had more than her own share of arrogance, for she had married the Dauphin of France who had duly ascended the throne, then died within the year. Francis, sickly and already dying from the disease which killed him, had adored Mary, his young and beautiful queen, and had showered her with every gift within his power.

He had repeatedly promised her the throne of England; when she had abruptly found herself a widow with a hostile mother-in-law and a newly crowned brother-in-law who did not intend to let her share in his new power Mary had decided to go back to her birthplace and sit upon a throne which was indisputably hers. But the conviction that she was also the rightful incumbent of the more glittering throne of England was by now firmly rooted in her mind.

Elizabeth Tudor, who probably knew more about the country her Stuart cousin had come back to than her cousin, had been pleased that almost as soon as Mary had landed she had managed to alienate her Scottish lords and her half-brother, James, inflame the papist haters in the shape of the formidable old John Knox, and commit a hundred petty solecisms against the touchy Scots.

Not so pleasing was the later news that Mary, not clever or experienced in government, had been shrewd enough to make herself over in a new mould and was now gradually winning her kingdom to her cause by using the only weapon at her disposal, feminine charm, and drawing as wide a distinction between herself and her Tudor cousin as possible.

Where Elizabeth ruled absolutely her ministers in the Councils, Mary sat quietly with her sewing, listening and deferring. She had denied her fondness for fine clothes, and wore sober velvets, ensuring that they covered her white bosom—in direct contrast to Elizabeth who had set the fashion in England for more and more exposure of this area of the female form.

Mary's virtue was beyond reproach, her four ladies— the four Maries—decorous daughters of Scottish lords; Elizabeth preferred to make her friends amongst the more raffish of her courtiers, and her own reputation had been sullied again and again by the liberties she allowed her gentlemen, in particular the infamous Robert Dudley.

All in all, Mary was a thorn in Elizabeth's side because, being intensely feminine herself, she recognised a competitor in this area who could play as good a game as she did.

Elizabeth moved restlessly again and this time the curtains were cautiously parted and Lady Sidney put her head in.

'May I help you, madam? Is there aught you want?'

'No. Go away.' The head was hastily withdrawn and Elizabeth went back to her thinking.

She pondered a few minutes, then thought, I believe it is that wedding that has unsettled me! George Latimar's marriage to that little nobody.

The affair had been partly engineered by herself, with the connivance of Dudley, but, strangely, on the day it had not pleased her. She had had the very definite impression that her presence and her former support were negligible; the couple were so *happy* in themselves.

Happy. Now that word needed some consideration. Was that what rubbed her? She frowned in the darkness. Why should it? She was happy, was she not? Queen of England, with the greatest nation on earth under her royal thumb, with all the riches and amusements she had dreamed of in her long years of captivity to be had at the snap of her fingers, and the love of the most handsome and charming courtier in the whole of Christendom. Her lips curved in a smile.

Dear Robert, dear Robin; how good he was to be with when he felt at ease. At court these days he gave the impression that she was withholding something from him that should be rightfully his. At Maiden Court, during their short stay, he had been a totally different person, treating her with a loving affection and no formal respect—as if he were her master and she not a queen. He had not been able to understand, when they had come back to Greenwich, that the love they had for each other did not conquer the fact that her ambition to rule her country did not allow for a consort—especially one which would have her share what was absolutely hers. 'The world is well lost for love', had been the phrase on his lips—

Now! She had heard that said before... Of course, George Latimar had said that to her when she had reprimanded him for not furthering his career by choosing a lady from noble ranks. His father, Harry, had obviously felt the same, for he too had given up a place at her father's, Henry Tudor's, side to marry his love.

Curious, thought Elizabeth, for surely power, adulation, great riches and authority should weigh more in the balance than. . .love.

Through the crack Lady Sidney had left in the curtains she could see the sinking red sun gilding her windows. It would soon be the supper hour and she must dress and make ready. Thinking of the Latimars reminded her of something else: Anne Latimar, she remembered suddenly, was to join the ranks of her waiting ladies this day.

She contemplated this with mixed feelings. She had met Latimar's daughter only properly when she had attended her brother's wedding, and had not taken to her. Too pretty, too articulate, and too slow to bend the knee—thus Elizabeth had summed up the girl.

And there was certainly no lack of ambition there! That had been all too plain in the demoiselle's manner! She would never give up the world for love—only a marquis would be good enough for her!

However, various favours were owed to Anne Latimar's parents, Elizabeth conceded, so she would welcome her. She sighed again, sat up and swept aside the velvet drapes.

CHAPTER FOUR

ANNE left Maiden Court feeling quite desolate. It was not the way she had imagined it. She should have been riding now with her mother and father. They would have had fun on the journey: her mother would have found sights along the way to comment upon and enjoy, and her father would have added his own unique charm to the proceedings. Instead, she was forced to take the dusty miles with a man she both disliked and found impossible to understand. She took a sideways glance at him.

Jack Hamilton rode easily upon his grey horse, but his manner was alert. His eyes constantly surveyed the road ahead in a calculating manner, making his companion conscious of the lonely places they passed through, for England could still be a lawless place even with the growing prosperity that a new regime had engendered. And he made no attempt at all to speak to her.

When they reached the crossroads and turned south towards the capital she said, 'Are we not to talk at all?'

Jack, who had been concentrating on the thick woodland—so convenient for bands of robbers—turned to look at her. 'I am sorry—did you wish to hold conversation?'

'It is usual, when two people are alone together.'

'Ah. . .well, please forgive me, but I am a little out of practice with such conventions—as you have already advised me.'

'But you must remember the required manners,' Anne said shortly.

It had come to her in the last few miles that she was suffering from homesickness—she who had so blithely looked forward to leaving! She was also more than apprehensive of what she would find at Greenwich.

All very well, she thought bleakly, to be full of confidence in her own dear home while entertaining others, or in the homes of neighbours who knew and respected her family. But when had she actually been anywhere, done anything, without the solid support of her family?

Never, was the answer. Before there had always been her father, her brother, her mother to help her take the leaps and bounds into any new situation. But today, on the most important day of her life, she had only Jack Hamilton! She was out of sorts and when Anne felt that way she showed it. She frowned.

Jack slowed his horse and leaned towards her. 'I have said I am sorry for my lack, Lady Anne. But your father has entrusted you to my care on this journey and I take my duties seriously.'

Anne had to admit that he had the right of it. Certainly, if old Walter had been assigned this duty he would have been equally concerned. But she could have talked to old Walter. They would have ridden together in amity; she could have discussed her fears and he would have demolished them, because he thought she was quite perfect in every way.

But Jack Hamilton did not think her perfect. Jack did not care for her; indeed he did not even like her—she was sure of that. He did not even *look* at her; when he turned in his saddle to address her his grey eyes were fixed on some point over her shoulder.

He is like a ghost; she thought, shuddering, like a half-alive man, living, breathing, but dead inside. Anne, who belonged to the warm and vibrant world, was appalled by another who could not join it.

The two horses and their riders were now almost at a standstill. To their left ran the river—for they had so far been following the Thames—and just ahead was an inn. She said, 'May we not pause a moment? I would like a cool drink and so, I think, would Jenny.' She patted her mare affectionately.

'Then by all means let us stop,' Jack said, raising his fine eyes to the sky. The weather was fair and they had made good progress. The girl at his side was a good horsewoman, he had noted appreciatively, her hands sure on the reins of her lively mare, her seat, even on rough ground, balanced and graceful. But he was eager to reach Greenwich before darkness fell. Still, a brief interval would not hurt.

The inn had no room within for lady travellers to rest and take refreshment, but the landlord indicated seats in the open overlooking the river. Anne sat and surveyed the sluggish water while Jack attended to their mounts, and she was provided with a glass of ale.

A few minutes later Jack joined her with his own mug of foaming beer in his hand. He drank, a creamy line forming on his upper lip. He brushed it away with his sleeve and began an awkward conversation about the scene around them, pointing out the row of little boys fishing from the bank.

Anne looked at him curiously. He was obviously making an effort now to entertain and amuse her and she had to give him credit for that, since he was no hand at small talk. When their mugs were refilled and the landlord had come out with a wooden platter of bread and cheese she said, 'Your own home is very different, I suspect, from the country around here. Please tell me about it.'

He thought a while, then replied, 'Yes, it is very different, as you say. The south of England is gentle; on the Scottish border it is harsh, uncompromising.'

She waited for him to go on.

'Conditions, I know, can be hard everywhere, but it is the whole of life there: the never-ending battle against the elements, the poverty, the land itself—which must be constantly placated before yielding enough food to survive.' He stopped, and gave a wry smile. 'This is probably not what you wanted to hear.'

'I am interested,' she assured him politely. 'Please go on.'

'Where I live—at Ravensglass Castle, which has been in my family since before anyone remembers—there is not the same distinction between so-called nobility and serf. Yes, I have gold and to spare, and rich furnishings and comfortable chambers, but one cannot eat French silk tapestries, and a night spent hungry in a feather bed is little different from one spent hungry on a straw pallet.

'Sooner or later even the most carefully stocked household needs supplies to replenish the store cupboard—and we can be literally cut off for months of the year. Animals, no matter how cosseted, die of disease as do their human owners. And the cold! You, I hope, have never experienced such...where a man, well clad and fortified, might venture out to see to his livestock and return minus fingers and toes—they literally snap off—'

He paused on seeing the expression on her face. 'Oh, this is not so every year—but I can remember several such winters. One Christmas I remember my mother smuggling the Yuletide pig into the castle and keeping him fat and snug before the hall fire, so that we might celebrate in style. My father was so outraged that they conducted an argument which raged for the full fourteen days of the festivities.'

'He was a Scot, your father, was he not?'

'By ancestry, yes, but his family had lived on the English side of the border for so many years that he considered himself to be of that nation. His allegiance was to the old King Henry, and mine to his children.'

Jack fell silent, his eyes on one of the fisher lads who had a fine silvery fish on his line and was attempting to bring it in. Jack got up. As the boy struggled with his flopping prize, Jack removed his cap and, leaning forward, scooped the glittering trophy into the crown and tipped it safely ashore. The boy looked up with a gappy grin and man and boy examined the bounty. The boys were not fishing for sport but for food, and this fine specimen would keep a family full fed for two days.

When Jack came back to her, Anne said thoughtfully, 'It must have displeased your father very much when you chose a lady from France to be your wife. The Scots are hand in glove with the French in their assaults on England, I understand.'

It was as if a shutter had been lowered behind Jack's grey eyes and his whole body tensed. But he only said mildly, 'Yes, well, that is as may be. Now, if you are rested enough, I think we should continue. I wish to see Greenwich before sunset.'

The remainder of the journey was spent in virtual silence. Jack answered Anne if she spoke, but in such monosyllabic terms as to be almost offensive. Anne again felt rebuffed. She supposed it had been her reference to the forbidden subject of his wife.

But goodness! she thought crossly. One would have thought he was the only one in the world to lose someone they loved. Why, she had been quite distraught five years ago when her maternal grandmother had died.

Joan de Cheyne, Bess's mother, had lived to a phenomenally old age. An indomitable old lady, she had lived with her daughter and son-in-law for years, had loved and cared for and interfered with all the Latimars. When she had passed quite peacefully away one warm summer's night after a riotous horkey supper in which she had taken full part, Anne had cried for three days—until her father had come to her chamber and told her sternly that to keep wailing against fate was to contradict the wishes of a higher authority than hers.

'It is God's will you contest,' Harry had said sternly, 'so no more of it, if you please.' Wise words, Anne had decided then, and thought now. Glancing briefly at her travelling companion's set face, she believed these words would be little comfort to him, and of course she understood that one could not compare the loss of a beloved grandmother with that of a wife and mate, but even so— Still, she wished she had not made the comment.

Their arrival at Greenwich was made just as the sky turned from blue to the shade of apple-green which told of a brilliant autumn day past and another to follow. The sun was just setting and threw its crimson glow over the two riders as they trotted into the main courtyard. Jack dismounted and helped Anne to do so.

He secured the services of a groom for their horses and ordered him to find a page immediately to take Lady Anne Latimar to her quarters.

Whatever his shortcomings, Anne thought drily, he could get things done, for within a quarter-hour she found herself in the care of Lady Allison Monterey in one of the chambers off the honeycomb of passages in the ladies' dorter. Of the royal residences Anne had only visited Windsor, and looked forward to exploring Greenwich at a later date. Just now she was anxious to meet and create a favourable impression on the women she would spend the next two years with.

There were four in her room, all her age and all from similar backgrounds: highly bred, but not of the great families. They all, in various capacities, served the Queen, but not intimately; such honour was reserved for such as the Ladies Warwick and Dacre.

The girls made her very welcome; any new face, any distraction, was desirable with the long winter months coming on. Within a few moments Anne saw the wisdom of her father's comments regarding the manner of her arrival. As she was unpacking her trunk and the others were exclaiming over her gowns—all new and in the latest fashion, as her father had insisted upon—Lady Allison said, 'Jack Hamilton brought you here, did he not? Oh, I think him most fascinating!'

'Do you?' Anne altered her look of amazement to polite enquiry.

'Indeed, we all do,' smiled Lady Frances. 'Is he a family friend, or—?' She paused delicately.

'Yes, a family friend,' Anne said firmly. 'He used to be my father's squire some years ago and he and my father have remained close. Mother and Father have seen him at various times over ten years, although I had not met him since I was a little girl. When my mother was taken ill and so could not accompany me to Greenwich, Father asked Jack to do so.'

She turned back to her trunk, lifting out a velvet cloak lined with fur which had been her parents' final gift to her a week ago. Holding the rich garment, she suffered another shock wave of homesickness.

'You will have your own maidservant who could do that for you,' Lady Jane pointed out.

'Oh, yes, of course,' replied Anne, scenting a sly criticism, 'but I thought I would do it and order my trunk removed.' She gave Jane a sweet smile. ''Tis a little cramped in here, don't you find? I am sure we all miss our own spacious homes.'

The other three looked at each other approvingly. And so it began—the endless game of scoring points. A game without winners, but which added some small spark to their lives.

They felt that Anne had already notched up a good score: she had arrived in the care of the enigmatic Hamilton, about whom speculation was rife—overtures to him many, but so far unrewarded—she had a sumptuous wardrobe, her family were well respected, and she had managed almost instantly to put little Jane in her place. She would fit in very well here.

They returned to the subject of Jack Hamilton.

'They say he has never got over his wife's death,' Clare said, with wide eyes. 'And that more than ten years since!'

'And my brother, Tom, told me that Jack has created a fantastic monument to her on his land at Ravensglass,' Allison whispered. 'The Hamilton vaults were not good enough for Marie Claire, so he built another from materials from Florence — Italian marble, and a statue at its side from the same fantastic stone.'

'Imagine the cost!' exclaimed Frances enviously. 'And all for a dead person.'

Anne continued laying her clothes in the chest indicated, a faint stirring of distaste in her mind. Whatever her thoughts on Jack Hamilton, something loyal in her nature disliked hearing his private hurt bandied about in this overheated room by these women.

'You must know all the eccentric details,' Jane prompted her. 'Do tell us.'

Anne folded the clothes neatly and closed the chest. 'I am afraid I know no details,' she said coolly, 'other than that Jack adored his wife and was desolate at her passing.'

There was an uncomfortable pause, then Clare said, 'Well, naturally, of course that must be so. . .and we all sympathise, but does it not seem to you that one cannot grieve for ever?'

Yes, it did seem so to Anne, but then she was not in a position to judge. She had never been in love, had no experience to draw upon. But one thing she did know instinctively was that she could not take part in any idle gossiping about the feelings of the grave-faced and bitter man with whom she had just shared the day. It would be a disloyalty.

'Well,' sighed Jane, 'he must come out of his ivory tower some time, and I could wish it were me who brought that state about.'

They all laughed, and, being only young and eager to enjoy themselves, began to experiment with the wealth of cosmetics on the dressing table, and chatter about other things. One full turning of the hourglass was completed, then it was time to go down to the evening meal.

The great hall at Greenwich was a huge area of smooth stone flags. At each end there was a vast hearth, lit tonight in a glory of scarlet and gold. Hundreds of candles in iron wall-sconces blazed wastefully between beaten silver plates, each a full two feet in diameter, which reflected an ever-moving picture of colour and light.

Anne sat with her room-mates, unable to eat for looking around. During her time at Windsor Castle, the year before, the Queen had only kept a small court; here at Greenwich the full complement of her courtiers was present. Anne had never seen such gowns and costumes, such fabulous jewellery or excesses of hair-dressing and decoration.

The Queen sat on a wooden platform with Dudley and William Cecil and others whom Anne did not recognise, and there could be no doubting that she was first lady in this assembly. She wore a gown of amber silk, embroidered with honey bees, the skirts wider than any other's. Around her neck a dazzlingly white ruff sewn with pearls rose a foot behind to frame her face. Anne strained her eyes to discover how this wheel of lawn was supported, for surely the weight of it must be considerable.

She whispered to Jane, 'How beautiful is Her Majesty's lace, but how, I wonder, is so much material remaining in place?'

Jane was a hearty eater. In later years she would be plump, but now, at only twenty, she was deliciously curved and feminine. Greedily consuming her portion of roast peacock, she wiped away the drops of grease from her white chin and replied, 'Oh, 'tis some Flemish

art, with something called. . .starch. Only the French
have so far perfected the art, and Her Grace has a
maid from there especially to tend her linen. Are you
not hungry?'

'Oh. . .yes.' Anne looked at the confusing array of
dishes before her. Selecting a little roast swan, she ate
it daintily; table manners had been very strict at Maiden
Court. Her father maintained that even the most lovely
woman lost beauty if seen at the board behaving like a
starving animal. But most here were, Anne noticed
disapprovingly.

She returned her eyes to Elizabeth. Her father had
given her a letter for the Queen, informing her why
he'd been unable to bring Anne personally to court,
and she had delivered it into the hands of one of her
ladies on arrival. Anne wondered if she would be duly
interviewed.

Jane had done with the savoury courses and, thirstily
swallowing two cups of wine, was trying to attract the
attention of a page with a great tray of sweetmeats.
'Mmm! Only taste one of these, Anne, dear. Her
Majesty keeps a pastry chef whose only duty is to
provide such concoctions as this.' She offered a square
of marchpane, a candied fruit placed like a dark jewel
in its centre.

'Thank you.' Absent-mindedly Anne nibbled at the
choice delicacy, but laid it down after a mouthful.
Unlike the mistress of this court she did not have a
sweet tooth.

'Lady Anne?' She looked up to find Jack Hamilton
leaning over her. 'May I escort you to the dancing
chamber? Her Grace is preparing to proceed there.'

Conscious of four pairs of interested eyes on her,

Anne said composedly, 'Thank you, Jack.' She rose and took his arm out of the hall.

'How went your first meal at Greenwich?' he enquired in the passage between the rooms.

'Quite well,' she said. 'Shall we go on in?'

They went to the door of the long chamber, filled now with dancing figures, and looked in.

'It looks a little complicated,' Jack said. 'Are you familiar with the steps?'

'My father engaged an Italian dancing master,' Anne informed him. 'I recognise all the movements.'

'Then wait for a moment and I will summon a chevalier to attend you.' Jack looked around the deserted corridor.

'No such thing,' Anne said, still holding his arm. He was the only familiar face here, she thought, reluctant to let him go. 'We will do well enough together.' She went in ahead, and he had no choice but to follow.

The steps were both unfamiliar and alien to Jack. Indeed, he had not indulged in this activity for years, but with grim determination and an instinctive grace and understanding of complex movements—mostly gained from studying warfare, which on a certain level was not unlike the stylised pattern of a dance—he held his own.

Glancing at Anne, he saw that she could be described as more than doing that. His beauty-loving eye was drawn impersonally to her swaying grace, and what did it put him in mind of? But yes, of her father's consummate skill in fencing. The years rolled back and Jack could see Harry Latimar now, turning, twisting, the light catching the silver foil in his hands, and himself a lowly squire holding his master's velvet cloak and admiring the man so much.

Long ago. Long ago, and before—Jack's heart contracted—before he had met Marie Claire. . .

He was suddenly opposite Anne and she was smiling
at him.

'You are doing *very* well, Jack,' she said happily. 'Is
it all not such fun?'

'Fun?' Jack asked bitterly. The room spun sicken-
ingly around him. 'I do not find it so.' He turned away
and left her, shouldering his way out of the crowd.
Anne stared after him.

Again! Again, this graceless man had left her
stranded on a dance-floor. She curtsied to the gentleman who had hurriedly taken Jack's place, smiling
brilliantly, then, as the dance swung into a different
rhythm, turned herself and followed the tall, silver-
haired figure out of the door, through the passageway
and out into the night beyond the palace doors. Jack
was walking quickly, but she caught up with him as she
descended the steps leading to the river.

'Jack!'

He turned, his face like stone in the moonlight.

'Lady Anne, I am sorry, I just felt suddenly that I
must have air.'

'You are rude, sir!' Anne said angrily. 'Somewhere
in your past career someone *must* have advised you
that when you invite a lady to be your partner it is
unforgivable to leave her halfway through the enterprise! Twice now you have left me.'

'I did not invite you either time,' he said gravely.
'However, yes, I admit I am in the wrong.'

His matter-of-fact statement took the wind out of
her sails. She felt a fool for chasing him out into the
night with her grievance.

She sat down abruptly on a low, mossy wall. The

night was warm, but she could feel the dampness through her thin skirts. Another attack of homesickness wrenched at her. She said wistfully, 'I do not suppose it occurred to you I might be feeling a little. . .homesick this evening?'

'Why, no, it did not.'

'Or that I might be overwhelmed by the company I find myself in, and so. . .nervous?'

'Not that either,' he assured her. 'For. . ."I have never been nervous in my life."' He quoted her words of that morning in neutral tones.

Anne hugged herself in the cool breeze blowing up from the water. The gesture, so spontaneous and childlike, was at odds with her appearance—the curled and adult hairdressing, the new and sophisticated gown.

Jack came and sat beside her. Used as she was to the two males in her family always offering comfort for all her ills, she leaned towards him and laid her head on his shoulder. He remained immobile, not putting his arm around her. After a moment she raised her head.

'I'm sorry, Jack. I know I must not trespass on your good nature in this way. On your past association with my father, I mean. But this evening I am feeling a little lost.'

How pale she is, he thought, and how small she seems beside me. But he knew that she would not be lost for long; he had not missed the dozens of admiring eyes upon her when they had danced earlier.

He said awkwardly, 'What has upset you, Lady Anne?'

'Nothing has upset me,' she said slowly. 'But the ladies in my dorter are so very confident, so well dressed and beautiful. Suddenly, I thought to myself,

Why, you are only little Anne Latimar from Kew! Not particularly beautiful or grand.'

She accompanied these words with a look full into his face. She had no thought of flirting; it was just her natural manner. She had been raised to consider men as friends and allies unless they proved otherwise, and to respond to them in an unaffected way.

In reality, she knew little of the games women played in a certain arena, but was by nature armed with the necessary weapons. At this moment she saw Jack only as a link with home; as a friend of her family and a familiar face.

Certainly, she could not have said that she liked him, and not just because he apparently did not see her as a personable female—more it was his way of standing off. Of refusing to be a part of any move to include him.

Anne had not fathomed this peculiar behaviour yet because, in her experience, everyone wanted to be liked and spent their energy in bringing this about. Jack seemed absolutely impervious to this very human conduct.

Others, she knew, had different perceptions about him. 'A sweet boy', her mother had called him. 'A good friend and the merriest boy I ever had to serve me', her father had said. 'Fascinating!' the ladies of her recent acquaintance had declared. 'Strange and unhappy', had been her brother George's summing-up, and it was this last that Anne felt most in tune with for it matched her own opinion.

Now Jack moved carefully away and stood up. He said thoughtfully and without emphasis, 'I would have thought you have all the advantages those other ladies do, for you are all the things you describe they are.'

Heavens! she thought, surprised. I believe I am being complimented! Complimented rather prosaically, it was true, but she was comforted just the same and rose with some assurance and smiled.

'Thank you again, Jack. I think I can go back into the palace now and feel less out of everything.'

'You are most welcome,' he said politely.

That was their last conversation for some weeks. The following morning Anne was summoned to the Queen's presence and advised of her duties. Elizabeth was gracious, but made sure her new lady understood that she was at court because of her parents' very special place in the monarch's affections.

'We are so sorry that Harry cannot be with us just now,' Elizabeth said sweetly, 'or your dear mother, Bess, for whom we have the utmost affection. Do we not, Robin?'

Anne was receiving her audience whilst the Queen was preparing to go hawking with Robert Dudley.

'It is as you say, madam,' Robert agreed, playing with the stout leather gauntlet that Elizabeth would wear for the sport she was about to take part in. He turned his full blue gaze on Anne. 'How was your brother when you left Maiden Court? Well, I trust?'

'George? He is quite well,' Anne said. 'At least, he is travelling at present with his new wife, but I think quite well.'

'We expect him, too, to favour us with his presence soon,' Elizabeth said. 'He is neglectful of his duty in that respect, you know.'

She gave Anne a sharp glance. Elizabeth had been prepared to show the handsome heir to Maiden Court the benefit of her favour, but George had made it all too plain that he shunned court life. These Latimars, she thought, were really no more than rural squires, but they managed to make an indelible mark on others more exalted, without ever having held high office or performed any particular great service for England's throne.

Her father, Henry, had loved Harry Latimar for thirty years; she herself had been more than enamoured with his son. Anne had her full share of this attraction, but Elizabeth liked her no better on this inspection than she had previously. The girl was beautiful in a striking and unusual way, and well dressed and elegant. But what was so desirable in a man—in Harry and George Latimar—was somehow not acceptable in the female member of the family.

Too much black hair, Elizabeth thought suddenly. It was rippling like dark silk in the sun shining into the chamber, and she especially disliked that hair colour on a woman. Why? Because her mother, Anne Boleyn, had had just that generous pouring of ebony hair, and those same dark eyes—for Anne's, so dark a blue, appeared black when she was discomfited, as she was now—and the same indefinable charm of manner.

Indeed, the little Latimar wench had been named for Henry Tudor's second queen, who had been disgraced and beheaded. Elizabeth's heart trembled in remembrance. However. . . She straightened her back and lifted her fur-lined cloak from a chair.

'You may go now,' she said to Anne. 'Robin, the game awaits us.' Robert opened the door and Elizabeth disappeared.

Anne crept out of the bedchamber feeling about three inches high. Elizabeth, she thought resentfully, had not been so distant whilst at Maiden Court! Oh, no, when the Kew manor had entertained her she had been sweet-faced and gracious, playing up to her host and dancing practically cheek to cheek with George!

She was in the passage now and looked up and down it doubtfully. She was not yet accustomed to the palace routine and had no idea where she should be at this hour. As she stood undecided, Robert Dudley came hastening back down the corridor and paused with his hand on the Queen's door.

'Lady Anne? I have been sent to gather up some important papers that Her Grace left behind. Do you come in and help me search for them.'

Anne followed him in.

'I thought 'twas to be hawking for you this day,' she said. Robert was looking through the piles of documents on one of the tables.

'What? Oh, yes, that is so. But after we are done with that we take up the cares of government again.' He gave Anne a laughing glance. 'The lady never ceases her work, you know. Ah—I think I have found what I am looking for... But no, this is something else again. Come, lady, please help me.'

'What exactly are you looking for?'

'The details of the projected marriage between young Fanshawe and his cousin Lizzie Butler,' Robert said distractedly. 'There is a great deal of revenue to the Crown at stake— Oh, really, I am no clerk!' He tossed up the papers and they fell in disarray on the vivid rug.

Anne had found a separate cache of parchments tied with a slim ribbon on a table by the window. She unrolled them and ran her eyes over the writing. 'I think I have it here,' she said, holding one of the stiff pages out.

Robert came and stood close to her whilst he examined it. He gave her his wonderful smile. 'You have found it indeed! Well done.'

They were so close that Anne could see how blue his eyes were, how dazzlingly white the surround to the pupil, and the faint smear of golden down on his cheekbones. He was very good-looking, she thought, but that was not his appeal. It was the aura of power, of knowing who he was, that was so attractive.

Jack Hamilton, too, had that aura, she thought suddenly, although two more disparate men would have been hard to imagine. Finding her eyes fixed on him, Robert smiled again.

'Why do you not join us today?' he asked, rolling the paper he held and pushing it into his sleeve. 'We are to hawk at the Monterey manor and enjoy their hospitality for the rest of the day.'

'I could scarcely do that,' she said primly. 'I am not dressed for riding and Her Majesty has not invited me.'

'Oh, invited...' Robert dismissed this convention with a wave of his hand. 'Elizabeth has no ladies to attend her today—she has allowed them to spend the day in getting ready for the masque planned for tomorrow night. I think she should have at least one in support.

'And dressed for riding? How long would it take you to rearrange that?' His tone became intimate and teasing. '*I* would like you to come...Anne.'

'If you think Her Grace would be ill attended if I did not,' she said gravely, 'then I will hurry now to change and join you in the stable-yard.'

In her chamber, hastily shucking off her gown and reaching for her habit, she knew a moment of doubt. The Queen had looked so disfavourably upon her earlier, she was quite capable of rescinding Dudley's invitation and sending her waiting lady back into the palace with a sharp word.

Well, what if she does? Anne thought rebelliously. I have been requested to join the party by her— What was the word? she wondered, pinching some colour into her cheeks before the glass, scooping up her hat and leaving the room. Consort he would like to be, of course, husband and equal ruler of England. Meanwhile, Elizabeth Tudor professed to love him, but treated him like a lackey. What proper man would relish such a situation?

Anne ran lightly down into the courtyard where the royal party was gathered and cursied before the Queen. Elizabeth frowned.

'Lady Anne? What do you here?'

'I asked her to come,' Leicester said easily. 'I was concerned that you had no lady to care for you, Majesty.'

'I see. . .' The Queen glanced at him. Robin had a penchant for admiring her ladies, some of whom became enamoured with him, to the sorrow of both parties. But, Elizabeth thought, with this girl he would get no further than admiration, and if it made him happy— She shrugged. 'Very well, let us get on. Be sure this lady is well mounted.' This last was directed at one of the hovering grooms.

Well mounted she was, on a spirited cream mare who was a handful even for a competent horsewoman. Anne concentrated on subduing this prancing bundle of horseflesh, but missed nothing of the beauty of the day and the country they rode through.

She loved autumn more than any other season—the vivid colours of the leaves drifting from the trees, the sharp clean air with its scents of peat and woodsmoke intensified as at no other time of year.

Others, her mother among them, preferred the spring, with its buds and green shoots and hopefulness, but Anne was constantly in a state of hopefulness; she always had the feeling that there was something new and good around the corner.

It was but a short distance to the Monterey estate and the host, John Monterey, a handsome man in his sixties, came hastening out to greet them. Close on his heels were his two sons, Ralph, the older, and Thomas, his younger brother, who spied Anne immediately and came to help her dismount.

'Anne!' he exclaimed delightedly. 'I had no idea I would have the pleasure of receiving you into my home today.'

'Thank you, Tom,' Anne said, looking anxiously towards the Queen. Would they go into the manor for refreshment? Should she take the Queen's cloak and offer to escort her to the close room?

But no; horn beakers of mulled wine were being handed round by the liveried servants and drunk there and then in the drive. Then the party walked through the copse of beech trees to a wide field.

Of all sports, falconry was Anne's least favourite. She hated the cruel birds which were kept hooded until the game began, then uncovered so that they could soar up into the sky where all too soon their close-set, sinister eyes would fall upon a tender partridge or wild duck fluttering, hover a moment, then bring the more gentle bird down, gripped in their iron talons.

Bred for murder, Anne thought distastefully, with no other function but to kill. She stood in the damp grass with set face and torn heart while everyone else enjoyed themselves immensely.

It was an unusually good day. Elizabeth's bird, Cardinal, was personally responsible for the capture of several wild duck, assorted pheasants, and—the greatest prize of all—a heron flying overland from its nest on the Thames in search of food for its family.

The Queen became quite shrill in her triumph. All the Tudors were cruel, or so Anne had heard her father say, in large or small ways. Today was a small, and acceptable, demonstration of cruelty, Anne thought, but she did not admire it.

At last the group walked, with their bloody count, back to the manor, and not a moment too soon. The sky had darkened and there was rain on the fresh wind and thunder in the distance.

'I think you did not enjoy that,' Tom said to Anne when they were seated about the fire in the hall with wine and cakes.

'You are right,' Anne admitted. There had been no need for her to fulfil any duty to the Queen once inside the house. The Monterey servants were smoothly efficient and had swept Elizabeth away to remove her bulky outer clothing and muddy boots, rearrange her hair and bring her down again to the hall to be enthroned in the best and most comfortable chair. She was now enjoying the good wine and sweetmeats, surrounded by her gentleman courtiers. If she had had her way, actually, she would have had no women about her at any time.

'But I know,' Anne went on, 'that I am deficient in this respect, for it seems that unless something is dead no enjoyment can be gained. It is the odds I object to, I think,' said the daughter of a gambler with a rueful

smile. 'They are always so uneven—the bear opposed
to a dozen dogs, the wild, darting forest creature
against hounds and men with cold steel, the defenceless
feathered bird no match for another with sharp
talons— Well, I am a squeamish invididual, am I not?'

Squeamish? Tom thought sentimentally. No, not
that. Rather so tender and lovely that her very feminine
side was uppermost in all her thoughts.

Tom had been in love with Anne for a whole year.
Her brother, George, was one of his closest friends—
he had stood usher at his wedding only six weeks since.
Her parents appeared prepared to be kind to him but
he had made no headway at all with her. She was like
the will-o-the-wisp seen by country folk on a sparkling
frosty night: always out of reach. One could not pin her
down, reduce her to ordinary status, catch and restrain
her in anything so mundane as a promise of marriage.
So thought Tom, who had proposed to Anne four times
in the last twelve months. Now he had her in his home
for a brief while, and was sure to be seeing her each
day for all of her years at court, and he hoped for some
resolution to the longing he had been enduring for so
long.

Well aware of Tom's thoughts, Anne sighed
inwardly. She supposed she should be flattered that
Tom, and so many of the other men who had courted
her, had been faithful for so long. But she was not. She
felt that he—they—ought to see as she did that if no
spark had been kindled by now it would not suddenly
be ignited.

Her eyes roved around the room, observing the rich
furnishings, the abundant silver, the general air of
prosperity. Tom Monterey was well-known to be the
son of a 'warm' father, and the Earl had made it clear

that his younger son would not suffer in terms of wealth and estate when he was gone. 'A very fine prospect', her father had said to her after Tom had declared his suit, and Anne had to agree that he was, but he was not what she wanted.

Her eyes alighted on Tom's brother, the legal inheritor of the Monterey title and this fine mansion she was seated in. She looked at him curiously.

Ralph, it was said, was something of a disappointment to the Monterey family. Certainly, she thought, he was in looks a young man to be proud of, very much the image of his handsome father and, since the Queen had shown him so much favour this day, obviously not lacking in charm either. She said, 'I have not met your older brother, Tom; perhaps you will introduce me later?'

'Oh...Ralph? Yes, of course I will do that. He is home in disgrace at the moment and I am surprised that Father allowed him to join the activities today. I expect Her Grace asked for him—she has always had a liking for him.'

'Disgrace? Why?' Anne accepted more of the excellent wine offered to her, although she knew she would not drink it.

'He is an inveterate gambler,' Tom answered heavily. 'He was sent on an important errand for my family, an errand which involved paying a large sum of money to a merchant acting for my father. Along the way Ralph fell in with a card game and—poof!—the gold vanished overnight.' Tom managed to look both disapproving and a full twenty years older than his age.

'Dear me.' Anne raised her eyebrows, but smiled a little. She had a soft spot for charming gamblers, for had not her darling father been the most reckless

gambler of his day before acquiring a happy marriage
and a much loved home to steady him?

She looked at Ralph with more attention, and pres-
ently he turned his head and found her eyes on him.
Excusing himself from the Queen, he came to the fire
and Tom rose to introduce him to Anne. She held out
her hand and Ralph bowed over it, holding it a little
longer than was necessary.

'Lady Anne Latimar! How delightful to meet you at
last! I have heard a great deal about you from my
brother.' Whilst Tom reseated himself, Ralph remained
standing, one hand resting on the hearth-shelf. 'I met
your brother two years ago at Richmond. I must say
you are uncannily alike.'

'We are twins, sir. It is unusual for boy and girl twins
to be so similar in looks, but so it is with us.' Anne
smiled up at him. 'But there I fear the resemblance
ends—George is the clever one.'

Thank God for that, Ralph thought. He had not
liked George Latimar at all—a very superior young
man who had, he remembered, been quite unnaturally
moral within the riotous life of the young male courtiers
at Richmond.

The plaque above the hearth at Abbey Hall was
carved with the Monterey cypher—that of a fox and
rose, for it had been the first Henry Tudor who had
conferred the earldom after Ralph's great-grandfather
had made a present of his hunting lodge to the King.
Ralph's hand caressed the pointed ears of the grinning
animal, smoothed the petals of the flower, as he contemplated the girl in the light of the leaping fire.

A lovely girl, he thought, with a delectable shape
and a charming smile. Pity indeed that Tom had seen
her first.

Anne's thoughts were also complimentary. Tom was tall and fair and blue-eyed, but beside his brother he seemed a blurred copy, for Ralph was stunningly blond, several inches taller and his eyes ice blue in an exceptionally fair-skinned face.

Elizabeth interrupted this moment of mutual admiration by joining them. Tom rose to his feet and Ralph straightened attentively.

'Lady Anne,' the Queen said sternly, 'the Earl has kindly invited me to stay here this night. You may not have noticed, but there is a rainstorm raging without and he refuses to allow me to risk a wetting. Pray despatch a note immediately to Greenwich requesting whatever I may need for my unexpected visit. You need not ask for any of my ladies to come: I shall be well attended by you, I am sure.'

With that, Elizabeth, who hated any other woman to command the attention of two personable males when she herself was available, turned away.

Anne stood up uncertainly. 'Don't worry, Anne,' Tom said kindly. 'Her Majesty often stays here. I will arrange for the message to be sent and at Greenwich they will know exactly what to send. What should I ask to be included for yourself?'

'I think your sister would know best.'

'It is already done, then,' Tom smiled.

'I'll go up and see to Her Grace's comfort in the bedchamber. Where—?'

Tom beckoned to a footman. 'Seton will show you where.'

Anne followed the stately figure up the stairs, and the brothers were left alone in the firelight.

'I must say I admire your taste,' Ralph said. 'Have

you furthered your cause at all since last we spoke of
it?'

'No. Anne is as hard to get to the starting line as any
of your frisky racehorses. But I have my hopes.'

Ralph looked into his glass. He was fond of Tom;
they had played together, fought each other as children,
then each gone their separate ways on the road to
knighthood travelled by all boys of the nobility. When
they had achieved this state, they had come together
again and found little in common.

Both granted good looks and deep purses, Ralph
had, as his sire put it, 'gone to the bad' and discovered
the lure of the gambling tables and the charms of the
opposite sex. Tom had fallen prey to neither of these
distractions and was as upright and exemplary a sprig
of English manhood as could be possible.

But Ralph remembered their shared youth and
wished he could offer the benefit of some of his new
experience; then he would have said, Forget her,
brother, she is not for you. I know women well enough
by now, and had she one thought in her head of a
romantic nature I would know it.

It was a shame all round that she had not, Ralph
thought, for she was both beautiful and wealthy. But
there it was, she was his brother's choice, although
obviously still not engaged in her emotions. Ralph had
known that in the instant he had approached her—no
lady gave that open-handed glance if she was.

He compromised by saying, "'Tis early days yet, Tom.
How stand you with her parents? I have heard that
Harry and Bess Latimar are quite eccentric as regards
their children.'

'They are indeed,' Tom confided. 'I have never met
a more liberal couple. George was allowed to choose

his bride from amongst the common people. Judith was, I believe, their younger son's nursemaid before elevated to the state of a future countess.'

Ralph raised his eyebrows. 'Indeed? Well, then, they should look upon you almost with relief.' He laughed and, putting out a long arm, embraced his brother. 'Tonight should be merry in any event. The Queen is out for some fun and we shall provide it here at Abbey Hall, eh, Tom? Come, put aside your cares and let us present a united Monterey front.'

his bride from amongst the common people. Judith
was, I believe, their younger son's unmarried before
elevated to the state of a future countess.

Ralph raised his eyebrows. 'Yes? Well, then, they
should look upon that union with relief.' He laughed
and reached out a hand ...... embraced his brother

CHAPTER FIVE

WHEN Anne eventually went to bed that night she had
fallen in love. Completely and irrevocably and for ever.
She had been given a small chamber adjoining the
Queen's larger one; when Elizabeth had finally been
settled for the night, Anne slipped into bed, drew the
curtain and hugged herself in the darkness.

Ralph! Magical name, magical person. All the years
she had been fending off this man or that he had been
on the same earth waiting for her. 'This is the one', her
brother had said about his love, Judith, and now she
could at last say the same.

She thought it had been love at first sight. Surely
when he had crossed the floor to her that afternoon,
with the rain lashing against the windows and the
lightning flashing across the room, she had known
then? But she had been certain during the long meal
which had begun as darkness fell and had lasted three
hours.

The Queen had been seated, naturally, at the head
of the table, with the Earl on her right and his lady on
her left. Anne had been put halfway down the board
and Tom had made sure he was beside her. But Ralph
had been opposite, the candlelight glinting on his hair,
blue eyes gleaming.

Anne had scarcely been able to keep her eyes off
him; in an inexplicable way he was both familiar and
excitingly a stranger. The familiarity was explained by
a habit Ralph shared with her father: they both had a

78

trick of turning the jewel in their left ear when listening intently to another's conversation.

The first time Anne had noticed him doing this, she had smiled involuntarily at him across the laden table and he had responded by dropping one of his clear-cut eyelids. Another habit of Father's, Anne had thought delightedly, and from thence had begun to look for more similarities.

They were there! Ralph was good-looking in an unusual way; he was very tall and thin and clean-shaven—almost all men these days had full beards, and Anne had often heard her mother tease her husband about his love affair with the sharp toilette knife.

Ralph was charming too; the Queen spent much of the meal directing laughing comments down the table at him, but he was also oddly dignified, never appearing to be overawed by her attention. How many times had Anne observed Harry Latimar combine respect with dignity. When the meal at last came to an end and the company stood about the fire, Anne was drawn like a magnet to Ralph's side.

He accepted her presence without comment, widening the circle and ensuring that she was given wine, and including her in the discussion.

'How long will you be at court, Lady Anne?' he asked later, when the Queen had been given Lady Monterey's lute and persuaded to sing, and her audience were seated in easy chairs.

'For as long as Her Majesty commands,' Anne replied. 'She has a great talent, has she not?' Elizabeth was singing a selection of popular songs, her sweet husky voice dominating the hall. She was a very accomplished performer. 'And not above entertaining her subjects.

'All women love to show off,' Ralph said dismissively. 'And she is but a woman, you know.'

'That is a strange comment!' Anne exclaimed. 'Most women could not begin to live the life she does—why, I could never do that, and she is but a few years older.'

'Thank God you could not,' Raph said lazily. 'If all women were to wake up one morning and wish to run Englishmen's lives, where would Englishmen be?'

Anne frowned, then laughed. 'Oh, but you are teasing me! I am sure you admire her as much as I do.'

'Do you? Admire her? Why? I could wager that she would change places with you in a moment, sweet Anne. What is there in life for her, after all? Dull conferences on the state of England, fat and boring advisers pulling at her sleeves: You must do this, madam! You must do that! And her never knowing who is friend or foe to her, never knowing if any man is seeking her company because she is just Elizabeth, or the Queen of England. Whereas you—'

'Whereas I?' Anne asked, her heart pulsing in her throat.

Ralph leaned towards her, so closely that she could have sworn that he must hear the beating of her heart. 'Whereas you could never, ever be in any doubt that the man by your side is in terrible danger of falling in love with your great drowning pools of dark eyes, your black silken hair, and the distracting little dimple which appears just here—' he touched her face with one long finger '—when you grant him the favour of your lovely smile.'

Anne, her breath constricted, looked away and found Tom's eyes on her from his seat the other side of the hearth. She flushed. Ralph, following her eyes, asked casually, 'Tell me, Anne, is there any…arrangement between yourself and my brother? He loves you, I know. May I know if you return the sentiment?'

'No. No, I do not.' She took a painful breath. 'Tom is my friend, but nothing more. Why do you ask?'

Ralph leaned back in his chair. She really was, he thought, a lovely creature—why, her response to his touch was quite delightful... 'Why? Come, Anne, I think it must be obvious why.'

Anne, lit like a torch by his words, settled back into her own chair. He feels as I do! she thought exultantly. Ah, we are meant to be, made for each other. Poor Tom, with his devoted eyes, poor Elizabeth with the long years ahead of nothing—why, she could not even acknowledge the man she loved—poor every other soul in this beautiful country! For I am in love, she thought. At last!

After Elizabeth's recital the tables were laid for cards. Lord Monterey cast an anxious eye upon his eldest son, but Ralph had no thought of playing deep tonight. His thoughts were fixed on Anne Latimar. As she had felt some sort of cataclysmic position of the stars when they met, so had he.

Tom's girl? his mild inner conscience asked dutifully. But no; for hadn't Tom himself declared that she had no fancy for him? And hadn't Anne said that he was a friend and no more? A very suitable girl in every way, Ralph decided. Lovely, and rich to boot.

This last was quite a critical issue for Ralph Monterey. Money he had, of course, but only at his father's discretion. When the Earl was gone his older son would be very wealthy, but at the moment his father held the purse strings and it was getting increasingly harder to get him to loosen them.

Ralph wanted for no luxury: his horses, his clothes,

his jewels were paid for without question. But the Earl would no longer give him large sums of cash simply to carry in his purse. All too frequently that money would cross the card table, be lost at the cock pits, or go rolling away with a pair of dice.

Ralph sighed now to think how dull life was without the joy of gambling. It had been so long since he had sat down at the tables with that unexplainable thrill of anticipation, for he considered himself an honourable man and would not offer his marker without funds to cover it.

His recent adventure, from which he had been lucky to escape with his life when his stern father had been apprised of the details, had been such a *sure* thing. Six wealthy merchants on the road to Dover, all amateurs in a sport he excelled at, but still he had been bested! And for the last time! his father had declared. 'Stay home awhile, my son,' he had also said, 'and learn some responsibility.' This gathering tonight had been the first small piece of fun he had had in a twelvemonth.

His eyes moved to his father now, sitting with an attentive expression as he watched Elizabeth. He was a hard man, Ralph mused; all the Montereys were—even young Tom with his simple nature—and most of them warlike as well.

But I have broken that mould, he thought, in spite of all efforts to the contrary.

Eight years ago the Earl had sent his older son to serve in the north under that most phlegmatic of all the Queen's commanders, Hamilton, and that had been the unhappiest phase in Ralph's life.

Presented with a tall, able boy, it should have been possible for a garrison famed for producing crack officers to make something special of a Monterey, but it had failed dismally. Within a year both Jack Hamilton and Ralph had agreed that he should go home and try another career. It had been the only point of agreement between them, and Ralph would not forgive Hamilton for the report he had made to the Earl on his heir's shortcomings.

'What are you thinking of so seriously?' Anne asked him, feeling that every moment he took his attention from her was a moment lost.

'That I might persuade my father to allow me to rejoin the court at Greenwich,' he said smoothly.

It would have been his next thought, he assured himself, for the idea had been forming in his mind all evening: here was a highly suitable wife, who would fulfil even his father's high ideals, and he wished to lose no time in setting the marriage machine in motion. He believed he would tackle the Earl that very night, indicating that he felt a mutual attraction had been established and it would be foolish not to be with Anne at court for fear that another, more determined gentleman would offer for her.

John Monterey had said several times that he wished that Ralph would look about for a wife, a steadying influence, an anchor, and now he was inclined to agree. This year he would be twenty-six years old, time enough for settling down.

'He might even allow me to accompany you,' he added to Anne, giving her the benefit of his attractive smile.

'Oh, that would be splendid,' Anne said breathlessly. And she had been making herself miserable for an hour at the thought of leaving him here! 'Shall I speak with him too?'

Ralph said, amused. 'Why should you do that?'

'Oh, come, Ralph,' she returned mischievously. 'I think you must know why.'

He laughed, then sobered, his eyes on Elizabeth. 'It really depends on Her Majesty. My father requested that I be released from my duties with her a year ago, and she agreed. To reverse her decision might be difficult.'

'I don't think it will be. I have noticed Her Grace is very partial to you.'

'You noticed that, did you?' he asked teasingly. 'That seems a little proprietorial of you, darling.'

Anne gave him a very straight look. 'In my family,' she said sternly, 'we do not bandy about endearments unless they are sincerely meant.'

'I assure you I am absolutely sincere,' he said. Inwardly, he raised his eyebrows. Harry Latimar's daughter accused him of insincerity? Those who knew the folklore of the Tudor court might have found some reason to laugh in that, for Anne's father had been legendary in the field of feminine seduction! Ralph was sure that he had showered a veritable snowstorm of insincere endearments upon ladies in his time.

However, Ralph also knew that Latimar's wife, Bess, was known for her prim ways; perhaps her daughter took after her. Ralph had nothing against that—he wanted his wife to be as pure and modest as was suitable for a future countess. But before any of this could happen he must talk first to his brother and then to his father.

When the ladies rose to retire and the gentlemen drifted into the parlour for a final glass, Ralph laid a hand on Tom's shoulder. 'Come out with me a moment, Tom. The rain has stopped and I wish to talk to you.'

Abbey Hall was graced with very formal gardens. So

much of the ground on which the house was built had surrounded the original monastic abbey and was consequently paved and walled to accommodate the stone.

'A fine night,' commented Ralph, turning the emerald in his ear and considering how best he could approach this.

'What is it you wish to say?' Tom asked, leaning against one of the grim cedars which stood sentinel to the manor.

'I wished to speak of Anne Latimar,' Ralph answered, then paused.

When his brother said no more, Tom said hesitatingly, 'I think I have seen how it is with you two tonight. I must say I take it hard that you could not resist adding the girl I care for to your list of conquests.'

'It was not like that,' Ralph said soothingly. 'But you said yourself she has no feeling for you of that kind, and she confirmed that to me earlier. I am sorry, Tom, but between you and me there is no need to mince words.'

Tom rubbed his palm over the smooth bark. Cedars were known as trees of Lebanon, and this fine specimen had been brought from that country by a crusading ancestor. What Ralph said was quite true, he knew, but had no desire to hear it.

He said, 'That may be so, but if I were in your shoes I would not have further made my cause hopeless. One does not do that to a friend, a brother, or so I believe. However, since you have raised the subject, what exactly are your intentions? She is no light girl, you know.'

'You need not tell me that! My intentions are, for once, strictly honourable. But first I felt I must be frank about the matter to you.'

Tom contemplated his brother in silence. It might be so—Ralph was no liar. But he was also quite wrong for Anne. Tom, despite his outward show of being simple, was actually an intuitive man. Anne had no love for him, very well, but he could not help but feel that she was making a grave error in fixing on Ralph.

He said abruptly, 'How much have her obviously comfortable circumstances effected this sudden attraction?'

Ralph laughed uncomfortably. 'You do like to call a spade an instrument for digging in the ground with, don't you, Tom? But I take your point. Certainly I would not be considering Anne as my future wife unless she were wealthy, and with the expectations of even greater wealth. Her father is rich, both Anne and her brother have unbreakable ties with present and future monarch—'

'What makes you think that?' Tom asked doubtfully.

'I know it,' Ralph said a little shamefacedly. 'Do you remember when I was sent home from the north in disgrace? And then attached for a time to William Cecil's household? Cecil was at that time adviser to Queen Mary, and now is the same to Elizabeth.

'Anyway, being handy with brain and pen, when in his employ I was assigned to catalogue the Crown's commitments. Amongst the papers left attached to old King Henry's will and testament—their content to be honoured by all his heirs in perpetuity—there was one making provision for Latimar's children—at least those two already in existence.

'Tom, Henry made provision for those fortunate children in the most extraordinary way! Any debt they incurred was to be settled immediately, any trouble they might find themselves embroiled in was to be instantly taken care of— In truth, Tom, I could not believe my eyes when I read this paper! Two more privileged human beings never roamed English earth.'

'You should not speak of it!' Tom exclaimed involuntarily. 'George, I believe, would be immune to such a guardian to his fate, but Anne... 'Twould make her quite irresistible to any suitor. And for all the wrong reasons.'

'I would never speak of it to any other,' Ralph assured him. 'But...knowing of the covenant does help me, naturally.'

'Yes, it would do,' Tom said ironically.

'So?' Ralph asked. 'I have stated my case honestly to you, brother. What have you to say?'

Tom looked out over the view beyond the gardens. Moon-dappled and fertile acres. If he had turned his head he would have seen the house, tranquil and beautiful, in which he had been born. But all this was destined to belong to Ralph. And so, apparently, was the girl he had set his heart on.

'What can I say? Except good luck in your endeavours.'

Anne returned to Greenwich Palace at the side of Ralph Monterey. The journey there was very different from the one she had recently completed in the care of Jack Hamilton. Along the road from Abbey Hall there were no awkward silences, no friction of personalities, only a shared harmony. She would remember that short ride all her life!

At the entrance to the palace's middle courtyard, Ralph sprang down from his horse and offered his arm to Elizabeth. Under the irritated eyes of Leicester, she allowed him to help her dismount and walked majestically inside. Ralph then turned to Anne and they went in together. In the small hall they looked at each other.

'We are to be together under this roof for an indefinite time, sweetheart,' Ralph murmured.

'I know,' Anne said breathlessly. 'I am so happy, Ralph. No woman has ever been so content as I at this moment.'

'Darling,' Ralph said. 'Oh—am I allowed to so address you?'

'You are. Now and. . .for always.'

Ralph hesitated. He had spoken with his father the previous night about Anne and had received an enthusiastic response. But, the Earl had said carefully, no further move in the matter would be possible until he had spoken with her father.

He and Harry Latimar had been young together in Henry Tudor's court. Since then Latimar had been absent from court circles, but had been recently honoured with an earldom by the present sovereign.

John Monterey was keen that the projected match should proceed according to etiquette. He had agreed that Ralph should go to Greenwich and spend time with the girl, but had adjured his son not to commit further until the two families had arranged the affair suitably. If the Queen was interested, then it was only politic to go slowly.

As Ralph hesitated, sharp steps sounded on the narrow stone staircase winding down behind the kitchen quarters and Jack Hamilton paused at the side door and bowed, then came to them.

'Lady Anne. Welcome back to Greenwich.'

'Oh. . .thank you, Jack. Do you know Lord Monterey?'

'I do. How are you, Ralph?'

'Well enough, Jack. We do not often see you at court.'

'I am here for a short while only—before taking Her Majesty back to Ravensglass.'

'Ah, yes, I have heard of this expedition. How goes it these days on the border? Still repelling the wild Scots?' His tone was that of a sophisticate for a man of action, but he was inevitably reminded of his time at Ravensglass—that God-forsaken place! During his tour there, there had been troublous times and the castle had been under constant fire...

Jack smiled grimly. He, too, remembered Ralph at Ravensglass. A likely boy, but no fighter, and he had been glad indeed to be relieved of his presence.

'I hear that madam's royal cousin is now upon the unstable Scottish throne,' Ralph said conversationally. 'For how long, one wonders?'

'*I* do not wonder,' Jack said gravely. 'I leave politics to politicians. I bid you good evening.' He bowed again to them both and, moving swiftly, stepped out into the gathering dusk.

Ralph laughed. 'What an uncomfortable man he is! And you had to suffer his company from Kew, you poor sweet.' Insufferable man! he thought privately. Every reprimand he had been dealt at Ravensglass came back to Ralph in full detail.

Anne frowned a little. ''Twas no hardship... He and my father are great friends, you know.'

'I know.' Ralph flicked idly at the dust on his gleaming sleeve. 'I cannot imagine what they have in common, can you? Jack is poor entertainment and your father, I have heard tell, the reverse.'

She was radiant again. No wonder she loved the

handsome man beside her—he even had the perfect
taste to compliment the other man she loved.

Ten days passed in a dream for Anne. As was usual
when the Queen planned any journey away from the
nucleus of her courtiers, she spent her days with them
indulging in as many frivolous pursuits as possible. The
northern provinces she was bound for were always
rather staid and worthy, very different from the company she surrounded herself with in the capital. Each
night at Greenwich saw a fresh entertainment: masques, plays, special performances of every variety.
Anne enjoyed everything.

Ralph was constantly at her side and she fell in love
a little more every day. The ladies of her dorter were
envious of her: Ralph Monterey, whom so many had
tried to permanently net and been disappointed, was
apparently quite smitten with a girl who had been at
court for less than two weeks! Anne's stock soared and
she was much sought after for private and public
gatherings alike.

However, an interview with the Queen on the last
day of September brought this idyll to an abrupt halt.

Thinking she had been summoned to discuss the last,
and most ambitious of the masques the day before
Elizabeth was due to leave, Anne came confidently
into the bedchamber and curtsied. She and the Queen
had become almost friendly over these affairs—Anne
was imaginative and always full of ideas, and her
sovereign must always be the most spectacular lady in
the hall.

Elizabeth laid down the book she had been reading.

'Lady Anne—pray be seated.'

Anne spread her silk skirts. She smiled timidly, for

however intimate the Queen became over their discussions of dress and fancy dress she was never less than a lady to be deferred to at all times. Bess Latimar's advice on this had been sound and to the point, for Elizabeth *was* always right and no one dared to contradict her in any way.

Elizabeth fixed her waiting lady with a penetrating look. Anne had changed subtly in the last month, acquiring a new and glossy perfection. Elizabeth had no objection to this—all her ladies were required to be impeccably turned out and up to the very minute in matters of dress and hairdressing.

Even so, Anne Latimar was almost incadescent in her aura. The reason for this Elizabeth rightly attributed to one source: the girl was in love, and with Ralph Monterey. The Queen did not even object to this; she believed that every maid should have a Ralph in their lives at some time, and there was no danger that anything untoward would occur—Bess Latimar would have brought her daughter up correctly.

But the pair were too obvious in their courtship! Nothing solid had been arranged yet and it was unseemly for two such favoured families to be making a link before she herself had sanctioned it! However, she said mildly, 'I have been sitting here musing on which ladies I intend taking to Ravensglass. It is not an easy decision.'

Anne looked suitably concerned. No, it would not be. Who attained intimate service to attend the monarch was a constant bone of contention amongst the ladies. The coming trip had been discussed at length between the high-born ladies-in-waiting for weeks now—not so much in Anne's circle, for they did not look for such favour, but they were aware of it and had even laid bets on the outcome. Anne waited for the Queen to continue speaking.

'As I say,' Elizabeth went on, 'a very difficult decision, but now my mind is made up. My Lord Hamilton has expressed the wish that the party will be small; easier, he insists, for our security to be maintained, and I would not argue with one who knows his business as well as he. So I will take only four ladies with me: Lady Warwick, Lady Dacre, Lady Fitzroy, and. . .yourself.'

Anne was astounded. She had never considered such an eventuality! Why, she had been in the service of the Queen for a mere two weeks! She had no claim to such an honour. Also, she did not want to go! Leave Greenwich, where the very walls vibrated with her happiness? Leave Ralph, the reason for this happiness? No, it could not be!

She said faintly, 'But, madam, I fear I have no possible right to such distinction. The other ladies more closely associated with you. . .more deserving—'

'No right?' Elizabeth raised her finely plucked eyebrows. '*I* decide, lady, who has rights in this place—or any other in my realm. Am I to understand that you do not wish to attend your queen?'

Anne flushed brilliantly. She swallowed. 'No, madam,' she said quietly. 'You know that is not so. Why, I, as any other, would follow you to the ends of the earth, if you so commanded.' She raised her dark blue eyes.

Dear me, thought Elizabeth, amused. The Latimar look! All Harry's children could produce it, even little Hal, who had sone so when reprimanded by her at his brother's wedding feast for behaving in too boisterous a fashion. It sat oddly on Anne's pretty face, and the

Queen was taken aback. But she was queen here, and said, 'Then pray leave us now and make ready.'

Anne rose and curtsied and left the room with dignity. This dignity was, however, impaired in the passage outside when she stamped her foot in frustration, and after, when she entered her bedchamber, tore off her jewelled cap and flung it onto her bed saying, 'I am to go north with Her Majesty!' The dramatic disclosure brought a chorus from her friends, who had been busy making ready for the evening.

'*You* are to go?' Jane said incredulously. 'Why, you fortunate creature!'

'But why you?' exclaimed Frances.

'This will set the cat amongst the pigeons,' said Clare. 'I have heard that Lady Wilson and Lady Simons are at each other's throats over the whole affair.' All four girls looked at Anne with an unflattering amazement.

Anne leaned to retrieve her cap. It was shirred silk sewn with garnets and had been made by her mother. Anne could see Bess now with the pretty thing in her hands. She recovered herself; it would not do to let her mother down.

'I am sure I don't know,' she said ruefully, 'why Her Majesty should so honour me, and I must confess I am scared to death by it!'

Her words touched the feminine nerve in her sisters. Dear Anne, they thought, she really has no idea of the stupendous honour involved in this. No ambitious thought!

The next hour was spent in supervising the packing of Anne's trunk. There were many generous offers of items to be included, and much and varied advice was given. Through it all Anne could only think, What of Ralph?

Their relationship had marched forward in a quite marvellous way in the last weeks, but was still fragile, she felt. At no time had he ever intimated that it was to be permanent. And now she must leave him in this place, where there were so many distractions and so many *women*, without being sure of him.

Why had he not spoken? His father, the Earl, had looked so kindly on her at Abbey Hall, and his mother positively eagerly. In truth, the Countess had been so afraid that Ralph might fix upon one of the many quite unsuitable girls he appeared to find so attractive that Anne Latimar was the answer to one of her urgent prayers.

It was such an ideal match for all concerned, Anne thought miserably, so why didn't Ralph speak? She went down to the Great Banqueting Hall that evening, dressed as Undine, quite determined to make him do so.

CHAPTER SIX

THE masque that night was an exceptionally grand affair, even for the standards of a royal palace. Anne looked about her with pleasure. So many beautiful and rich costumes, such an abundance of exotic food and wine. Each courtier, knowing the Queen was to be taken from them shortly, had resolved to give her his or her best effort.

Looking over the assembly, Anne immediately found Ralph, caught his eye and waited by the door for him to come to her. Jack Hamilton arrived first. He bowed. He had made no concession to the evening and was dressed, as always, very plainly in black.

'Lady Anne, I have heard that you are to come with us tomorrow morn.'

'That is so,' Anne said, her eyes still on Ralph who was completing his measure.

'It will be the greatest pleasure,' Jack said stiffly, 'to receive you into my home.'

Anne turned impatiently. 'The Queen insisted I go with her, Jack. I have to say it will be no pleasure to me.'

Jack's face did not change. 'Is it so? Well, I still am honoured to welcome the daughter of my friend into my home.' His grave dignity made an impression on her and she was ashamed to have made the comment.

'Thank you,' she said, colouring. 'I value your words. Will you wish to take some refreshment?'

'I might, but see another gentleman has come to

claim you.' Ralph was in crimson, his doublet sleeves slashed in scarlet. Jack looked him over. 'What do you represent, my lord?'

'Fire,' Ralph said, smiling. 'I see you are water, my dear Anne—I fear we are an ill-matched couple. Nevertheless, let us chance the floor.'

Jack looked after them. He liked Anne no better than he had on first meeting her; her conduct in the last weeks had confirmed his opinion of her as a shallow creature, of which there were so many in this assembly. But his ties with the Latimar family entitled her to some protection and Ralph Monterey was a man no gentleman would wish to see courting an innocent lady of his acquaintance.

He had not liked the boy at Ravensglass, and thought him unimproved with age. Ralph's aversion to military life did not condemn him in Hamilton's eyes—it was not to everyone's taste. But Ralph Monterey had set the place on its ears during his brief stay, for he had been a mischief-maker, a barrack-room lawyer, and not above the self-seeking lie if it suited.

He had also been disgracefully involved with one of the innocent maids from the village—not an unusual occurrence, of course, but the girl had not been of the type that most of the young squires chose for their escapades. She had been a decent girl, ruined by the attentions of the worthless young man.

Jack supposed that Ralph had moved on to more sophisticated prey now—certainly he had a reputation in that area—but surely he did not consider Anne Latimar to be a fair quarry?

Jack pondered upon how best he could serve his old master in this and came to the conclusion that the Queen might have solved the problem by determining that Anne would be out of reach for at least a month. By the time she was returned to Greenwich, no doubt Ralph would have fixed on another demoiselle.

Even so, watching the couple on the floor, Jack could see that they were physically well suited. Both stood out in a crowd, both had a light and amusing way with them—in Ralph, rather experienced and studied. Jack spent some time following them with his eyes as they laughingly executed the steps with matched grace, and it did not occur to him that this was the first time in ten years that he had paid any attention of any kind to a woman.

Anne found it as hard as usual to rise the next morning. Fortunately, the other ladies in her room had her welfare at heart and roused her early enough to dress, eat a sketchy meal and be ready to join the party bound for Northumberland. Anne followed their instructions in a dream. Her last thought before sleeping had been, Ralph! Her first on waking was, Ralph!

Last night he had been as surprised as she to hear that she was to go north with the Queen. Indeed, mixed with the amazement had been annoyance—very sweet to Anne.

'I don't want to go,' she had told him. 'How will I live without seeing you for a whole month?'

'The time will soon pass,' Ralph had said absently.

His preoccupation had worried Anne. She had seen the way the other women looked at him; how soon would it be before one or more of them moved to console him in her absence? She had longed for some definite word from him to reassure her.

'Will you truly miss me?' she had asked, managing to make her voice light but failing to control her eyes.

They had wandered out into the night air at the very end of the evening, and Ralph had shivered in the chill. He was not an outdoor man, or a very active one. The skills of combat and hard exercise to gain his knighthood had been both tedious and irksome to him and only a natural physical aptitude had sustained him.

Once knighted, he had given up all such so-called manly pursuits and now confined any activity of that kind to hunting and hawking as befitted a gentleman of his rank, preferring the infinitely more attractive and less dangerous sport of the gaming tables.

He said, 'You know I will—and Anne, what I am about to say I have no right to, but—'

'Go on,' she said, her eyes dilating in the moonlight.

He took one of her hands in his and bent his head, examining it, noting its smooth whiteness. On the forefinger there was a great aquamarine surrounded by diamonds.

'I think,' he said slowly, 'we are in like mind over the way we feel for each other. I spoke with my father before leaving home and he made no objection to our making that feeling a lasting affair. But in matters such as this both families must be in consent. I cannot do what I wish to do now—ask you to be my wife— without first applying to *your* father.'

'Oh, he will agree!' Anne said impulsively. 'How could he not?'

'I am happy you should think so, but nevertheless. . .' He let go of her hand and drew her into his arms. As yet he had not presumed on her obvious love for him in any physical way; now he did. Quite deliberately he kissed and caressed her, a little surprised that she was obviously a complete novice. He drew back first.

'Oh, Ralph—' Anne's head was spinning '—must we

let a technicality stop us from committing ourselves to each other? I would do anything, anything you asked of me.'

A technicality? Ralph was too young ever to have known Harry Latimar in his days at court, but old gossip was occasionally revived, and he knew Latimar had a reputation for a flashing rage, always detrimental to whoever that rage was concentrated upon.

Thus, in the interests of self-preservation he said, 'It must be done right, darling. But I will say privately to you now that I love you and wish you to be my wife. But I would also say that nothing will go ahead until I have spoken with your father.'

'Oh, it is enough!' said Anne. She pulled off the ring and pressed it into his hand. 'It is the only jewel I am wearing this night—I thought it appropriate to my costume—but I would give you everything I possess, my love. Let it be yours.'

'An exchange of rings?' Ralph smiled. 'So be it.' He considered his own rings—rubies and garnets—and slid off one of the inferior—a garnet set with seed-pearls— and gave it to her. He wished to make the gesture, but the rubies were saleable. Who knew when he would fall from grace, attend the tables, and need ready cash?

But Anne was delighted with what he gave her. She put it on the forefinger of her right hand and doubled the other hand over it. She was content. She could go riding off tomorrow and know that this entrancing, absolutely right man would eventually be hers.

His words about her father were also right, and appropriate, but she saw no difficulty there. How could there be? If Ralph had doubts, they were only those of a man brought up in the confines of arranged marriages between the nobility.

She was not so confined, she felt, and had he been from any class she would have loved him. Her father thought the same, she reasoned, for had he not married the lady of his choice, when he could have had an heiress? Had he not allowed his son and heir to marry a nursemaid, when that son could have had any aristocratic daughter of any nobleman?

Anne was convinced that her father had only to set eyes on Ralph to know why she had chosen him, and he would approve that choice. She listened to Ralph's next words in a daze.

'Whilst you are away,' he said consideringly, 'I will go to Maiden Court and lay our case before the Earl. If all goes well—'

'Yes? If all goes well you will ride for Ravensglass!' Anne looked at him with shining eyes.

Ralph was taken aback. Kew in this season's weather was possible, but the wildness of the north when the year was drawing to a close? And Ravensglass—that terrible place! He had sworn he would never go back there! But what could he say? He kissed each of her hands in turn, and so it was decided.

When the royal party bound for the border was nearing its destination the weather turned bitterly cold. It had been fair travelling so far, with every noble house along the way throwing wide its hospitable doors to its sovereign, and even the occasional night in a public inn not too uncomfortable.

But it was October, after all, a notoriously unpredictable month in England. Anne, clad in her fur-lined cloak and sturdy other garments, was warm enough, but raised anxious eyes to the sky. The day had begun with cloudy skies and intermittent sunshine, but more clouds had come, which now had a different look to them—a purplish hue which was strange to see before December.

Surely it would not *snow*? thought Anne. She recalled Jack Hamilton's words on how his home could be cut off during the snow season. But she had known Octobers so brilliant with sunshine that it had been possible to lie out on the Maiden Court lawns! And it had been generally thought by those at court who knew about such things that the weather was set to be unusually mild this autumn—otherwise Elizabeth would not have planned the short excursion.

Fate could not be so cruel at this most important time to allow such an aberration of nature. . . Anne's thoughts were purely selfish at this time.

Since beginning the journey, she had been entirely wrapped up in her own concerns. A week after leaving Greenwich she had pictured Ralph mounting his horse and riding to Maiden Court. She had imagined her parents' delight in the reason for his coming—at last their dilatory daughter had decided upon a man!—and she had imagined him then turning his horse and spurring it on to Ravensglass, arriving soon after they did.

It was all beautifully imagined, but if the weather *had* conspired against them how was he to come galloping to the fastness of Ravensglass Castle with his glad news?

Of course, she knew, no fall of snow could affect the ultimate outcome, but she wanted to *know*. She wanted her future settled.

Human beings were designed for many tribulations, many hardships, but waiting in uncertainty was the hardest of all states, and Anne the least equipped for that state. As the royal train wound majestically along the northern roads towards the border, she hunched her shoulders against the biting wind and thought herself unlucky indeed.

In the late afternoon they moved through a dark wood, the leaves like deformed hands curling under the horses' hooves, and followed the bridle path in single file for a mile or so. Then they left the sheltered semi-darkness, emerging again into the harsh wind. The riders streamed over the bare landscape and in an hour were within sight of a grey mound of stone which was Ravensglass.

Anne drew up her horse and paused to re-tie the hood of her cloak, thinking that she had never seen such barren country. There were no trees now to soften the wind-swept landscape, only the bleak structure of the fortress rising into the leaden sky.

Huddled to the left in the far distance a group of low buildings crouched on the plain, but there was nothing else to be seen. This must be the loneliest place on earth, thought Anne.

Jack Hamilton, at the head of the small cavalcade with the Queen, glanced back, his soldier's instinct telling him that one of his troop had fallen out of line. He made a sharp gesture with his arm and the four gentlemen behind closed up around the Queen. Jack then turned and trotted back to Anne.

'What is wrong?' he asked peremptorily.

'Why, nothing. I was just adjusting my hood and looking at the castle—it is very lonely here.'

'Which is why the Scots have always thought it a propitious place to make their forays into English land—' He stopped and stood up in his stirrups. The drawbridge of the castle had been lowered and a body of riders was racing out. They were riding light horses bred for speed and came swooping down the slope, arms raised above their heads, shouting into the wind. They strung out in a long line, then dismounted, caps in hand.

'Those are my men,' Jack said. 'Come, let us rejoin the others.' He trotted back to the Queen's side and watched as his men, clad in the Hamilton colours of green and gold, formed two half-circles and knelt, heads bared, as Elizabeth rode graciously on to Ravensglass. Anne followed, noticing that the kneeling men were all young and tough-looking, but not above giving her a curious glance as she passed by.

Ravensglass was an Edwardian castle, one of those built in the time of Edward I. It had no central keep, but used the contours of the terrain it was built upon and relied upon an arrangement of walls and towers for its strength. It consisted of two concentric rings of walls, inner and outer. The outer wall, some feet lower, was defended by half a dozen towers; the inner—its walls fifteen feet thick—had cylindrical towers on the corners and two gatehouses.

Both gatehouses contained the accommodation: suites grand enough for royalty. The vast ward contained within the walls allowed ample space for barracks, stabling and all other offices. Above the main gatehouse on the weatherbeaten stone terrace was carved the Hamilton motto, and Anne raised her eyes to read it as she rode under: 'Pure thoughts, honest tongue, faith in Christ the King'.

The entire household waited in the courtyard for their sovereign. Elizabeth, denied any contact with her rustic subjects along the journey through England by Hamilton's order, made the most of this moment. She had her father's touch with all the English, great or humble, and had a word for all.

Anne remained mounted while Her Majesty acknowledged each stammered greeting. As always, Robert Dudley was elbowed aside in the proceedings and he handed his mount over to a groom and came to Anne's side. He lifted her down.

'A grim stronghold,' he observed, glancing up at the manned battlements, at the array of arms lining the parapet between the towers.

'Yes.' Anne had never been in a castle such as this before. After the Reformation, the southern castles had mostly fallen into decay or been modified into dwelling places; a gentler, less defensive style of establishment was now fashionable in England. 'Lord Jack is young indeed to command such a place.'

'But well fitted to the task. I declare that at each stopping place along the way here he posted himself as personal guard to Her Grace.' He asked suddenly, 'What do you think of Hamilton?'

Anne shrugged. 'I scarcely know him, but he does seem somewhat. . .serieux.'

Dudley laughed. 'And you prefer a less intense gentleman! Such as Monterey? Well, you will get your fingers burned in short order there, my dear.'

'Why do you say that?' Anne flushed.

'Why? For no reason.' He looked with interest at the girl beside him. He had a fancy for her himself, but had made no headway. He had decided that she was virtuous in the way her mother was, until she had taken up with Ralph Monterey. . .

'Ralph and I have an—understanding, you know,' she said hesitantly. She should not have said that, of course, but could see by Robert's expression that he did not believe her anyway. How frustrating it was not to be able to say, This man is mine, and I am his!

'Well, if you say so.' Dudley took her arm. Elizabeth had completed her inspection of the household and was now progressing through the wide oak doors of the gatehouse proper.

'I love him!' Anne said suddenly. 'And he loves me.'

'Is that so?' Dudley looked at her again with some compassion.

'We have exchanged both promises and rings,' Anne rushed on ingenuously, 'and he is to speak to my father. Maybe has already done so. Father will be favourably disposed towards us, don't you think? Father will like Ralph, don't you agree? Sometimes I think I fell in love with him because he is so like Father. Wouldn't you say so?'

Robert steered his charge in. Organised chaos was usually the form whenever Elizabeth of England visited, and today was no different. He looked up the winding stone stairway where the Queen was being escorted by her ladies and a dozen servants, all jostling in the narrow space.

He said, 'It would be pleasant to think that, Anne.'

'But it is so!' Anne too looked upwards. Everything was grey in this place, and hard and unyielding, she thought. She supposed she ought to join the rush to show Elizabeth her quarters, but stayed a moment longer.

'*Don't* you think that?' she demanded.

Robert considered. Did he think Ralph Monterey was like Harry Latimar? No, was the instant answer to that. Gamblers and womanisers both, they had those two traits in common — but their personalities were quite different.

For one thing, Harry had had an insecure early life—Robert recognised that mark on a man because he bore it himself—whereas Ralph had been indulged to the point of pampering. Also, Ralph was an ambitious opportunist—Robert also identified with this characteristic—and that Latimar had never been.

'You are not going to answer me?' Anne asked.

Robert smiled. 'I am not a connoisseur of men, Anne, but I am of women.' He leaned closer and said softly, 'Ask me about yourself and I will give you my opinion.'

'You are joking with me,' she said sulkily, 'and I am so serious!' She turned up the steps in Elizabeth's wake.

If anyone from the court at Greenwich had been expecting life at Ravensglass to be dull, they were to be pleasantly surprised in the next few days. It was a garrison filled with fighting men, but those men were young and youth was always merry given the chance.

The evening entertainments were lacking in sophistication, naturally, for it was rare for any visiting player to venture so far away from civilisation to engage his trade. And women—even wives—were not permitted to share a Ravensglass soldier's tour of duty unless that soldier was a senior officer of long standing.

But the contingent could and did put on for their queen fine shows of jousting and wrestling and fencing. They were also only too pleased to play any sporting game she wished and the shortage of feminine competition was the last circumstance to worry Elizabeth.

Those ladies she had brought with her—with the exception of Anne—were matrons and approaching middle age. They were good women, devoted to their young mistress, but not lively company and they certainly had not the looks to disturb a body of young males. Anne had, of course, but was so distant and aloof and preoccupied with her own thoughts that even Elizabeth noticed. She spoke to her young attendant one morning a week after their arrival.

'May I ask if there is something troubling you, Lady Anne?'

Anne started. 'I beg your pardon, madam?'

Elizabeth had been dressing and now sent her maids away. 'Really,' she said sharply. 'I expect a small measure of your attention, lady!'

Anne blushed. 'If I have failed in my duty to you, Your Majesty, please forgive me and tell me how.'

'Tut! I am not talking of your duty to me, but of your manner with our young hosts. Modesty and restraint pleases me, as you know, but your conduct is little short of insulting.'

'Insulting?' Anne was outraged. She had never been accused before of poor manners, let alone insulting behaviour. How had she offended? Any more than my Ladies Fitzroy or Dacre, who always looked down their long noses at any attempt by a man to speak with them!

'Well,' Elizabeth said, 'perhaps insulting is too strong a word, but, my dear, 'tis this way: these young men are far from their homes. They defend our border valiantly that we might sleep easy in our beds inland, and it is an event in their lives to see a pretty girl. You might, I think, relax a little and be. . .kinder.'

'I had not thought of it that way,' Anne said, frowning. 'But you are right, of course, as you usually are.' There was no attempt to flatter, and the smile she gave Elizabeth was sincere.

'Well, then.' Elizabeth was standing by the narrow

window overlooking the area enclosed within the stalwart castle walls. She beckoned to Anne. 'Have you noticed this, Lady Anne?'

Anne opened the window a little and looked where the long finger pointed. 'What is it? Oh, yes, the Hamilton burial vaults.' She had seen the grey stone block, and its adjoining smaller one of palest marble, but not at close quarters.

''Tis a statue which stands as monument to his dead wife,' Elizabeth said. 'It is beautiful, I think.'

Anne stared at the square of coral, on which there was poised a graceful statue. Yes, it was beautiful; even under grey skies it caught and held the light. Narrowing her eyes, she could see that the stone figure was female, dressed in flowing draperies, its face turned up, arms outstretched in a pose of supplication.

'He is a strange man, Jack Hamilton,' the Queen mused. 'So apparently straightforward and, not to put too fine a point upon it, almost brusque in his dealings with others. Yet underneath it seems there dwells a romantic soul. It must be so, don't you agree—for a man to so honour his wife's demise with such a shrine, and poetry too?'

'Poetry?'

'Why, yes, whilst I was conducted on my inspection of the castle I viewed the Lady Marie Claire's monument and on the base there is a most evocative verse.'

'What does it say?' Anne's attention was caught. Elizabeth frowned.

'Oh, I disremember the exact words.' Her own interest had waned. In truth, Elizabeth Tudor was not very interested in anything which did not touch the affairs of her realm, or her personal life.

'Now, what I wished to say to you, Lady Anne, is

this. Tomorrow eve Lord Thaxton and a small party from his manor will visit Ravensglass. His is the nearest noble house for many miles and he is taking the opportunity to renew his allegiance to myself. I believe my Lord Hamilton intends to put on a brave show and I shall expect my attendants to support the enterprise in every sense. I shall expect *you*, lady, to descend from your pinnacle and not shame me.'

'I will not,' Anne assured her. 'And shall be very interested to see how this particular outpost of your kingdom manages to entertain us.'

Elizabeth returned Anne's smile. 'As shall I. But I would put nothing past Lord Jack.'

The next morning, obeying the Queen's instructions, Anne took especial care with her toilette. She put on a gown she had not yet worn. It was of heavy velvet, its full skirt divided to show a silk underskirt, and was also a colour she had not worn before: bright scarlet.

When shown the material, Anne had liked it and her mother had ordered it made up without comment. But, parading the dress for her father, Anne had seen that he did not like it and so had left it unworn since coming to the court. But the weather was so chill here that the warm fabric was ideal.

Nevertheless, looking at her reflection in the glass this night, she could see why her father did not favour the gown for it made her looks, already distinctive, positively bold. However, it was too late to change now; she could hear horses in the courtyard and Elizabeth and her ladies leaving the royal chamber. She took a last look in the mirror and hurried out to join them.

Anne and the Queen had pondered on how

Ravensglass would entertain in a grand way, but it had been managed. With no large town near, no extra servants could be brought in for the evening, nor professonal musicians. But amongst the young men had been found those willing to change their battle dress for that of servant, and every well-bred boy was brought up to play a musical instrument and to sing— if possible in tune.

To give the obligatory feast, Jack had ordered his stores plundered, but not extensively. Ravensglass had its men to feed through the winter and Jack, reading the signs well, thought this season would come early to the border country. But the plain food was well cooked and served and, with the sweet dishes which Elizabeth so adored, Jack had had a stroke of luck.

One of his batch of prisoners taken in the spring had been a Frenchman. This was not unusual—many Frankish soldiers were to be found employed as mercenaries in the Scottish ranks. But this one, Villeau, had once trained as master cook in a great house in France. Forced to a more lucrative occupation, he had not forgotten his skills and this night had produced the kind of mouthwatering delicacies loved by the English Queen.

The pièce de résistance was borne in with ceremony at the end of the meal. Anne, seated next to her host, who had placed the visiting noblemen beside their sovereign, looked at the spun-sugar edifice in amazement. It represented a crown, the golden sugar strands strung with preserved fruit to imply jewels. Elizabeth, having admired the confection, was served first, then a page brought the remainder to the rest of the diners.

'Thank you, no,' Anne said. 'Although it is very

splendid,' she added. The page proferred the crumbling sweet to Jack.

'I think not.' Jack waved it away.

'You do not like sweet dishes?' Anne enquired. So far, throughout the meal, they had had no conversation, Anne having been fully engaged by her other neighbour, who had just excused himself to take up his temporary position as lute player on the dais in the area reserved for dancing.

'No, I do not.'

'My mother holds that 'tis bad for the teeth to indulge too often in sugary foods,' Anne offered, when it appeared that he had nothing more to add.

'Oh? I cannot see the connection,' he said dismissively.

No more could Anne, but she had noticed that people who shunned sweetmeats generally had a good set of teeth, even if elderly. Jack Hamilton's were unusually fine: white and even. She also noticed that he had obviously made a great effort with his dress tonight—black, as was his custom for formal occasions, but very fine velvet and patterned with diamonds on his doublet and silk slippers.

His hair could not be curled and primped as was common now, for it was too closely cropped to his well-shaped head. He wore no jewellery either, except for the now familiar gold earring and ring.

There was another long silence, which she finally broke by saying, 'You have, as they say, done Her Majesty proud this night, Jack. I think she is enjoying herself very much.'

'I hope so.' After another pause he added thoughtfully, 'She is a very intelligent woman, her grasp of military matters quite extraordinary for a woman, and she is hardy too. I took her out to view the various stations along the perimeter today and we were unlucky enough to attract the attention of a band of marauders. We were too small a force to engage so we ran for cover and Her Grace showed mettle in both her calm and her horsemanship.'

'I had heard nothing of this!' Anne exclaimed, her eyes large.

'Naturally not. I am sure you were fast in your apartments curling your hair and making ready for the festivities.'

'My hair curls of its own accord,' she said, stung by his tone and the way his grey eyes flicked over her dismissively.

'Indeed? How lucky for you.'

Anne laid down her knife and wiped her lips. Really, it was impossible to hold civilised conversation with this man! She said heatedly, 'Had I known my mistress would be in danger taking the air with you, then I would have insisted on being with her.'

'She was in no danger,' Jack countered. 'But what would you have done, I wonder? Set about the enemy with your frivolous tongue?'

Anne jumped up angrily. Jack put out a hand and encircled one of her wrists. 'Sit down, lady. No one may leave the board before Her Grace without express reason or permission.'

Anne sat down again. 'I know that,' she muttered. 'But I resent your implication that I am a silly woman who thinks of nothing but her toilette! And your comment that my tongue is frivolous! I can speak of weighty things, you know, if the occasion demands it.'

'I had not noticed that tonight,' Jack said ironically.

'Nor, I think, has young Chantry.' Will Chantry had been Anne's supper companion.

'Her Majesty requested me to be. . .kind to the young men under your command here. She held they were in need of a little feminine attention, and I was but anxious to provide it.'

'So anxious that the young fool is probably even now tuning up his lute and thinking of how he may apply to your father for your hand.'

'There was nothing in our conversation to make him think that!' Anne said defensively. 'Indeed, we were speaking of his home in Kent. He told me of his mother and sisters and of his sweetheart, whom he intends marrying as soon as he is released from Ravensglass next spring.'

Jack laid down his own eating utensils. Once again he hardly knew why he always wished to goad her in this way, except that she always annoyed him so much.

Until tonight, when she was seated in the hall next to him, vivacious and gay, dressed in scarlet and attracting the eyes of every man in the assembly, he had seen little of her in his home. He had not heard what she and Chantry spoke of but, glancing sideways, had seen the expression on that young man's face. Perhaps he had misread the situation.

He said uneasily, 'I am sorry if I have offended you, Anne. Again. But the commander of a force of young men must naturally be concerned for their state of mind.'

'Their state of mind is the same as yours! Fixed upon duty and on. . .death.'

'Why do you say that,' he demanded, 'and in such an accusing tone?'

'You may have eschewed all human affection,' Anne

said angrily, 'but if Will Chantry is an example your battalion has not. But his mind does not wander far from his duties; you run what is known as a tight ship here, my lord.'

'Should I not? This is not a French dancing class, Anne, but an armed garrison.'

Quite oblivious now to tact, Anne said, 'These boys under your command are just that—boys, in need of care and attention, and the odd diversion. Even Her Majesty saw that.'

'I have no knowledge of what the Queen saw,' Jack said bitterly, 'but cannot believe she criticised my effort on her behalf in this remote place.'

'She did not!' Anne said, frustrated. 'Only pointed out to me that all men need a softer side to their lives. Tonight I have tried to provide that and do not expect to be abused by you for *my* efforts.'

'If you could remove yourself from the centre of this argument for a moment, I would like to tell you something. Of course I know all these young men need. . .affection. But here, now, in this place which is effectively a battlefield, such feelings are out of place. Or do you believe that a man can march to war, maybe to be killed, certainly to witness his friends slaughtered or maimed, and have his mind on romance?'

Now he had shocked her. She did not show it outwardly, but her eyes became even larger and he read gentleness and compassion there. . . But she was not silenced. 'It is not quite like that here,' she said slowly.

'No, lady, it is not quite like that here. But here is a—a rehearsal, if you like, for what I describe. And I would that any lad I have had a hand in training acquit himself well—better still, stay alive—when he finds himself in the real situation.'

'Yes,' she said. 'Yes, I can understand what you say.' She smiled suddenly. It was the kind of smile which turned young men's heads, made them think of the romance she advocated, Jack thought. At twenty-one, perhaps he would have been one of those young men, but now it simply annoyed him afresh.

'I am sure you don't,' he said harshly.

Anne's smile faded. She had been interested in what he was saying and, for a time, he had seemed almost human. 'Nothing I say or do pleases you, does it?' The question was asked before she had time to wonder why she wanted to ask it. Except. . .except that when he had just spoken his voice had been so passionate, his eyes so vivid when he had spoken of his men.

It occurred to her suddenly that any mother or sweetheart handing over a beloved son or lover to such a commander might well do worse. She had not needed to be longer than a day at Ravensglass to know that Hamilton's entire command worshipped him.

He was strange, yes, they would concede that, hard, yes again, for many of them had had the rough edge of his tongue and frequently the even rougher feel of his hand, but one and all they seemed to reckon that my lord would stand up alongside them on the field of battle, and go into battle for them in any other troublous event in their lives.

The meal had come to an end before Jack could reply. Elizabeth was rising to leave the table and everyone else following suit. He bowed to Anne. 'Excuse me, please; I must escort Her Majesty.'

Anne followed on, fuming. He was so aggravating, she thought crossly. She had held out the olive branch

enough times now for him to realise that she wanted to
be his friend, but he always chose to ignore it and, not
content with that, trample it into the ground with his
attacking comments.

In the brightly lit hall, lively with music, she danced
and smiled and tried to carry out the grand ideals she
had spoken of both to the Queen and to her dour host.
At midnight, she fell into bed and fell asleep
immediately.

She awoke to a quiet world. Turning over in the
narrow bed, she glanced at the closely draped windows.
Before she was halfway across to draw them she knew
what she would find on parting them. She recognised
the odd, hushed effect that a heavy fall of snow
produced and, looking out onto a totally white landscape, had only one thought: Now how will Ralph
come?

Travel in these days, on poor roads, was difficult
enough in the fair months of the year. In the rainy
season, the roads were muddy and clogged; in snow, no
one would even attempt it! Ralph would not, could not
come, she decided.

CHAPTER SEVEN

DESPITE the dismal thought of Ralph not coming, once she had washed and dressed Anne felt curiously exhilarated. Memories of the snowball fights she had had as a child with her brother and the other youngsters at Maiden Court came back to her and made her smile. Beauty, too, was wrought by the coating of white on the walls and towers she could see from her window. She had the urge to get out into the sparkling day and see how Ravensglass looked, transformed by a fairy wand.

In the hall there was no evidence of the feast and revelry of the previous night. All was cleared away and the hall was tidy; even the sparse furniture had been polished. She opened the main door and stepped out. In the distant barracks she could hear male voices and the clank of steel as the battalion came to grips with another day. Before her, on the flags of the ward, was an unbroken expanse of glittering and dazzling snow. She would visit the tombs, she decided, hugging her cloak about her and raising her fur-lined hood.

The Hamilton crypt was set away in one corner of the inner wall. She did not look to it, but paused before the tomb dedicated to the last Hamilton wife. She looked up at the graceful statue, its eyes blinded by snow, before descending the five deep steps into the crypt below.

Then she drew back, shivering. At Maiden Court, her home, the dead were buried in decent fashion

117

under a canopy of stone, shelved in stout coffins. But here, on a granite square, lay in morbid splendour the remains of Jack Hamilton's wife treated in the new way. A sheet of lead had been laid over the out-stretched corpse so that—in time—the covering took on the features and appearance of the body beneath.

Anne struggled to remember the exact name for the treatment, but failed and could only think, 'Tis not decent! When one is dead, one should be granted the dignity of decay.

Moving closer, she could see the outline of the slender body, even the very features of the dead woman. A movement on the steps behind her caused her to turn, her heart missing a beat.

Jack Hamilton came carefully down the slippery steps, a spray of spindleberry in his hands. He too started when he saw that he was not alone. He glanced briefly at Anne, then proceeded forward and laid the tribute at his wife's feet. The vivid red of the berries, succulent and bursting with life, and the bright green of the leaves, was somehow horrible in this macabre place.

One of the squires at Ravensglass had told Anne that in the appropriate season fresh flowers were packed in ice, and rushed from the nearest farm to the castle. In this barren time for blooms Jack had only been able to take a piece of the wild winter shrub which grew in such profusion just beyond the fortress walls.

He put his two tanned hands on either side of the dark slab which Marie Claire lay upon. He bowed his head and Anne turned away in embarrassment. She hastened up the steps, on the top one slipping and losing her balance. Two strong arms from behind caught her and supported her out into the white day. Jack released her immediately and she looked up at the statue.

'It is very beautiful,' she said, 'your tribute to... Marie Claire.'

'So I think,' he returned gravely. 'But no monument could ever express what I feel.'

Anne bent down and loosened the drifting snow from the base of the statue. Here, on a square plaque, were the words of poetry Elizabeth had mentioned. She read them in silence.

'Not dead, but only sleeping.' This I have read on many graves. I would dispute this: no sleep could be so long-lasting, no rest so final. I say waiting. My love is but waiting for me to come to her.

Anne straightened up. She could think of nothing to say. She was more shocked that he should have chosen those bitter words to keep his dead wife's spirit alive than that he should have planned the preservation of her body. At length she said, 'I have not heard the lines before. Who made them?'

'I did,' he said briefly. In one of his swift, vital movements he put a booted foot up on the plinth supporting the statue and, reaching up, brushed the snow from the upturned face. Once again, Anne's warm heart turned in impulsive pain. It should not be, she thought, that the living must be so tied to the dead.

'I am going back into the hall now, Jack. Do you come with me and we will talk a little by the warm fire.' Her voice was very gentle, but he did not even look at her.

'Thank you, lady,' he said coldly. 'But, as you mentioned last night, I run a tight ship here and must

ensure that my—er—sailors have not been affected by
the tempering wind from the south last night.'

He stepped down and strode away in the directon of
the barracks and Anne made her way back to the hall.

Within, the central fire was blazing, sending great
billows of smoke up to the already blackened rafters.
Elizabeth and her ladies were grouped about the fire,
their discussion no hotter than the crackling logs.

'We may well be marooned here until the spring,'
Lady Warwick was saying distastefully. Her tone
implied that no worse situation could have arisen.

'It is barbaric!' Lady Fitzroy protested. 'Snow before
November!' Her tone implied that it was the fault of
this barren place that she was so inconvenienced.

'Early snow, early thaw,' Elizabeth said placidly. 'We
had not intended leaving anyway for a sennight, and,
English weather being what it is, it may well be fair
again by then.' Her voice expressed a proprietorial
pride in the vagaries of her country's climate.

She looked up then and saw Anne at the door. 'Take
off those snow boots and that dripping cloak, lady. You
will take cold.'

Anne did so and sat down in a chair slightly apart
from the others. She had been concerned that the
snowfall prevented Ralph from joining her here; now
she must consider the fact that she would be tardy in
being reunited with him at Greenwich. . .

'My maid informs me that the last time they had
snow in this month here was twenty-two years ago,'
Lady Dacre said crossly. She rose to lay a fur lap-robe
over her mistress's knees.

Elizabeth thanked her and then said to Anne, 'You
have not complained, Lady Anne. Is this place to your
liking, perhaps? Or maybe its commander?'

There was a general laugh, and Anne forced herself to smile too. Her conversation at supper last night and her walk in the snow with Jack this morning had obviously not passed unremarked by these women. If you only knew what I am really feeling, she thought.

'Jack Hamilton,' Lady Dacre said thoughtfully, 'is an extremely wealthy young man, with a proud heritage. And he has shown scant regard for any lady in the last decade who may have helped him forget his sad loss. Certainly I am sure he has never shown any of them to Marie Claire's grave.'

'He was not showing *me* there,' Anne said mildly. 'I fancied a walk, was intrigued by the monument, and so met him there.'

'Even so,' Lady Warwick said judicially, 'it may be a step in the right direction for him, poor boy. Upon the path to recovery, I mean.'

Jack has no desire to step down that path with any woman, least of all me, Anne could have said. And, even were I heartfree, we would be an ill-matched pair. She resisted the impulse to say this, or, I fear his heart is in the grave with his dead wife, knowing it would produce more sentimental speculation. She contented herself with silence and another noncommittal smile and looked over her shoulder at the glittering day.

Oh, these women, she thought. With no other thought in their heads but others' business. She had a sudden longing for her mother. Lady Bess Latimar would have put these ladies to rout in short order, she thought idly, with her dignity and common sense.

Anne also wished her mother there so that she could tell her how she felt about Ralph Monterey, feeling sure that she would get support and understanding. Perhaps, even at this moment, Ralph was at Maiden

Court and her father and mother judging for themselves how well their daughter had chosen.

She sighed, wishing for a magical ability to see over the miles to her home.

By chance Ralph was to visit Maiden Court that very day. The weather was still fair in the area of the capital and Ralph felt that he could no longer put off riding to visit Anne's parents.

As he approached Maiden Court he checked his horse and viewed it critically. Anne had spoken of it, as had his brother, Tom, both with affection. But it is not a grand place at all, Ralph thought. Well kept and pretty enough, certainly, and obviously old and steeped in tradition. But small! Abbey Hall was ten times its size.

He rode into the stable-yard and was courteously greeted by a very bent old man who took his mount and called for a groom to take him into the hall. Once there, Bess Latimar came running down the stairs and curtsied as Ralph introduced himself.

'How very kind of you to call on us,' Bess said, rising and surveying her visitor.

Very good-looking, she thought, susceptible as always to handsome looks, and obviously very much a part of the élite assembly of the Queen's court. Now why had he come? Tom Monterey's brother, he had said on introduction; perhaps that was the connection.

She took him to the fire and ordered wine and cinnamon cakes to be brought, then seated herself opposite him and looked politely enquiring.

'You must wonder why I have come here,' Ralph said, with his attractive smile. 'Then I must explain. I very much wish to speak to the Earl—about. . .your daughter, the Lady Anne.'

Ah, so that is it, Bess thought. She smiled encouragingly, but the young man drained his glass and looked into the fire. She said, 'My husband will return at the supper hour, sir. I pray you will join us for the meal and also be kind enough to accept our accommodation for the night.'

Ralph allowed the servant to replenish his glass. It was very good wine, he thought. In fact, he had tasted no better for many a long month. 'Thank you, my lady,' he said, flashing his charming smile again. 'I greatly look forward to meeting Anne's father. I have heard much about him.'

Harry returned home as the night closed in. Bess had been well entertained by her unexpected guest in the intervening hours and the two were already good friends. Hearing her husband's horse outside, she instructed Walter to put the meal on immediately and invited Ralph to the table. So Harry came in to find an extremely attractive young man settling his wife into her place.

He paused in the doorway, peeling off his gloves and throwing down his fur-lined cloak. The young man came swiftly towards him.

'My lord earl, I am Ralph Monterey. I present my compliments.' He bowed and waited deferentially for Harry to extend his hand. The two men came to the table together.

When the servants had served the meal, Harry asked, 'It is a great pleasure, naturally, to see you here, Ralph. Have you business in this area?'

Ralph had helped himself liberally to the good

food—as he had the wine; he had rarely tasted such delicious fare. He wanted to enjoy these pleasures before entering into any serious discussion. 'My own personal business, sir. My brother has so often spoken of your home, and Anne—whom I had the pleasure to meet at Greenwich—has become my friend and has also spoken fondly of her home.' He left it there and Harry asked no more questions.

When finished the three left the table and went into the parlour. It had always been a custom for the family to retire to this pleasant room in the evening. It was generously proportioned for a house built in the period of Maiden Court and had begun its life as a second dining hall for the first owner's intimate family when they were not entertaining in the great hall. Bess had furnished it most comfortably and always kept a good fire in this room.

At his host's invitation Ralph sank into a chair and looked around, noting in appreciation the delicate French tables bearing bowls of dried herbs and vases of late roses, their petals curled and blackened by a recent frost, the richly brilliant rugs beneath his feet, and the shelves of silk-bound books.

He raised his eyes to the only picture on the wall— that of a man in grey standing behind a table on which was spread brightly coloured playing cards. The man depicted was his host. He asked, 'That is your portrait, my lord?'

Without looking at the painting Harry said, 'Indeed. Made long ago in my distant youth.'

Ralph smiled. 'You were the most talented gambler of your day, or so it is said.'

Bess spoke from the fire. 'But has moved on from such pursuits now.'

Ralph sampled his wine, again excellent. Every physical comfort in this house was exemplary, and its master and mistress so interesting and attractive too. His decision to take a wife was becoming more and more appealing to him.

The night drew on and Bess rose. 'Please forgive me, Ralph, but I think I will retire now.' Both men stood and bowed as she left the room, and Harry poured more wine.

'So,' he said. 'Perhaps we should get now to the matter in hand.'

'I agree,' Ralph returned. But he let a long silence develop before saying, 'I have come here to tell you I love your daughter, sir, and with your permission wish her to become my wife.'

Harry had not resumed his seat by the fire, but had gone to sit on the window-seat. 'Indeed?'

'She is in agreement, my lord,' Ralph continued. 'Before Anne went north, we agreed—'

'Went north?' Harry interrupted.

'Yes, forgive me, of course you will not know. . . Her Majesty has gone to Northumberland to visit Ravensglass, Jack Hamilton's fortress, and Anne went with her.'

'Is it so?' Harry digested this information. What a singular honour for Anne! 'But, I am sorry—you were saying?'

'Before Anne went, she. . .indicated to me, in the strongest possible terms, that she would accept me as her husband. If you agree.'

'I see.' Harry reached behind him to draw the drapes. He wished Bess were still in the room. She was so sensible, so worldly, despite her innocent demeanour. He himself scarcely knew what to think of this young man. Except that he recognised a fellow traveller. He had been so much like Ralph Monterey two decades ago, they might have been brothers.

'I have the patronage of my sovereign,' Ralph had said modestly at the supper table. 'She interests herself in me not a little.' So, thought Harry, could I have claimed: Henry Tudor had had a great partiality for young Latimar. 'I admit I am a profligate gambler,' Ralph had also said, with charming self-deprecation. So might I have described myself in those days, Harry thought uneasily.

'What are your thoughts on my proposal?' enquired Ralph now. Harry had no idea what to say. It was not the first time—or even the tenth—a suitor had come to him to apply for Anne's hand, but it was the first time she appeared to have agreed that he should do so. He only had Ralph's word for that, but was inclined to believe him.

'I feel I can say nothing until I have spoken with my daughter,' he hedged. 'What, if any, are your own father's thoughts?' He knew John Monterey and had respect for him, both as a man and as someone who could be relied upon to show good judgement in such matters as this.

'My father looked kindly on the idea,' Ralph said. 'He met Anne some weeks ago—at Abbey Hall—and was greatly smitten with her.'

Harry raised his eyebrows, wondering how far this affair had gone if John had acknowledged it.

'My reason for coming here alone, and not waiting for an opportunity when Anne could have joined me,' Ralph went on, 'is that she was so eager it should be settled swiftly that she persuaded me to ride to Northumberland with the news of your blessing. Or otherwise,' he added. 'She is impulsive, as you will know, and I hardly liked to deny her.'

Harry got up to refill their glasses and also to think on this. A marriage between these children, of comparable estate and birth, was probably the only kind that allowed a little freedom of choice to the two concerned.

Considering the facts as he went to the fire and added another log, he thought how pleasant it must be for Anne to have chosen for herself. Ralph was an older son, he would be extremely wealthy when his father died and he would inherit a title and a handsome manor house.

It was very ideal, but Harry wished to like his future son-in-law, and he knew without doubt that this would not be the case if Ralph Monterey assumed the role. He was surprised that he did not, for surely there was nothing against the lad, other than the rumours of too much gambling and too many women. And, given his own past, Harry felt that he should overlook these facts, knowing from his own experience that rakes frequently made the best of husbands once bridled by the woman they loved.

So, why the almost immediate distrust and dislike he felt for Ralph? Bess, he could see, had felt the reverse. She had been instantly drawn to their visitor, and she was very acute about others.

Ralph began to be a little annoyed by the long silence. After all, he could have left it to his father to approach Latimar. The matter could have been arranged between the two older men quite properly. Instead, he had made the effort to come personally, to admit his love for Anne squarely and invite inspection by his prospective in-laws. Now he felt he was being subjected to a humiliating lack of appreciation.

He said, 'Perhaps you have some objection, my lord?'

'Objection?' repeated Harry thoughtfully. 'None that I can think of, no.'

'Then?'

'Do you really intend making the long journey to Ravensglass? Could it not wait until Anne returns?'

'It could, if I were prepared to hurt her feeling in this,' Ralph replied coolly. 'And to break my promise to her. Perhaps if I am to bear disappointing news it would be better to do just that,' he added pointedly. He had actually decided that he would not journey the wearisome miles to Northumberland, but now felt that he would.

Harry sighed. 'That will not be the case,' he said mildly. 'You may tell her I favour her choice, with the proviso, naturally, that nothing will be definite until I have had an interview with your father.'

Ralph relaxed. He got to his feet and gave Harry his hand. 'I am happy to hear that, sir, and may I presume to say I will be delighted to be accepted as a member of your family?' He glanced up at the portrait again. 'I have long admired your reputation, my lord.'

'What reputation might that be?'

Ralph half laughed. 'Well, in all areas, of course, but especially in that of your prowess at the card tables. I am a dedicated gambler myself.'

Harry sipped his wine without speaking.

'Someone told me once that the hand laid before you in that picture won you this lovely house.'

The log Harry had placed on the fire began to burn in earnest now; a shower of orange and violet sparks flew upwards into the dark chimney. He moved away, saying, 'You have been misinformed. I did indeed win

Maiden Court in a game of cards, but won something far more precious with the hand shown in the picture.'

Long, long ago he and Bess had seriously endangered their happy marriage in one way and another and Harry, off balance for the first time in his life, had lost his home to money-lenders. It had been reclaimed by the old King and presented to Bess, who lost it in turn back to her husband. What had happened that sultry night twenty years ago had been no mere game of chance, however, but a fundamental reaffirmation of their love which had endured ever since. . .

'Please tell me the story,' Ralph said. 'It sounds most intriguing.'

'I am afraid that would take some time,' Harry said vaguely. 'And you will be weary. May I take you to your room?'

As they left the parlour Harry thought, It would only take a few sentences to describe the circumstances, but I don't believe this man would understand them if I used a thousand. It was a depressing thought for a father who had just agreed to part with one of his dearest possessions.

The days at Ravensglass assumed a pattern in the next week. The snow had cut the castle off from any contact with the outside world, but within its walls the company was merry.

Elizabeth, always eager to throw off her regal cloak, was enjoying herself immensely. The young regiment was denied its usual regime of hard training by snow-clogged practice fields, and conditions no man would take any animal out into, let alone the highly bred creatures Ravensglass maintained. So the young men found other amusements and games, and mock trials of

strength and displays of fencing and indoor archery and
bowls were the order of the day. And there was no one
more eager to join in than the Queen of England.

Anne, too, seemed to have thrown off her earlier
reserve. This was not entirely due to the hint from
Elizabeth, but rather because Anne had found that the
only way to get through the days of waiting to know if
she was to be happy for ever, or the reverse, was to
fling herself whole-heartedly into the atmosphere of
gaiety prevailing in a place used to hard work, but quite
willing to take advantage of an unexpected holiday.

She was ideally suited to the endless games of sport,
the games of chance, the dancing and the little plays
put on frequently. Although her father had retired
from palace life when she was a small child, he had
brought back with him a love of all sophisticated forms
of amusement and Maiden Court had entertained his
friends in the way they were accustomed to, and the
Earl had expected his family to join in.

Both Anne and her brother, George, were superb
musicians and dancers, naturally talented at all athletic
pastimes and exceptionally fine riders. George had an
aversion to gambling, particularly cards, but Anne
more than made up for him, loving the tables. At
Ravensglass she could have greatly enlarged her private
purse, but would not take money from the reckless
young men, remembering her father's words: 'If one
excels at this particular sport, 'tis as easy to lose when
appropriate as to win.'

The other waiting ladies felt that in theory they
should disapprove of a young girl who was as popular,
as sought after and as abandoned to merriment as the
Latimar miss, but found they had little to disapprove of.

Anne was completely impartial in giving her favours; with half the company now in love with her, she showed no favouritism, but chose a different gentleman each day to be her partner in the archery or bowls, another again to take her in to supper, yet another to lead her out into the first dance.

And she did not neglect her duties in this rush of popularity, but made the necessary chores so amusing and delightful to be a part of that the other ladies were infected with her laughter and began to think that it would not be a catastrophe if this isolated state of affairs went on indefinitely.

All this is very nice, Anne told herself. I really am enjoying myself and am glad to play my part in these people's lives. But her thoughts returned like a homing bird to Ralph. His image was constantly with her, and when alone she often cried in frustration that they must be separated. She had pinned her hopes on him coming to her here, and now it seemed impossible. It was strange, she thought, that she could be outwardly so gay and inwardly despairing.

This thought brought another about Jack Hamilton and also a mischievous little smile. For Jack was no good at all at dissembling. He showed plainly in those days that he greatly resented his well-run garrison being turned into a playground. Coming upon one or other of his lieutenants winding wool for one of the ladies, or tuning his instrument preparatory to accompany the little orchestra, he would utter a sharp exclamation, then quickly remember himself and turn away.

Anne could see that the long evenings, with their music and singing and the sound of dancing feet in the old chambers, were a constant torment to a man who believed so strongly in the night hours being solely for sleep to refresh the body for the onslaught of a day spent in training that body for combat.

She took a malicious delight, when he tried to absent himself in the early evening, in recalling him to attend herself or another lady in the dancing, or at the card tables. He obviously hated to play cards, which he had little talent for, apparently finding it impossible not to reveal his hand and strategy upon his face.

At games there was little enjoyment for him either; he was so much better at all physical sports than any other competitor that the contest was over before it had begun.

On a dark night two weeks after the first snow fell Anne had a very disagreeable interview with him.

She had been dancing with a young man called Mark Bolbey. She did not much care for this young man; he was a bully in the physical games, frequently injuring less able boys, a cheat at the card tables, which she despised, and had too masterful a way with him with her in the dance, often overriding younger and more courteous officers in partnering her.

This night, to avoid any display of this, she had spent the latter part of the evening with him. As the musicians tuned up for their final set, and Elizabeth was already ascending the stairs to her bed, Mark persuaded Anne out into the stables to view, he said, a beautiful foal that one of the mares had produced.

The stables were warm and well lit. Mark's mare had indeed produced a fine son and she stood admiring him. But when she and Mark left the foaling stall for the outer area something quite horrible occurred. Saying that she must return now to the main apartments, Anne smiled and held out her hand to thank her escort for an enjoyable evening. The next moment she was seized and crushed against him. His lips sought hers with deadly intent, his hands with a familiarity that was quite terrifying.

Anne was instinctive in her response: she wrenched herself away and smacked his face. Mark then said, 'You would assault me? I will teach you, lady, that no woman may do that!'

What followed was even more horrible, and, desperately afraid, Anne cried out. The stable door opened and closed and Jack Hamilton was suddenly beside them. He first looked to his liegeman.

'Bolbey? What is the meaning of this?'

Mark shuffled his feet in the straw underfoot. Younger and easily overcome young men were one thing; a slender girl, with no more strength than a bird in his hands, too. But his commander in chief, with his record of real violence, was another. He hung his head.

'Leave now, sir,' Jack said roughly. When the door had opened and closed again he said, 'Are you all right, lady?'

'I believe so,' Anne said haltingly. She was trembling from head to foot. No man or woman had ever laid rough hands on her. Her father disapproved strongly of the rule of brutal treatment either to his family or servants. Her brother, whom she had fought in childhood, had always given way immediately his sister was under real restraint. Anne was quite unaccustomed to any physical violence.

'I can only say you brought this situation upon yourself,' Jack said sternly. Foolish girl, thinking she could play her silly games with a hundred young men! Every evening he had seen her drawing the boys to her side like moths to flame with her loose ways. Those great luminous eyes which promised ecstasy, that graceful body, undisguised by the rich material of her gowns, and that shining cape of sweet-smelling black hair— why, a man could turn mad just imagining his fingers entwined in—

Jack caught himself up in dismay. He had not realised he had even noticed all this. . .

'I have brought this on myself?' Anne queried tearfully. 'How so? Mark wanted to show me the foal his favourite dam had given birth to. I came here only for that purpose.'

'Alone in a secluded place? With a gentleman you must have known had taken too much wine?'

Anne could not deny any of what he said. In retrospect she had to admit that she had acted unwisely. Knowing it, however, did not stop her from resenting the reprimand in his voice. She said coldly, 'You will have to excuse my ignorance in these matters. In the past I have been quite safe with any *gentleman*, whatever the circumstances.'

Jack's eyes were on the faint bruises beginning to show at the base of Anne's white neck. This sight filled him with an inexplicable rage. Inexplicable because, as the girl had freely acknowledged, she had invited the horseplay that had occurred: Ravensglass was not the garden of her country manor home. Young Bolbey had acted inexcusably, of course, but humanly surely.

He said stiffly, 'The young man will be punished in the severest way for behaving so. I will see to it myself.'

At that moment Jack felt that he would like to personally boot the boy around the snowy interior, and that again was an unexplainable reaction. He knew all the men in his command, knew that Bolbey had his drawbacks, but he was also the stuff of which great warriors were made. Given an order, Mark would carry it out to the letter; given an inch of ground to defend, he would do so with his life. He came from a great family renowned for their soldiering skills.

Women, Jack thought bitterly, at least a certain kind of woman, could play havoc with even the most likely man.

'Pray don't bother,' Anne said, seeing the irritation on his face. 'If you are willing to condone such behaviour, I would not wish to disturb—'

'I do not condone it!' Jack said, exasperated. 'But, lady, you have been free with yourself during the last weeks here. This is the result and now I give you instruction: do not invite such an occasion again.'

Anne had been shaken by Mark's attack, and now was under a different but equally distressing attack. Free with herself? Why, she had gently turned away a dozen overtures from Mark Bolbey's fellows, and not a one of them had pressed her. She found her handkerchief at last and wiped her eyes, then pressed it to her mouth, swaying.

'Are you going to faint?' Jack asked. Surely she was not usually so white? Had that young ruffian seriously hurt her?

Jack felt a pain like a blow above his heart. All that was sturdy in him rushed up to protect her. Along with this feeling was another, less easy to define as the accepted reaction of a man confronted with a female under duress. It sprang from a part of him that he had thought long dead. To his astonishment he had a quite shameful desire to take her in his arms, to kiss and caress away the expression on her face, remove that lost look from her eyes.

'I never faint,' Anne said icily.

Struggling to control emotions he had thought with-

ered a decade ago, which indeed *should* have died with
their rightful recipient, Jack said coldly, 'You are never
nervous, you never faint and your hair curls of its own
accord. You are certainly a woman in a thousand!'

'And how would *you* know that?' Anne asked
insultingly.

There! Now she was back on course, and daring to
taunt him for his lack of masculine obsession with the
opposite sex, for his loyalty to a lady whose name she
was not worthy to have upon her red lips! He took her
by the arm and hustled her out of the stables.

'Go back inside now, Anne, and remember what I
have said.'

'I will remember *all* you have said,' Anne assured
him, hurrying across the white ground towards the hall.
She did not look back and that was just as well, because
Jack, his hard features illuminated by the lantern hung
to throw its light on the path from the stable to the
hall, had an expression in his eyes which she would not
have been able to interpret.

When the hall door shut behind her, Jack reached
up and extinguished the candle within this lantern.
Then he went back into the stables and moved around,
closing the stalls and thinking.

Anne's final words did not disturb him so much as
his desire to continue speaking with her. As she had
flown across the icy cobblestones he had longed to call
out, Anne, come back! Come back and talk to me.

Talk? What was there to speak of with such a girl?
He remembered the hours he had spent in conversation
with Marie Claire, her clever way of making him feel
that he was the only man alive who could entertain her.
This had never been done with the tricks Anne Latimar
had at her disposal—Marie Claire had been the least

provocative woman he had ever known, and certainly not the most beautiful.

Jack had married her at twenty-two years old and had not been inexperienced when he met her. Before leaving England he had been courted by some of the beauties of the English court, and had not been slow in taking advantage of the offers they had made. Before that, as squire to Harry Latimar, he had constantly been rebuked for his escapades in this area.

Then he had been sent to France, to the court of pleasure, where the ladies had been more sophisticated than any he had encountered before, and he had swiftly lost his heart to the unusual, modest, doe-eyed Marie Claire Lauren.

It was not physical looks, Jack thought now, leaving the barn and standing in the cold wind outside, but personality which decided matters of true love. *Love*? Why did that word come into his mind now? And also Harry Latimar's scarcely heeded words on leaving Ravensglass after their acrimonious discussion on his erstwhile squire's drinking habit.

'I know you do not wish to hear this,' Harry had said that day, 'and I am not sure I am qualified to say it, but the world is a curious place, Jack, and those living in it also curious. You feel you are dead to all human love in the future, and I might understand that feeling and agree with it.

'But consider this: the good Lord saw fit to put you and Marie Claire together. Out of all the men and women roaming around this earth, he brought you together. If he could do that once, and, as a gambler, I marvel at the odds involved, could that have been his last throw on your behalf? I don't think so.

'She is gone now, the perfect one, the one woman in

the world for you, but is that all there is for you? I
think not. In fact, given your youth and worth, I do not
choose to think so.'

Jack remembered those words now, standing out in
the biting wind. At the time he had ignored them,
allowed Harry to mount his horse and ride away
without commenting upon them, but now they came
back to him with a certain meaning. Anne had
reminded him of those words, had made him feel they
had a meaning.

'Tis lust, he decided as the swirling wind sought to
penetrate his clothing and chill his heart. That is the
explanation. The girl is so beautiful, so sexually allur-
ing. I am no better than Mark Bolbey, to fall victim to
it, and I am, he thought ruefully, long overdue for the
wares plied in places I too seldom visit—as we all are
here in this isolated place!

This thought made him more sympathetic to what he
must do, he decided as he crossed the yard and made
his way to the barracks.

Mark was abed when his commander came into the
spartan room he shared with twenty others. He had
taken to his bunk with mixed feelings, abruptly sober.
He came from a good family, his father and brothers
were also soldiers in the ranks of the Queen's bat-
talions, and he was in no doubt as to what those men
would say of his conduct tonight. When the rough
wooden door to his sleeping chamber was thrust open
and the starlight blocked by a tall figure, he knew
exactly who it was.

Jack trod quietly between the sleeping figures and
stood over Mark's bed. 'Bolbey, a word with you, if
you please.' He spoke softly so as not to wake the
others, but penetratingly.

Mark hesitated a second too long. Jack reached down and upturned the rough sleeping pallet Mark lay on. He fell with a thud to the earthen floor. In a moment he had regained his feet.

'Yes, sir?'

'Outside. Now.' Mark followed his master out into the night.

'It is cold tonight,' observed Jack, raising his eyes to the sky. 'Bitter weather indeed. But more bitter is my task at this moment. You have assaulted a lady who is a guest at Ravensglass. One of our queen's ladies.' Jack ceased looking at the sky and looked at Mark. 'What have you to say? You felt she tempted you, yes?'

Mark dropped his eyes before the candid grey stare. He considered his options. He had wanted Anne Latimar earlier, had not been surprised she had agreed to go out with him from the safety of the hall, for he had thought her an insouciant and flighty woman.

But, once in the stables, he could not honestly say that she had responded in the way he had expected. Touching and kissing her, he had been able to determine that she was quite innocent. It would pay him to deny this knowledge now in the face of Hamilton's address, but found he could not do so. Did not wish to do so.

He said humbly, 'I understand what you are saying, sir, but can only plead that I misread certain things.'

'Misread? How so?'

Mark straightened his shoulders and looked squarely at his captain. 'My Lady Anne gives certain promises, my lord. She has a way with her which goes straight to a man's head. . . She is so very *excellent* at everything a man admires, and I believed her to be acute in other. . .

areas. I was wrong, sir, and am willing to be punished for my fault.'

It was not what Jack wanted to hear. He had come prepared to understand and sympathise with his young lieutenant. Instead that lieutenant now appeared determined to take all the blame for what had happened. 'What exactly are you saying, boy?' he asked shortly.

'I am saying, sir,' Mark said candidly, 'that Anne Latimar shamed me this night with her dignity and innocence. Shamed me in a way I hope, and believe, my sisters would shame any gentleman who attempted to treat them as I did Anne tonight. . .' His voice tailed off but his meaning was clear.

Jack sighed. 'What, then,' he asked, 'would you suggest I do with you? In the face of your explanation?'

'If you are asking me,' Mark said bravely, 'and bearing in mind what *I* would do had the lady in question been one of my sisters I mentioned earlier, I might counsel some violent display from you.' Mark took a step back so that he was ranged against the stout wall of the barracks.

'I see,' Jack said thoughtfully. 'You would advise that I take my fists to you?'

'Indeed, sir,' Mark said gravely.

There was a brief pause. Within it each man considered the consequences of the encounter. Mark thought, I will not be able to rise from my bed for a month. . .I might even be maimed and unable ever to rise again in the service of the Hamilton force.

He was not afraid of the pain, or the aftermath of such, but he greatly regretted that he might not be able to serve again the man he so admired and who would cause this.

Jack thought, I don't want to do this! The boy has

admitted his mistake in an honest way and has not tried to lay the fault at another's feet. He said mildly, 'Women are quite unaccountable, are they not, Mark?'

'Indeed,' agreed Mark fervently. 'But in this case—'

Jack interrupted him. 'I am inclined to let you off with a reprimand this night, my boy. That and a month's worth of punishment duties. That is not to say,' he added sternly, 'that I take this matter lightly. Only that I wish not to disturb the peace whilst our gracious queen is visiting. You will not approach this lady again?'

'No, sir,' Mark said instantly. 'But I must say again that she was in no way to blame—'

Jack interrupted again. 'Very well, then. Go back to your bed and think on this: I have my eyes on this particular lady. Do you, or anyone else, interfere with her safekeeping in the future and there will be no lenient outcome.'

'I understand absolutely,' Mark declared.

'Then you are dismissed,' Jack said quietly, 'and may choose to spread the word amongst your peers of what I have said this night.'

Anne had spent a restless night. Like all articulate people, she was furious with herself for not winning the honours in the disgreement she had had with Jack.

The man grows more impossible each day, she thought, getting up and retrieving her red gown from the floor where she had discarded it the night before in her haste to get to bed and end a disagreeable day. It was early yet, and she could hear no sound from the other rooms which housed her sisters-in-waiting.

It was another coldly dazzling day; looking out of the window, she could see the light sparkling on the frozen snow. It had not snowed for several days, but what lay was as hard as iron.

She tried to calculate the date. They had been at Ravensglass, she thought, three and a half weeks and the thaw that Elizabeth had spoken of seemed remote: it was far too cold. It had been planned that the royal party would leave Ravensglass in ten days' time; unless there was a dramatic change in the weather, Anne thought this unlikely. It would also prevent Ralph from coming.

If Ralph had been here last night, what would he have done about Mark Bolbey? she wondered, looking into her washing bowl and discovering a crisp layer of ice. Gingerly, she tapped at it with the handle of her silver brush and it splintered. She splashed the freezing water on her face, shivering, dried herself and looked discontentedly into the glass. Perhaps he too would have felt it was she who had transgressed.

Pulling the ribbon she had plaited her hair with last night, she released her hair, which instantly gathered the glittering white light. I know very little about Ralph, really, she thought. And of course I would not like him to begin laying about his fellows each time they admired his lady, but I had expected it of Jack Hamilton. Why?

Having bound back her hair, she went again to the window. She was restless not only because she had not seen the man she loved for weeks, but also because she had been cooped up in one place for too long. From here she could see the stables; the Hamilton men were leading their horses out into the wide yard. As she watched, the drawbridge was lowered with a grinding of the old chains and the men rode out.

That is what I need, Anne decided, a brisk ride in

the open air, and Jenny would appreciate the exercise too. She quickly dressed in a riding habit, and, taking her fur-lined cloak from her trunk, hastened down the stairs.

Jenny was delighted to see her. She showed her affection with nuzzling and the trilling neigh she reserved only for Anne. But her coat was dull and her eyes less bright than usual. Anne patted her, murmuring endearments, then found her rig and proceeded to saddle up. A groom came to her side.

'My lady? Is there anything I can do for you?'

'I wish to ride a little. Is there a man who can be spared to go with me?'

The ancient groom's face creased in anxiety. 'It is not permitted to leave the boundaries of the castle without my Lord Hamilton's permission.'

'Oh? But Jenny needs exercise, and we will not venture far.'

'My lord has inspected the ground and issued instructions that all the visitors' mounts will be exercised in due course.'

'Well, I wish to go now,' Anne said briskly. 'I have just observed a great number of riders leaving the castle, and if the conditions are satisfactory to them I will come to no harm. If you cannot provide an escort I will go alone.' Without help she swung into the saddle.

The groom grasped her bridle. 'It is not just the snow, my lady, but the danger... If you will wait, of your kindness, I will apply to my lord.'

Anne jerked the bridle from his hands. 'Oh, poof! I have been here weeks and seen no sign of danger. Kindly get out of my path.'

The groom stood helplessly back and watched her

leave the yard and trot briskly across the wooden
drawbridge. I'm a dead man, mourned old Jacob, when
my lord knows of this. Nevertheless, he made good
progress across the icy cobbles to tell him of it.

NO RISK, NO OBLIGATION TO BUY... NOW OR EVER!

CASINO JUBILEE

"Scratch'n Match" Game

Here's how to play:

1. Peel off label from front cover. Place it in the space provided opposite. With a coin carefully scratch away the silver box. This makes you eligible to receive two or more free books, and possibly another gift, depending upon what is revealed beneath the scratch-off area.

2. Send back this card and you'll receive specially selected Legacy of Love novels. These books have a cover price of £2.50 each, but they are yours to keep absolutely free.

3. There's no catch. You're under no obligation to buy anything. We charge nothing for your first shipment. And you don't have to make any minimum number of purchases - not even one!

4. The fact is thousands of readers enjoy receiving books by mail from the Reader Service, at least a month before they're available in the shops. They like the convenience of home delivery, and there is no extra charge for postage and packing.

5. We hope that after receiving your free books you'll want to remain a subscriber. But the choice is yours - to continue or cancel, anytime at all! So why not take up our invitation, with no risk of any kind. You'll be glad you did!

*Prices subject to change without notice.

YOURS FREE!

You'll look like a million dollars when you wear this elegant necklace! It's cobra link chain is a generous 18" long and its lustrous simulated pearl is mounted in an attractive pendant.

(Pictured larger to show detail)

CASINO JUBILEE
"Scratch'n Match" Game

SCRATCH HERE ?

PLACE LABEL HERE

CHECK CLAIM CHART BELOW
FOR YOUR FREE GIFTS!

2A6M

YES! I have placed my label from the front cover in the space provided above and scratched away the silver box. Please send me all the gifts for which I qualify. I understand that I am under no obligation to purchase any books, as explained on the back and on the opposite page. I am over 10 years of age.

BLOCK CAPITALS PLEASE

MS/MRS/MISS/MR _____

ADDRESS _____

_____

——————————— POSTCODE ———————————

CASINO JUBILEE CLAIM CHART			
🍒	🍒	🍒	WORTH 4 FREE BOOKS A FREE NECKLACE AND MYSTERY GIFT
🍒	🍒	🔔	WORTH 4 FREE BOOKS
🔔	🔔	🍒	WORTH 3 FREE BOOKS CLAIM Nº 1528

Offer closes 31st August 1996. We reserve the right to refuse an application. *Terms and prices subject to change without notice. Offer not available for current subscribers to this series. One application per household. Offer valid in UK and Ireland only. Overseas readers please write for details. Southern Africa write to IBS Private Bag X3010, Randburg 2125.
You may be mailed with offers from other reputable companies as a result of this application. If you would prefer not to share in this opportunity please tick box ☐

◆ DETACH AND POST CARD TODAY! ◆

MILLS & BOON READER SERVICE: HERE'S HOW IT WORKS

Accepting free books puts you under no obligation to buy anything. You may keep the books and gifts and return the invoice marked "cancel". If we don't hear from you, about a month later we will send you 4 additional books and invoice you for just £2.50* each. That's the complete price, there is no extra charge for postage and packing. You may cancel at any time, otherwise every month we'll send you 4 more books, which you may either purchase or return - the choice is yours. *Terms and prices subject to change without notice.

Mills & Boon Reader Service

FREEPOST

Croydon
Surrey
CR9 3WZ

NO
STAMP
NEEDED

If offer card is missing, write to: Mills & Boon Reader Service, P.O. Box 236, Croydon, Surrey CR9 3RU.

CHAPTER EIGHT

ANNE was enjoying her exhilarating ride. Beyond the confines of the fotresses, on the open ground, the snow was crisp but not unduly hazardous. She kept to what was obviously the highway, following the tracks of the previous riders, and also kept the castle in full sight behind her.

She was not a fool, and appreciated that Ravensglass was a fort, its purpose to repel marauders. She had no wish to become the victim of any border chief foolish enough not to stay home in such grim weather.

The wind in her face, she let Jenny have her head and finally intended turning back, when her attention was distracted.

A few miles beyond Ravensglass there was a low-lying settlement. She had seen the rough buildings on clear days from one of the high towers and, on asking about it, had been told it was the village of Transmere—a very small community of only twenty or thirty people.

Anne rode nearer, puzzled that no smoke rose from the cottages. She guided Jenny slowly between the poor dwellings; as she did so, a flurry of snowflakes swept down the wind tunnel created by the facing cottages. She paused, looking up at the sky. It had changed from grey to dark purple.

'We are in for a storm, I think, Jenny,' she murmured. 'Best get back, but first I believe we might ask for refreshment.'

She dismounted and walked carefully over the frozen ruts to the nearest hovel. She raised her crop and tapped on the door. There was no answer and no sound of life from within.

She trod on to the next; again there was no reply but the door of this little place was open and she looked inside, then drew back sharply. What a stench! Her mother, she thought disapprovingly, would never allow such an offence on the Maiden Court estate.

She progressed to the next hut, and this too was open and also malodorous, but now she was determined to make her presence known. She ducked her head in and looked about. There was evidence of habitation: on the scarred table a meal of sorts was laid out—bread, chunks of cheese—but, leaning closer, she saw that both were covered in green mould. Frowning, she went through a curtained alcove and stopped in horror.

On the one bed in the chamber lay three bodies. A man, a woman and a little child, all blue-white in death. In spite of the cold, decay was already present and explained the smell.

Various thoughts crowded into Anne's shocked mind. A ghost village, a place of death! What had happened here she had no idea, but her one desire was to leave immediately. She half ran across the mud floor, caught her foot in the pathetic rag rug and fell heavily. She regained her feet in an instant, but a sharp pain shot up from her right foot. A twisted ankle, she thought, limping to the door and out into the road.

The delicate sprinkling of snow had now become a blizzard; freezing particles beat against her as she peered into the veil of white for Jenny, who was standing patiently a few feet away. Anne reached her side with difficulty and hoisted herself back into the saddle.

'Ravensglass, Jenny,' she said. 'Back to the castle with all speed.' She urged the mare down the almost invisible road, but before the end had been reached Jenny pulled up, half fell, and toppled her mistress onto the ground.

The newly laid snow saved Anne from more injury. Bruised and shaken, she got up again, trying to ignore the now agonising pain in her ankle. She reached out for Jenny's bridle. 'What now?' she asked. Jenny shifted, one of her forelegs doubled. Anne ran her hand over it, noting the swelling, her heart sinking. 'Dear me,' she said, rallyingly, 'you and I are in similar case, sweet. We must find some shelter now and wait out the storm.'

She looked up the road. As the wind parted the curtain of white for a moment she saw a wooden building with a crude iron cross pinned to its walls. 'A church?' she murmured. 'Let us seek sanctuary there, then.'

Horse and rider limped in mutual pain to the place which implied safety to any Christian.

Jack Hamilton did not receive the information that Anne Latimar had left the castle until four hours after she had done so. He had risen at dawn to see the noble guests of the previous night well breakfasted and well provisioned for their journey. He had then escorted them for several miles, before making his way back to Ravensglass.

On arrival he had been informed that the Queen wished to see him, and spent an hour in her company discussing the possibilities of the royal party being able to leave on the agreed date. By the time he made his way from the Queen's apartments to his own apartment to change his clothing for the midday meal, the blizzard outside had reached howling proportions.

Changed and ready for another afternoon of—in his opinion—nonsensical frivolity, he was descending the stone steps at the rear of his hall when he was accosted by old Jacob. He listened to his tale in disbelief.

'And you let her go?'

'I had no choice, sir,' Jacob said humbly. 'She is a lady of some spirit... But she has not returned; I have watched for her.'

Jack let out an exasperated breath. 'Perhaps she came back with the party who were riding the boundaries?'

'No, sir. I have asked them, and not one of them saw the lady. They were driven in by the storm, and that was hours since.'

They were in the great hall now. Elizabeth and Leicester were seated at the head of the table enjoying their meal. Above their heads behind them the windows were a blur of white.

'Where could she be?' Jack asked irritably. He ran his eye over the assembled ladies, but there was no shining black head, no white-skinned woman. Even so, she might be in her chamber. But a page sent running came back with the news that one of the maids had told him that the Lady Anne had not been seen all morning, and Lady Fitzroy was much annoyed.

'One of the grooms told me she asked yesterday about Tranmere,' Jacob offered. 'She had seen it from her window.'

Tranmere... Jack's heart faltered. Tranmere occupied a dark place in his soul and had done for ten years since Marie Claire had died there. He had wanted the place razed to the ground when the tragedy happened but, of course, common sense had prevailed and he had continued to support it, to encourage produce to be supplied to the castle from the village, as had been the custom for a hundred years. But he had not been back there.

Two weeks ago, one of the villagers had tramped the ten miles to the castle and told of a sickness within the village. Jack had immediately despatched one of his physicians to care for it and the man had reported comfortably that they had the sweating sickness but it was not critical. Dr Rawley had left two of his deputies to deal with it and, as Jack had had his hands full entertaining the Queen of England, it had been some days before he had enquired again about Tranmere.

The doctor had been doleful on this occasion. The disease, he had said, had swept like fire through the tiny community. Everyone had died from it, even both of the young physicians from Ravensglass. Tranmere had been declared a plague village and no one must enter its precincts for fear of the infection.

Jack had received this information with a bitter heart. He hated Tranmere—the very name sent a cold chill through him—but he had been a good landlord and had a real care for his tenants. However, there was nothing to be done, other than to make a note that eventually his men would go down there, bury the dead with honour and burn the village.

If Anne Latimar had gone there today, with her wide eyes and young heart, and seen the dreadful sights that must meet those eyes, Jack felt that he would never forgive himself. His thoughts were reflected in Jacob's faded eyes and he laid a swift hand on his shoulder.

''Tis not your fault, my friend. As you have said, the lady has spirit and would not be denied. Go back to your fire and forget it.'

When the man had gone, Jack considered. He hoped Anne was not at Tranmere, but if she was at least there would be shelter there. He called to his second-in-command, gave him careful instructions, then hurried out to the stables. He saddled Valiant and ordered the drawbridge lowered once more.

Anne was truly frightened for the first time in her life. She had managed to get to the church with Jenny in tow. It was a poor place, comprising one large room and another adjoining to serve as the vestry. She had rubbed Jenny down in the latter with one of her petticoats and laid her cloak over the trembling horse.

In the main room she looked around. The church was really no more than a roof and four walls, an altar, some rough benches and a few decrepit wooden chairs. She sat on one of the benches, until the chill forced her to move about—a choice of two evils, for now her ankle was throbbing unmercifully.

She was cold, colder than she had ever been in her life before, and hungry too, for she had not broken her fast that day. It was now, she judged, beyond midday and she had eaten nothing since last night. And who knew where she was? No one. The groom would report that she had ridden out, but would probably decide that she had returned. Perhaps no one would come looking for her at all until tomorrow.

Well, I shall be frozen to death by then, she thought grimly.

Don't panic, she told herself sternly. You must think now how you may keep yourself warm.

Limping painfully around the primitive place, she saw a circle of stones placed centrally between the benches, the smoke-blackened rafters above indicating that here was the means of heating the house of God.

There was a pile of dry kindling within the stones. Thank God, she thought, glancing at the bare altar, but where was the means to light it? Another painful hobbling search revealed no tinder-box or flint. There would be one in any of the shacks, she knew, but she would rather freeze to death than go back there.

She went disconsolately out into the vestry again. Jenny turned patient eyes on her mistress and Anne looked enviously at the fur cloak covering the mare. Lifting one corner, she laid it over her shoulders and put her arms around Jenny's neck, grateful for the small warmth.

She had no idea how long she stood there, on one leg to ease the agony of her injured ankle, but the chill had crept up from the ground to invade her whole body when the door was thrust open and Jack Hamilton came in, shaking the thick layer of snow from his cloak.

Removing his hat and knocking it against the wall, he gave her a swift assessing glance. 'Is there no end to the trouble you are determined to cause me?' he enquired. His eyes travelled over Jenny. 'Well, at least you have had the sense to care for your mount. I must do the same.'

As he turned back to the door, Anne moved. The leg she was standing on was numb, so she put down her injured foot, cried out with pain, and all but fell. Jack crossed the space between them and caught her. 'What have you done to yourself?'

'Twisted my ankle,' she said, biting her lip. 'I am

indeed glad to see you,' she added through chattering teeth.

'Really? Surely you were not at all nervous or in danger of fainting? And your hair, I notice, is still in good curl.'

Her lip quivered. 'I was very much afraid,' she said with dignity. 'I thought I might not be found until too late.'

He picked her up and carried her back into the church, setting her down on one of the benches. He looked around. 'There used to be — Ah, there it is.'

'I found the fire, but had not the means to light it.' The chill had receded when his arms had been about her; now it returned, and with it the full horror of what she had seen in the village.

'Well, I have.' He strode to the fire and opened a slim leather bag slung over his shoulder, and a moment later she heard the strike of tinder and then the crackling of dry sticks. 'But this won't last long.'

He straightened up and, grasping one of the wooden chairs, put a booted foot through the seat. It fell to pieces and he shoved them onto the blaze. 'Now I must get my horse in out of that storm, then I will see to that ankle. Come, sit nearer the fire.' He dragged a bench over and she limped to it.

When he came back she was mesmerised by the leaping flames, a feeling of unreality competing with the pain in her ankle, and the recurring images of what she had seen in the cottage in her mind.

The light had failed outside now, and the chapel was shadowy and mysterious in the red glow of the fire. Jack lit a taper from the flames and went silently about igniting the candle stubs. They were made of inferior animal fat and smoked and smelled vile, but they illuminated the church.

'Now, that ankle. . .' He knelt before her, taking out his short dagger. 'It must come off,' he said.

'My foot?' She looked at him, horrified.

'The boot. That way the swelling will be free and it will hurt less.' He reached into his leather jerkin and took out a silver flask. He gave it to her. 'Brandywine. Take some now.'

'I don't need it.' No lady drank brandywine.

'You will,' he said laconically. He took the heel of her boot firmly in his hands and she gasped. She unstoppered the flask and drank as he cut through the top of her soft leather riding boot.

'More,' he said, without looking up. She took another mouthful and half choked as, in one swift movement, he removed the shoe of the boot and a searing pain made her dizzy enough to disprove what she had claimed about fainting.

'Brave girl,' he remarked. 'I will fetch some snow to pack around the swelling. Fortunately, there is an abundance of the stuff just beyond the door.'

When he returned, his hat filled with snow, Anne was staring at her foot. The ankle had doubled in size within the few moments he had been gone; it was purple and red and still increasing in size.

'A nasty sprain,' he said, running gentle hands over the foot, 'but no bones broken, I think. How did it happen?'

Anne took a breath without speaking and he looked up. 'Down in the village,' she faltered. 'In one of the little homes. . .'

'Yes?' He had taken linen from his jerkin and was

soaking it in the melting snow. He bound the cold compress carefully around her ankle.

'Jack. . .something terrible has happened here in this village—'

'I know,' he said briefly. He tore the bandage neatly, tied a knot and got to his feet, looking down at her. 'What did you see?'

'Three. . .people. All dead. A little child. . .no older than my baby brother—' She broke off, tears filling her eyes and rolling down her face. She made no attempt to dry them and, after a moment, he sat down beside her and brushed them away with his fingers.

'Hush now, there was nothing you could do.'

'I did not even say a prayer for them, though. When I reached this holy place I could have done that.' She gulped and pressed her hands together in a childlike gesture.

'We will say one now, shall we?' He and his company had already done this, in the chapel at Ravensglass, but he wanted to comfort her. He put an arm about her shoulders and said gravely, 'Dear Lord, please accept the souls of your servants of Tranmere, and grant them Your everlasting peace.'

Anne sniffed. 'Amen,' she murmured, comforted as much by his warm arm as by the prayer.

There was a small silence, apart from the snapping of the fire, then he asked, 'Are you hungry?'

'Yes. . .no. . .I don't know—I have not eaten this day.'

He got up and picked up his bag. Reaching into it, he produced a wrapped package and offered it to her. She opened it and looked doubtfully at the flat grey biscuits, the portions of dry-looking meat. Both looked unappetising. 'Thank you, but I think I am not that hungry. What exactly is it?'

'Soldiers' provisions. Hard tack bread and smoked beef. You ought to eat—liquor lies badly on an empty stomach.'

Her head was certainly revolving in the most alarming way. Anne knew she was no drinker and so dutifully nibbled at one of the biscuits, finding it had no taste at all. She laid it down again. 'I will make up for it at supper,' she said.

'When do you expect this supper to take place?' he enquired gravely. 'Not tonight, that is certain.'

'What do you mean?'

'I mean we are stranded. When I brought in Valiant the snow was already inches up the door. And had I not called to him I would never have found him in the dark, so blinding is the storm without. Also, your own mount is lame.'

'I know; she fell in the snow... But we cannot stay here alone—unchaperoned! Why, my reputation will be worth nothing!'

'Perhaps you should have thought of that before setting out. Before causing yet another of my household to be reprimanded through no fault of his own.'

'Mark Bolbey *was* at fault!' she returned angrily. 'But not your groom. I am sorry if I caused him any trouble. But surely we are only a few miles from the castle? You must know the way back well.'

'Of course I do,' he admitted. 'And might attempt it in this blizzard were I alone. But with two lame females I dare not.'

'You could go and bring help,' she suggested.

'You are very free with others' safety,' he said ironically. 'If I had wished to risk mishap to any of my men for such a dubious cause, I would have brought several with me. Then your reputation would have been even more compromised.'

His negligent words belied his efforts in the last two hours. Jack had left Ravensglass after an interview with his trusted second-in-command, Kit Mandrake. Jack's instructions had been most explicit: no one was to leave Ravensglass in his absence. No search party was to be assembled if he did not return.

Captain Mandrake had received these orders impassively, knowing that if any man could find the missing woman Hamilton could, and then she would be safe. If he did not find her, Hamilton would see to himself—there was no other soldier of the captain's acquaintance more able to survive in conditions that another might find perilous. Meanwhile, as Jack had impressed upon him, the first duty of Ravensglass was to their sovereign.

Jack had then left the castle and travelled a circuitous route. No tracks had been evident because of the snow, but he had ridden around in a circle, searching in the blinding snow. Finally, Tranmere had been the only remaining option.

'If you feel like that,' Anne said sulkily, 'I wonder you came at all. Why did you?'

'I owe your father a number of debts which can never be fully discharged,' Jack said simply.

'I would have been perfectly all right here on my own!'

Jack rebuckled his leather bag. 'Strange words from someone who had not even the good sense to light a fire already laid.'

'To light it I would have had to go into one of those cottages again to seek tinder, and I couldn't do that.'

'The dead cannot harm you,' he said, disarmed by her candour. 'Only the living can do that.'

'But I am afraid of dead people,' she said, swallowing. The alcohol was working in her now, loosening her tongue. 'You know, when my grandmother died I could not bear to look at her corpse, and she had been so kind to me when living. Besides, I preferred to remember her alive... I cannot understand anyone who makes a fetish of worshipping their beloved dead.'

'You are speaking of me?' he asked, his eyes suddenly dark in the combination of fire and candlelight.

'Can you not remember Marie Claire as she was when alive?'

'Do you think I do not?' he asked violently. 'Every waking moment for ten years, six weeks and two days!'

She was silenced. There was such a change in him now. All at once she saw the youthful lover of Marie Claire blaze out from the self-contained shell.

'I am sorry,' she said hesitantly. 'I did not mean to trespass upon your grief. Please forgive me. Would it further offend if I asked you to tell me about her? I would like to hear—to know her.'

He was rigid at her side. 'I never speak of her.'

'No...but as I have asked, and with kind intent...'

He relaxed a little, but did not speak. The fire had burned low now, its fuel almost exhausted. He got up and broke another of the ancient chairs into pieces. He threw in the dry wood and stood looking down at the flames.

'She was not beautiful,' he finally said slowly. 'If you and she were in a room together, every man must be looking at you. But she held a magic for me. After I met her I saw no other woman...ever.'

He paused, a little confused. After so many years of

being unable to speak of his dead wife to another living soul, now, in this unlikely place—for hadn't his love been struck down not a hundred yards from where he stood?—with this unlikely listener, he found that he could. A little of the iron around his soul shifted.

Anne did not speak, but linked her hands on her lap. The pain in her ankle was reduced to a dull ache; she gave her full attention to the man staring into the makeshift fire.

'She was very innocent,' Jack went on; his voice could hardly be heard in the quiet church, with the wind beating against its walls. 'Untouched by life, although she could be shrewd enough about others— but in such a kind way that they responded to her as they would not have done to a more worldly woman.'

He raised a hand to his lips. When bringing in his horse, the animal had shied in fright and forced his master back against the rough wall, scraping his knuckles.

'She sounds,' Anne said thoughtfully, 'very like my mother.'

'Lady Bess?' Jack shook his head. 'Oh, no, for your mother was—is—beautiful. When I was your father's young squire, half the court was in love with her dazzling looks. Marie Claire was never like that. 'Twas one of the many things I loved her for—she reserved herself only for me. . .' He stopped again and silence fell.

'And so you lost her,' Anne said. 'And your child too—a double tragedy.'

'My child?' Jack gave a bitter shrug. 'I would have exchanged that unimportant life for hers at any given time. If she had not been so heavy with. . .him that day, perhaps what happened would not have.'

Anne was silenced again by the expression on his face. To say that about his own child, she thought, when she had heard tales of men who, when having to make the fearful choice at childbirth, which sometimes happened in these days, had decided for their heir. . .

She should not have raised the subject in the first place. Jack Hamilton was frightening in his grief—a grief which should have been tempered by ten long years, but somehow was not.

She got up and took a painful step towards him, laying a hand on his arm. 'Gently now,' she murmured, as if he were a hurt and frightened animal. Indeed, he was rather like some highly bred and aristocratic stallion: a danger to others when roused, but an even greater danger to himself. 'I am sorry I made you speak of it.'

He looked down at her with a twisted smile. As earlier Anne had gained comfort from the pressure of his arm around her, so he was now calmed by her slim hand. Curious, he thought, because Anne was so absolutely the antithesis of his ideal of womanhood, yet he felt more intimate with her than with any other woman he had come into contact with since—since— He relaxed.

She moved away immediately, saying, 'Well, I suppose I must try with the dried meat again, for frankly I am starving!'

It was a long night. In spite of Jack's denuding the place of all available wood, the church grew unbearably cold. Anne protested loudly, but when dawn came to Tranmere she was warmly wrapped in Jack's wool shirt, his jacket and his fur-lined cloak.

She had even slept a little; he had not. The new day's

light penetrated the shelter to find him shivering and blue and knowing that this place would not serve for another twenty-four hours: they must try to make for Ravensglass.

'You go,' Anne said. 'And—if you can—bring back help when conditions improve.'

'I cannot leave you here,' he said angrily. 'Try to think clearly, woman!'

'I will not be a drag upon you, Jack!' she said with equal spirit. 'You are swift to point out that all this is my fault—well, I admit that! Why do we always have to *argue*?'

'Because you're a fool,' he said brusquely. 'This weather is set for days now. You thought last night was bleak? In the border country that was a mere taste of what there will be today and tomorrow. Now stop distracting me with your prattle and let me think how best I may go about getting you back to safety.'

'I'm a fool?' she said hotly. 'I return the compliment! If any one of your men—one of your hand-picked élite men—got themselves into such a predicament, would you have any hesitation in leaving *them*?'

'You must see it as different,' he replied, trying to think practically, to assess the pros and cons of the situation.

'How is it different?'

'Because I must get you back safe! Because—' Jack, befuddled from lack of sleep and never having had to plan any stratagem with an intransigent woman railing at him, was less than sure in his response '—I *care* that you get back safe!'

It was hard to tell who was more astonished by this declaration—the speaker or the hearer. But both knew in that moment that something significant had been forged between them with those words. Anne half smiled.

'Why,' she asked, 'do you always pretend to me that you are so tough, when 'tis obvious you are a very nice man?'

'For the same reason, presumably,' he answered, 'that you prance around pretending to be a brazen, hard-faced little baggage when you are actually a very nice girl.'

Her face lit up, and her laugh rang around the bare chapel. 'Well, then, we are agreed at last. We are both very nice people! But in rather desperate circumstances. Let us try to combine our forces now.'

She stood up, testing her weight on her injured foot. It was not too painful—Jack had continued applying icy compresses throughout the night, considerably reducing the swelling. She could certainly manage to sit a horse. But Jenny could not possibly bear her mistress; she must be led.

'We must both ride Valiant and spare Jenny. And we must share what warm clothing we have between us.' She stripped off his cloak and jacket and handed them back to him.

Five hours later, they arrived at Ravensglass. It had been an arduous journey, through deep and drifting snow, and through an almost impenetrable snowstorm.

Jack had done all the walking. He would not allow Anne to give up her place astride Valiant's broad back, Jenny's bridle looped over one frozen arm, despite all her protests. Doggedly he had led them, his inbuilt compass guiding him always towards his home. At the gatehouse Jack found the breath to shout his demands for entry, and the drawbridge was lowered and they were immediately surrounded in help.

Anne was lifted stiff and frozen from the stallion's back and carried bodily to her room. Jack was similarly cared for, after giving minute and passionate instructions regarding all three of his charges. Both sank into sleep, a pint of scorching ginger cordial inside them, and both had similar thoughts.

Anne thought, If, at any time in my life from henceforth, I should have the impossible to do, then give me Jack Hamilton as friend and helper.

Jack thought, My God, were I required to go out and fight the French this very day, I could ask for no more than I be granted a handful of men with Anne Latimar's heart!

When Anne awoke the next morning, she turned over in her bed, bewildered for an instant as to where she was. Her sleep had been so deep, so totally dreamless, that awakening was like pushing her way up through dark clouds. She sat up.

'Ah, you are awake at last.' Lady Fitzroy laid down her needlework and came to the foot of the bed. ''Tis almost noon,' she added disapprovingly.

Anne pushed back her long black hair. She smiled tentatively. 'You have been watching over me, Lady Maud? How very kind.'

'I was so instructed,' Maud said, sniffing. 'Lord Hamilton's instructions were that you be attended during the night, and indeed until you awoke.' And the fire regularly rebuilt, and hot bricks wrapped in flannel put into your bed at intervals, she thought resentfully, having missed some of her night's rest.

She lifted a cloth from a mug on a table by the bed

and put it into Anne's hands. 'Here, drink this; it is still warm, I think.'

Anne sipped the concoction of milk and honey and cinnamon. 'I have put you to trouble, my lady. I am indeed sorry.'

'Sorry you will be,' Maud said drily, 'when Her Majesty has had her say. Whatever can have possessed you to do so foolish a thing and shame Her Grace?'

'I had no notion that my little ride would result in danger or inconvenience,' Anne said placatingly.

'I am sure you did not, but to leave the castle at all, without permission... Madam does not expect such conduct from her ladies.' Maud took the empty mug and swept out of the room, leaving Anne to dress and contemplate the coming interview.

I ought to be trembling and distraught, she thought, washing and dressing and wishing she had a maid to tame her hair. Pushing the long, shining strands untidily under a cap, she knelt on the window-seat and looked out at the violent white storm. In spite of the high-banked fire, and the warm clothing she had put on, she was still bitterly cold; Jack had spoken true—they would have had no chance of survival exposed in the poor shelter of the church at Tranmere.

But I am not! I am neither trembling nor distraught! she discovered, breathing on the icy pane to give herself a little circle to peer through. I could have died yesterday, and probably would have were it not for that extraordinary and stubborn man! A brush with death rearranges one's perspective, and I really cannot fear a few sharp words from Elizabeth.

But those words had to be faced and she went slowly down the stairs towards the sounds of the midday meal already in progress in the hall. As she turned the winding stone steps a man was coming lightly up and they met in the narrow curve just before the foot.

'Lady Anne.' Jack bowed his head and looked up at her.

'Good day, Jack,' she smiled. 'How are you? None the worse for our adventure?'

He mounted the couple of steps necessary to bring him level with her. The area was so confined, they were only inches apart. 'I am none the worse,' he replied shortly. 'And nor, from your looks, are you.'

His tone dismayed her. Surely now they were on such terms that this cold behaviour from him was inappropriate?

Her smile vanished. Surely this could not be the same man who had so gently encouraged her over those treacherous miles from Tranmere? Who had walked waist-deep in icy snow that she might sit safely astride his horse? Who had, when her spirit had faltered, lifted her briefly from that horse and embraced her in the sparkling white ocean, and murmured endearments against her frozen cheek?

She said, 'I have received one lecture on my conduct already this day, and am shortly to receive another. But do, by all means, add yours.'

Jack, who remembered every part of that journey they had taken together, including those endearments, flattened his back against the rough stone wall. He had not had a dreamless night; on the contrary, it had been filled with bewildering phantoms.

Marie Claire had been with him, shadowy and insubstantial and quite unable to compete with a more vivid and vibrant personality. Anne, her pale oval face framed in jet-black hair, her red lips smiling, had dominated the misty night dreams and Jack was furious with her for doing so.

He could even, he thought now on the cold stone stairway, smell the perfume rising from her skin and hair, which he had been so aware of all the miles from Tranmere.

He said, 'Thank you, but I will leave that to Her Majesty, who has been simmering for some hours.'

'Has she?' In spite of her brave thoughts earlier, now Anne looked crestfallen. Perhaps it was because Jack had apparently withdrawn his support, appeared to have retreated once more to that unreachable place he chose to inhabit, but Anne limped on down the stairs full of apprehension.

Elizabeth did not disguise her annoyance with Anne, who was interviewed after the meal in one of the small cold ante-rooms off the hall. She expected high standards of behaviour from any lady attending herself, and made that fact abundantly clear.

However, during his report to her that morning, Hamilton had somehow managed to convey an impression of Anne's courage and fortitude during the affair, and, as the Queen admired both these qualities, this tempered her reprimand.

Even so, Anne left her mistress's presence feeling very chastened. And, as she did so, it struck her that she had not thought of Ralph Monterey in two whole days.

CHAPTER NINE

THE thaw came suddenly five days later. The natives of Ravensglass had been expecting it: snow so early in the year was always followed by a dramatically swift thaw. Within two more days Hamilton adjudged the roads fit for travelling, his scouts having informed him that the worst of the snow had been confined to a relatively narrow radius, and the Queen instructed her small entourage to prepare to leave for Greenwich without delay.

The day before their departure, while the other ladies were in a fever of packing and fussing, Anne took the opportunity to walk around outside. It was slushy underfoot, but she was warmly clad and shod and her foot—raised at regular intervals in the last days—was very much improved.

A watery sun had appeared today and she was grateful for its dim radiance. In the small enclosure of Marie Claire Hamilton's statue she paused, hearing footsteps behind her. Jack Hamilton, who for the first time since the snow had come had been able to drill his troops, had dismissed them for the meal hour and so was free.

He bowed to Anne. 'You are taking the air, after so much close confinement?'

'As you see, although not so disastrously as the last time, I hope.' If he had been trying to avoid her since their return from Tranmere, she thought, he had been most successful. She had not seen him in the hall, nor had any word with him.

He was not listening to her now. His eyes were fixed on the statue commemorating his dead wife. He was dressed in the colours of his regiment, was bare-headed, and had received a cruelly close haircut some time in the last few days.

'You will be glad to be back to soldiering now, of course?'

'Hmm? Oh, yes, it is all too easy to become soft playing indoor games.' His eyes were fixed on the pale marble features.

'Well—' she turned '—I imagine you will see us off tomorrow, Jack, but I would like to say thank you now—for your hospitality and for rescuing me from my foolishness.'

At last he looked at her. 'Your farewell is premature, lady. I will be accompanying you to Greenwich.'

'You will?'

'Naturally. I brought Her Majesty here—of course I will see her safely back again.'

'Oh.'

'I hope that does not displease you?'

Why must he always be so aggressive? she wondered. Why must he hide the vulnerable part of him she had seen at Tranmere and, indeed, during her stay at Ravensglass, when it was obvious that he was a deeply caring commander, whose least valuable recruit received his careful, if brusque, attention?

'Of course it doesn't. Why should it? But can you bear to be parted from this place so soon again?'

He gave her a stormy look. Anne had merely been making reference to his duties as general here at the fortress, but he had obviously taken her remark to be a reference to his lost love's grave.

He let his eyes measure her in the pale sunlight. He had, indeed, been avoiding her lately. It was a matter, he thought, of loyalty: this girl was taking up his thoughts, his dreams, and that was nothing short of treason! Treason to the one who had occupied his life for so long—

'Sir?' one of his men interrupted, respectfully. Jack looked at him enquiringly. 'A gentleman at the gate requests leave to enter.'

'His name?'

'Sir Ralph Monterey.'

Anne's heart gave a great leap. Ralph, here! Jack, glancing at her, thought she looked as if someone had lit a flame behind her eyes. His tone was brusque as he gave his man the order to lower the drawbridge, and Ralph's handome horse came mincing over the slippery surface and into the courtyard.

Ralph had set off from the south in fine weather. He had been assured of a comfortable passage—there were a great many gentlemen's manor houses along the way. At the last stop the weather had turned poor and Lord and Lady Glenning had extended a warm invitation that he stay until it was more clement.

There had been quite a large house party and Ralph had enjoyed himself. He had been assured by Tom Glenning that the party from Greenwich had reached Ravensglass in good order and Tom had suggested that they both ride there as soon as there was a thaw. When the day had come, however, Lord Glenning had been indisposed, so Ralph had taken the road alone.

Now he manoeuvred his dancing mount towards Anne, dismounted and swept off his hat.

'Anne, my dear, how good it is to see you again. Such a time I have had in coming. Had you quite despaired of me?'

Anne thought guiltily that she had scarcely given him a thought at all for days. But she made up for it now, raising her face for his kiss.

Jack watched them in silence. He had been fretting indoors for too long, in the company of women, and unable to keep his men from the inevitable softening process induced by too much wine and playing, late nights and overindulging at the table. That no doubt explained his intense irritation as he witnessed this reunion.

Having covered Anne's face in kisses, Ralph turned and offered his hand. 'Jack, I must, I am sure, thank you for taking such good care of this lady. She looks absolutely radiant, does she not?'

Jack gave the hand cursory pressure. 'No looking after was involved,' he said drily. 'She has been the perfect guest.'

'I am sure of that.' Ralph looked about him. 'Well, nothing has changed here, I see.'

'Nothing has changed,' agreed Jack. 'Excuse me.' And he turned and walked away.

'And he changed least of all,' Ralph laughed, looking after him. 'I don't think you know, sweetheart, that I used to be one of Hamilton's merry band at Ravensglass?'

'Why, no, I didn't.' Somehow Anne could not imagine Ralph being part of this fraternity, but then his father had been one of the old King's famous soldiers— where better could he have sent his older son to learn the knightly arts? 'They are a very likely bunch of boys—you must have been in your element.'

'Thank you for the implied compliment,' Ralph said, smiling. 'But I was perfectly miserable for an entire twelvemonth, as might be expected with such a joyless captain.' He turned inside, not noticing the little pucker forming on Anne's white brow.

Elizabeth received Ralph Monterey with pleasure. A handsome face was always attractive to her and, combined with a witty tongue, irresistible. On hearing that he had been visiting the Glennings and, being advised that she was at Ravensglass, had ridden specially to join her escort home, she was doubly pleased.

This slight deviation from the truth on Ralph's part was not entirely self-seeking—if he had told the Queen that he had journeyed all the miles from Greenwich to pay court to her youngest waiting lady, Elizabeth would not have favoured him, and she would almost certainly have made Anne's life miserable. If anyone was making an effort in Elizabeth Tudor's vicinity, it was necessary that it was for her. She felt it fitting tribute and an appropriate end to an interesting if rather extended visit to Ravensglass. So, dressed in brilliant emerald-green embroidered with diamonds, Elizabeth invited Ralph to sup with her so that she might hear of the messages of goodwill he had collected on the way north, and also to tell her again of his undying allegiance to herself.

Robert Dudley watched Ralph's manoeuvring and the Queen's response to it with sardonic amusement. He had seen enough prospective rivals spring up in the last few years to know that Monterey would be one of them, and he accepted this as the lot of a man in his position. But he did not care for Monterey; there was something essentially cold-hearted about the man.

Personally, he was not much interested in the liaison that was apparently to be formed between the Latimar girl and Ralph, but he liked Anne, and her brother George was one of his dearest friends, and he thought that whatever woman got Monterey would have a sorry marriage.

When Elizabeth had been invited to take the floor in one of the lively dances, he said maliciously, 'My dear Ralph, what pretty speeches you have been making all evening! And here was I thinking you had ridden all those arduous miles to see little Lady Anne.'

Ralph gave him a cool look. 'Why should you say that?'

'I believe the lady herself mentioned it—in the strictest confidence, naturally. But of course your coming here has made it more formal.'

Ralph turned the ring Anne had given him on his finger. It was so fine a stone that even the thrifty use of candles at Ravensglass could not dull its blue-white splendour. 'Not at all. The arrangement is not formal until all the details are definite. So I would be obliged to you, Leicester, if you would not mention it.'

Robert fondled his glossy beard. 'Details not definite. . .? In that case you will have to be vigilant of the wench until they are: she has attracted a great deal of attention during her visit here.'

Ralph looked contemptuously around the hall. 'Naturally she would do so here—amongst the women-starved boys of Hamilton's regiment. Unless, of course, you are including yourself in that remark?'

Robert watched Elizabeth being lifted high by Captain Mandrake. He was adept now at pocketing the kind of sly insult that Ralph had just delivered, but he would not forget it. 'I was not speaking of boys. Jack Hamilton's youthful looks belie his age.'

'Hamilton?' Ralph laughed. 'I fear no competition from that quarter. The man has been encased in a block of ice since losing that mousy little wife of his.'

'Indeed. But I believe he and Anne managed to light a small fire during their enforced seclusion at Tranmere, and perhaps some of that ice you speak of is now melting.'

Ralph gave him his full attention. 'I am afraid I don't understand what you are implying.'

'Implying? Why, nothing at all! Of course, had it been any other gentleman, I might be speaking of more than implication, but—as you say—Hamilton is the kind of man who can be trusted with even such a tasty dish as Anne Latimar.'

'I wish you would just tell me what you are talking about.'

'I beg your pardon. . .I felt sure the lady would have acquainted you with the details. . . However—' Robert told the story, concluding with a mock-sentimental sigh. 'Truly, it was a splendid sight to see them come in safely—she half-frozen on his brave horse, he almost dead from supporting her over the weary miles—and he not content with such effort but still ranting about how she must be cared for with warmth and cosseting—'

He had the satisfaction of seeing Ralph's fair face darken. 'My dear fellow! No need for such an expression, I am sure—' But he was talking to the air, for Ralph had risen abruptly and gone onto the floor in search of Anne.

When he found her he cut in on the blushing squire who had been looking after her and making sure she did not tax her sore ankle, and led her away into an alcove. It was an unfortunate choice, for it was the same place where Anne had had to listen to the Queen's lecture over her absence from the castle a week ago.

Without preamble he demanded, 'Is it true you spent a night in some place alone with Hamilton?'

'Why, Ralph, there is no need for such a stern tone! The whole affair was a misadventure, very easily explained.'

'Then pray do so.'

Anne launched into an explanation, greatly resenting the need to do so. Someone had obviously been making mischief, but, even so, she felt that Ralph should not look at her in that accusing way, or use that aggressive tone with her. After stopping and starting several times, and becoming slightly entangled in her discourse, she stopped.

'But you did spend the night alone with him?' Ralph asked, scarcely listening. 'Why so? I know Tranmere — 'tis a few short miles away.

'I know, Ralph,' Anne said, with an attempt at a reasonable tone. 'But each one of those miles could have been a hundred in the conditions prevailing that day. I assure you that during that time the road from Tranmere was quite impassable. I really had no option.'

'Perhaps you wished for no option.'

Anne paled. She could see now that she should have told Ralph immediately of what had occurred, but they had been so happy in their meeting, so intent on discussion of what her father had said with regard to their match... Besides, the whole matter had simply been an unavoidable accident, and— What exactly was he suggesting?

'I cannot think what you mean by that! My father's daughter should not be accused of what you are obviously suggesting, and especially not by the man who pretends to love her and want her for his wife!'

'My wife must be above reproach!'

'You are the only one doing the reproaching, Ralph!'

It was true. Anne had been rebuked by the Queen and her ladies, but not one of them had implied for a moment that they thought her guilty of any impropriety.

They had both raised their voices in anger and were attracting interest from the company around them. A tall shadow detached itself from one of the walls of the hall and came to their side.

'I do not know the reason for this altercation,' Jack Hamilton said quietly, 'but would ask you to please take it elsewhere. My hall is not a bear garden.' He drew aside the curtain behind them to reveal an anteroom to the alcove, and all three moved into it.

'The reason for this altercation,' Ralph said furiously, 'is your recent conduct with this lady, Hamilton!'

'My conduct—? Ah, I imagine you speak of the unfortunate circumstances we found ourselves in a week or so ago. I am sure I do not have to advise you that you have nothing to rebuke the Lady Anne about.'

'I am afraid you do have to so advise me.'

'Ralph!' Anne cried. 'What are you saying?'

'What any gentleman in the situation would. I do not blame you, my dear. Obviously the fault is entirely Hamilton's and he must answer for it.'

'Oh, that is not true,' Anne said passionately. 'If you had only listened to what I said—that I was foolish enough to leave the castle—that I placed myself in harm's way and Jack *rescued* me. Really, Ralph, you should be shaking his hand and thanking him for it!'

'I have no intention of doing either,' Ralph said coldly. 'Instead, I have quite a different activity in mind.' He bowed to Jack. 'I think you know what I mean, Hamilton, and at a more suitable time, and in a more suitable place, I expect you to accommodate me.' He gave Anne another angry glance and left them.

Anne looked blank. 'What? Oh, surely he does not mean—?'

'I fear he does,' Jack said. Ill-mannered young cub, he thought, to challenge me in my own home! His sympathies were not with Monterey, but he also thought, It is truly amazing the amount of damage a woman like Anne Latimar can wreak.

Anne had discovered a chair in the sparsely furnished room; she sank into it, looking tragic. 'Oh, no! It must not come to that.'

'And will not,' Jack answered briskly. ''Twould be nothing short of murder. The young fool has no idea of what he would be involving himself in. I—were I sufficiently interested to engage with him—would not give up my life for such a trivial cause.'

His statement was not quite the insult to Anne that it might have been considered to be. It was simply that Jack, who had risked his life so many times for genuine and honourable causes, had a contempt for duelling, thought it no more than the occupation of men with no real and serious thing on their minds.

As a young man he had seen men called out for no greater sin than tripping over another's feet on the dance-floor, or wearing an identical colour of costume for a masque. Needless to say, it was strictly forbidden in his regiment at Ravensglass.

Anne looked at him in silence. Of course, she was glad to hear him say that. She had no desire to be the reason for two men meeting on the field of honour, particularly since no honour was involved here, but she could understand in part Ralph's feelings, and resented Jack's casual dismissal of them.

'Don't worry,' Jack said caustically, misinterpreting her silence. 'I will find some acceptable reason for not meeting him—you will not suffer any loss of prestige.'

Anne stood up. 'I did not provoke this!' she exclaimed angrily. 'Why must you always assume that I am at the root of disharmony?'

'Because you usually are,' he said drily. 'At least that has been so in the short time I have known you.'

Frustrated, Anne said bitterly, 'You always think the worst of me! None of it is ever my fault.'

'Dear me, no,' Jack said. 'Not your fault that you so inflamed one of my young officers that he must assault you! Not your fault that you must defy common sense and decide to ride about the countryside during a snowstorm. And definitely not your fault that you managed to convey to your ardent sweetheart that I had somehow compromised you.'

Anne swallowed, near to tears. 'I did none of those things!' she said indistinctly. 'At least, I did go riding and that was rash, but—oh, I don't know why such things should always happen to me.'

Jack ran a finger inside his tight pleated ruff. All formal dress was uncomfortable to him; he was more at home in practical clothing. Tonight, the last of the royal visit, he had made a special effort and now the stiff satin costume and flashing jewellery he wore on hands and ears irked him.

The jewellery had belonged to his family and Marie

Claire had loved to see him wear it. The Hamilton diamonds were famous and he had put them on tonight as much as a mark of respect for her memory as for his queen. Normally he wore only his wedding ring, converted to an ear adornment, and hers, which he had, on that terrible day on her funeral, removed from her slim finger.

Thinking of Marie Claire, he was suddenly ashamed of his jeering comments to Anne. She was nothing to him, he assured himself; he was foolish to think of his budding friendship with a girl he was unlikely to see in the future as being in any way treacherous. Anne could take nothing away from Marie Claire—she possessed it all and unconditionally.

'I suppose, Anne,' he said more kindly, 'it is this way: if one is so very—er—outstanding, so beautiful and talented at so many things, it should bring a certain responsibility. If you have the ability to draw others to your side, to make them notice everything you do, there is inherent in the gift a. . .duty to take care. Can you understand at all what I am saying?'

She nodded. Without loss of modesty she was aware that she had the gift he spoke of. In the past, it had brought her only happiness, but her life was different now, lived with diferent people. She was as much interested by his unexpected analysis of her character as by the thought that here was a man who had the imagination to notice it.

'Then,' continued Jack, 'knowing all this to be so, perhaps you will recognise the dangerous occasion in the future?'

'Do you really think I am beautiful?'

Perhaps he should have saved his breath; she had picked out the one word she was really interested in. 'I have said it on at least two occasions. Do you doubt it? "Hair like polished ebony, skin like cream, eyes like the stars a lifetime's span away from ordinary mortals, of so deep a blue a man could be lost in their oceanic depths"— Not my words, but seen by me on a paper confiscated from one of my men who was wasting daylight hours composing a poem to you.'

Anne, her eyes still on his face, said, 'I am more than that, you know. What one looks like, what one can achieve with inherited skills, does not denote the real person. What counts is the person beneath all that.'

There was a hushed pause. The illumination in the room was fading and he was only able to see the pale oval of her face and her great dark eyes. Jack remembered the puzzling but unforgettable dreams he had experienced the night following their return to Ravensglass from Tranmere, and his mind shied from that remembrance.

He offered his hand. 'Let me take you back to the festivities.'

She smoothed her crumpled skirts. 'As to what you have said about Ralph's challenge—I appreciate it. Why do you suppose he issued it in the first place?'

What Jack supposed he had no intention of saying. He thought Monterey an egocentric and posturing fool, who had fought and decided fatally five duels in the past—all against very young men and all in circumstances Jack considered less than honourable; but he had no wish to come between Anne and her love.

He said, 'I have no idea. Pride, I suppose. The Montereys, a fine family, probably have an excess of it.'

* * *

The party from Ravensglass arrived at Greenwich in the following week. It had not been a hazardous journey. Once they had left Northumberland, with its covering of slush and mud, they had found the rest of the terrain quite gentle. But Jack, lifting his eyes frequently to the unsettled sky, had thought it not unlikely that the weather which had begun its course in the north would proceed south eventually.

He rode beside Elizabeth and Dudley, and was quite stubborn in his insistence of this position in the entourage, for he felt strongly that on this particular expedition his sovereign was his own special responsibility.

This was very aggravating to Dudley, who, as Master of Horse, was officially responsible for the Queen on all her journeys, but he did not dispute the matter. Indeed, he found it impossible to hold such absolute commitment against Hamilton, for Jack was so obviously lacking in ambition in the ways most courtiers were; he simply made it clear that he was just doing his duty.

The rest of the group chose their travelling companions amongst their friends. The ladies of Elizabeth's attendants rode together, with their outriders of hand-picked men from the Hamilton regiment; the guards from Greenwich selected the front and rear of the train for their place. Only Anne Latimar rode apart, too miserable to hold conversation, her eyes fixed on the road ahead.

Ralph had not yet relented towards her. At breakfast, before they had left the castle, he had sat near the Queen and had not looked her way; after the meal, amidst the bustle of departure, she had not been able to catch his attention and he had not even offered to mount her on her horse, although he had made a great show of assisting the Ladies Fitzroy and Warwick. It had been left to old Jacob to put her up and as he had done so she had given him her charming smile.

'Thank you, Jacob. I am sorry to have made trouble for you with Lord Jack.'

Jacob had crinkled his faded blue eyes. 'Don't you worry about that, lady. He's not a man to lay blame where it's not warranted.' He had checked her girth and saddle then stepped back to allow her to follow the others.

Really? Anne had thought. In my case I *always* get the blame from him!

It was not a happy trip for Anne. They stayed at various nobles' houses on the road and were royally treated, but she could take no pleasure in any of it because still Ralph made no attempt to speak with her. As they neared Greenwich, Jack Hamilton relinquished his position at the Queen's side and reined in his horse until Anne came alongside him.

'You look very tired, Anne,' he said. 'Did you not enjoy the hospitality? Were you not well housed?'

Anne turned her cloak collar up against the driving wind. 'I was well housed, Jack.'

'Then. . .?'

'If I looked tired it is because I am sick at heart. Ralph has spoken no word to me since the last night at Ravensglass.'

The road was churning mud now, near to the palace and its consequent traffic. Jack reached out and caught Anne's bridle as Jenny sank into the mire to her fetlocks and all but fell.

'Thank you. I was not paying attention. . .' She patted her mare. When they were in progress again she asked abruptly, 'Have you and Ralph talked of what happened that night?'

Looking up, Jack could see the grim spire of the palace pointing at the sky. 'Hmm? Oh, no, I imagine he will want to inform his friends—seconds—and do all formally. But don't worry; it will come to naught.'

He hesitated, looking at her now and thinking how frail she looked in the grey light, then said haltingly, 'It occurs to me, Anne, that what I said myself that night—regarding—er—trivia— I did not mean to have you believe I felt your...honour to be trivial. But I expressed myself badly as usual.'

Anne gave a little lopsided smile. The phrase reminded her of her father, as nothing else about Jack did, because the Earl was fond of declaring himself inarticulate when no one was ever in any doubt of what he was trying to say. The same could be said of Jack Hamilton. 'I understood you then, Jack, and I agree with you now. Neither of us was at fault.'

'Well,' he said, 'we are in agreement yet again. If we are not careful it will become a habit. And here is Greenwich.'

He felt the usual apprehension about going into a society he had no use for. The close confinement with men he had little in common with, the noise, the constant jockeying for position and for favour, the endless discussions about clothing and hair and the latest dance step—for men were no different in this respect in court circles than women—and, most of all, the impossibility of finding any place in the mêlée where a man might be alone with his thoughts did not appeal to him at all.

He had insisted upon seeing Elizabeth safely home, knowing the English climate might prevent him from returning to Ravensglass until the spring, and had no regrets about his decision. But it would be hard for him.

Jack rode over the grassy lawns to the palace, the lowering clouds gathering force above him, with resignation.

Her fellow ladies in the outer royal bedchamber

been invited in all amongst the Ravens...

George said

whom he had always

trip he had queried his

CHAPTER TEN

ANNE, too, re-entered the life at the royal residence
with mixed feelings. If it had been Richmond or
Hampton, within easy reach of Maiden Court, she
would have been happier. She desperately needed the
counsel of her mother and father at this time.

Her fellow ladies in the outer royal bedchamber
greeted her cordially, exclaimed over her tales of what
had happened at Ravensglass — although she omitted
to mention the Tranmere affair — and generally made
her welcome.

Lady Allison said one thing on the first evening
which cheered her considerably: 'Your brother,
George, is at Greenwich, you know, with his new
bride,' and by chance he and Judith were in the crowd
at the foot of the stairs as she came lightly down to
supper. George looked up and saw her.

'Anne!' He caught her as she ran into his arms and
the three linked arms into the hall.

'You look so happy, George,' Anne said, a catch in
her voice, as they sat at one of the long tables and
helped themselves to food.

'Why not, sister?' George asked, with an ardent look
at his wife. 'I am happy. And you? I returned to
Maiden Court to find Mother in a great taking over
one of your suitors finally being granted your approval.
We both want to hear about the matter, so pray put us
out of our misery. It is Ralph Monterey, is it not?'

'Yes, 'tis Ralph,' Anne said, inspecting her food and

wondering why she had chosen it. 'He is the Earl of
Monterey's son, and. . .we met. . .fell in love. . .and—'

'Is he here tonight?' Judith asked. She and her new
sister-in-law had had rather a stormy passage over her
marriage with George—Anne having been totally
opposed to it—but in her new-found happiness and
security she was prepared to let bygones be bygones.
'Can we meet him?'

Anne abandoned her attempt to eat and glanced
about her. 'He is on the top table,' she said composedly,
'beside the Queen.'

Judith looked up to the dais where Ralph was
engaged in conversation with Lord Cecil. He had
greatly furthered his ambitious cause with Elizabeth on
the journey from Ravensglass and had consequently
been invited to sit amongst the favoured few tonight.
He had seen Anne come into the hall, but yet again
had not acknowledged her. His anger over the affair at
Tranmere had cooled now, but he was not averse to
keeping her anxious for a little longer.

'Oh, he is handsome!' Judith said happily.

George said nothing. He knew Monterey, of course,
and was a good friend of his younger brother, Tom,
whom he had always hoped might win his sister's hand.
Ralph he disliked, thinking him a charming waster.

At Maiden Court, on his return from his marriage
trip, he had queried his father's acceptance of the
match, but Harry Latimar would not be drawn. He had
made one telling remark, however, and that was that
close association with Ralph at Greenwich might
change Anne's mind. George hoped that might be so;
meanwhile, he planned to keep Yuletide at Greenwich
and also have an eye on his twin.

Anne ate little at the meal. She had appreciated the

plain food at Ravensglass and found the food at Greenwich—especially rich tonight in honour of the Queen's return—over-sauced and over-spiced. Anyway, she could think of nothing but her estrangement with Ralph. Surely he could not avoid her for the rest of the night?

From being upset and miserable she found herself becoming angry that he should treat her this way. For what had she actually done? Been a little foolish, but her nature was impulsive—his suspicions were the insult in this, not Jack's actions, and Anne felt that nothing would do but to tell him so at the first opportunity.

It came at midnight. The Queen was in her element. At the most ordinary of times she was a poor sleeper and could sustain energy all through a long night. Tonight, with her return to her court, to the nucleus of the élite of English men and women, she was even more highly charged than usual, and launched into an evening of dancing and revelry, expecting all to join her.

Anne, a little unsteady on her feet for her ankle was still unreliable, joined the merry crowd on the dancefloor, and within moments she was partnered by Ralph.

In the required steps of the dance she curtsied and he offered her his arm. They progressed down the line and, as the next pair followed suit, were able to talk.

'Well, Ralph! she said, her eyes snapping. 'You cannot ignore me now.'

'Why should I wish to do that?' he asked. Actually, she pleased him very much at this moment, dressed in her red gown and obviously one of the most attractive women in the assembly.

'You have spoken no word to me since the night we discussed my sojourn at Tranmere.'

This was carrying the battle into the enemy camp with a vengeance, and Ralph did not quite like it. He had not forgotten their discussion, or his challenge to Hamilton, and was quite prepared to stand by and further it, but his feelings about the affair had changed.

For one thing, the Queen had touched briefly upon Anne's escapade during the ride from the north and Ralph had not gained the impression that Her Majesty would hold the matter against her lady-in-waiting. Also, during the nights spent with the young men of Hamilton's outriders, it had occasionally been discussed and Ralph had learned that Anne was a great favourite with them. Sweet and pretty, they had all agreed, but also kind and modest.

They all knew the details of the incident, but had put no emphasis on it other than to say that the lady had wished to exercise her mount. She was a rare one with horses, they also said, so it was small wonder that she would not tolerate Jenny's incarceration.

As to their commander going out to bring her home—that too was quite natural. No question of anyone being compromised had been spoken of, or apparently thought of. In fact, Ralph felt slightly the fool for making an issue of it.

What had annoyed him in his interview with Anne had been her partisan defence of a man he could not abide. However, he had no wish to disturb the arrangement he had with Anne and put an arm around her waist to draw her to the side of the hall.

'I was hasty,' he said placatingly. 'I realise that now. But I at no time blamed you and made that clear.'

Anne looked up at him. Surely she had missed him

dreadfully whilst away from him? What if she were to lose him? 'I should not have said what I just did, darling; please forgive me.'

He smiled. He had half apologised; she had put all her generous spirit into retracting her own words. This was how it should be, for Ralph wanted no domineering woman for a wife. His mother was inclined that way, and he had witnessed his father—an otherwise self-assured and imposing man—often made to feel discomfited and even guilty by a female half his size.

He took Anne's hands and kissed each of her fingers in turn. 'Of course I forgive you.'

'And Jack? You will not pursue your argument with him?'

Ralph frowned. 'That is none of your concern. It is a thing between he and I. He understands that—or should.'

'But no!' Anne cried, disregarding his expression. Her relief at being back on good terms with Ralph made her want the rest of the world to be similarly at ease. 'I did not fully *explain*, because I was a little taken aback by your attack—but anyway—'

'I do not wish to hear it.'

Jack, pacing the dance chamber, wishing he could get to his extremely uncomfortable and crowded bedchamber but knowing that no one could leave the proceedings before the Queen decided to take herself to bed, chose this unlucky moment to approach Anne and ask her to dance. Whilst at Ravensglass during Elizabeth's visit he had been forced to dance many times and had now given up his self-imposed rule to reject the activity. He even found he enjoyed it—as much as he enjoyed anything these days.

He bowed before Anne and extended his hand in the approved way.

Ralph gave him an outraged look and struck the hand away. It was nothing more than a testy brush of his fingers but Jack straightened up with a face of thunder. Insulting words between gentlemen in these circles was one thing, but actual physical contact was another, he felt. 'How dare you strike me, sir?' he said harshly.

Anne saw, with a sinking heart, what appeared to be another confrontation forming. Someone touched her arm and she turned with relief to find her brother there.

'Good evening.' George bowed with casual grace. His arrival, however, was not casual; he had been irresistibly drawn across the room by the inexplicable link which existed between himself and his twin. He knew Anne was in trouble and had come to help her.

Before Anne could speak, Ralph said, 'Ah, George, I am glad to see you here. I had intended visiting you later tonight on a serious matter.'

George turned courteously and the two men shook hands. 'Well met, Ralph. What may I do for you?'

Ralph lifted his hand palm upwards towards Jack. 'This man has insulted your sister, and my future wife. My intention was to ask you to stand second to me while I extract satisfaction.'

Anne gasped. She had thought that Ralph's relenting towards her would put an end to the whole affair. Oh, why did these distressing things keep happening to her? Was it, as Jack said, all her fault? She looked at the floor in painful self-doubt.

'Indeed?' said George smoothly. 'May I ask what insult was given?'

'My Lady Anne,' Ralph said heavily, 'chose to give

her horse a run during her stay at Ravensglass. Whilst doing so there was a sudden fall of snow and her return to the castle was impeded. She took refuge in a village chapel and Lord Hamilton followed her there, and, instead of escorting back to safety forthwith, kept her there the night, thereby impugning her honour.'

Anne thought, But it was not really like that!

A fair assessment of events, thought Jack judicially.

What a very disagreeable man Monterey is, George thought. He must have been responsible for compromising at least a half-dozen women that I know of, and now would take the moral high ground and attempt to cast aspersions upon a man he is not fit to valet! He said mildly, 'It sounds quite dire, Ralph. But there are always two sides to any question. What is your side, Anne?'

Anne hesitated. Whatever she said would be wrong. 'It is how Ralph describes, but he does not—could not—know the weather during that time. If we had, during darkness, tried to take the journey we were forced to the following day I doubt we would be standing here discussing it now.' She raised her eyes to meet Jack's and he sent her a faint glance of approval.

I could not have summed up the situation better myself, he thought. A little more of the iron casing around his heart, so carefully erected and maintained throughout a decade, sounded before Anne's warm support, and their friendship, reluctantly acknowledged by himself, was granted another link.

He said, 'Whatever the circumstances, Ralph, I believe you should trust your future wife. Apparently, you do not, so I must assist you in this.' He was a man used to speaking with great authority, and did so now. 'You could have been present in that dismal place—

the church in the graveyard of Tranmere—for the whole of the time Lady Anne and I were together and not been dismayed by anything which passed between us. I give you my word upon that.'

'Naturally you would say that,' Ralph said quickly. This situation was fast slipping out of his control. Firstly, Anne's brother must come with his damnably reasonable talk. Then, this—this barbarian presumed to try to overbear his rights.

Still young enough to wish to put aside sense and score off the man for both past and present slights, he said offensively, 'I find I cannot accept it. Come, man, let us settle it now—the time and the place.'

But Jack had dealt with too many hotheaded young men in the past to be forced into a position he did not care for. 'I cannot do that,' he said quietly.

'You refuse to meet me?'

'I do.'

'Then I will make your name stink in these quarters, and you will have no defence because it will be obvious to all that you are a shameful coward.'

Anne whitened. Ralph was angry, she understood that, but surely—? Besides the patent absurdity of his statement, could he not see it was dangerous to provoke a man like Jack?

When she would have spoken, she paused. Ralph would hate her for it, and Jack didn't need any help.

'No defence?' repeated Jack thoughtfully. 'On the face of it I suppose it might seem that way. Although, as to the charge of cowardice,' he added with a rare flash of humour, 'I could always show my war wounds.'

George turned away to hide a smile. What had happened to the man? He appeared suddenly so human, after all these years of bitter apathy.

George sincerely hoped that the change had nothing to do with Anne. As her brother, he scarcely approved of Ralph Monterey as a prospective brother-in-law, indeed thought that he might possibly break her heart in a thousand ways. But Jack Hamilton would be an altogether different kind of heartbreak, for, although a man worth loving, he must surely be incapable of returning the sentiment. No human being could devote a decade to a dead love and have any love left to give, and Anne needed love so badly.

'Latimar?' Ralph said impatiently.

'I fear I cannot act for you in this,' George said quietly. 'For one thing I believe Hamilton, if only because not to do so would be to name my sister a liar—and I would not do that, or allow any other man to do so. For another, I am strongly averse to duelling and would not hesitate to say so in this assembly, and give my reasons.

'Now—' he bowed '—Her Majesty has expressed the wish that my wife and I join her for late supper. She wishes to be apprised of all my news. . .'

It was a delicately veiled threat, and Ralph flushed. Elizabeth's views on duelling within her court were well-known, and rigorously enforced. George left them.

'Ralph—' Anne began, but he stopped her.

'It seems I am not to be allowed to stand for you, my dear, surrounded as you are by. . .gentlemen who feel differently from myself about these things. I must obviously rearrange my thoughts.' He turned on his heel.

'Well,' Jack said, 'we are all neatly in the wrong.'

Anne's eyes filled with tears. She could not speak and Jack took her arm and steered her out of the hall.

'Don't cry here; you'll spend the rest of the month explaining it.'

He took her down the passage, looking for the impossible—somewhere private. At the end of the corridor there was a small writing-room, used occasionally by courtiers wishing to despatch short messages with the riders whom the palace kept especially for that purpose. It was unoccupied at this time, being a place usually frequented in the early morning. He led her in and she went to the window and sat down.

'It is snowing,' she discovered as the fluttering white pieces were blown against the dark panes. The wind was restless tonight; having torn the last of the leaves from the trees, now it probed at the palace walls and rattled its windows.

'Yes, and has been all evening.' Borne on the howling wind were his hopes of returning to his home; he wondered why he was not more desperate at the thought of remaining in this uncongenial place for at least several months more.

'Oh, dear,' Anne said, trying to soothe her hurt by comforting him in his. 'I know how much you wished to go home.' She turned again to the window, her profile clear and lovely against the darkness, saying wistfully, 'I wish I too could go home.'

'Surely not! This season at court—why, I have memories of it being quite magical.' Those memories included the last time he had been part of these festivities. His parents had been dead for six months and he had brought Marie Claire to present her to Edward, the boy king, and to receive acknowledgement that he was now master of Ravensglass. She had been so happy, his gentle wife, when her beloved husband

had received honour from his sovereign... His heart
contracted in remembered pain.

Now I have reminded him again of Marie Claire,
Anne thought bleakly. Really, I am becoming a menace
to those about me.

Mistaking the reason for her mood, Jack said quietly,
'I should not take what Monterey said too much to
heart, Anne. He'll come round.'

'But it is all so unnecessary,' she cried. 'All this
dissension.'

Jack had found a book of poems, left on one of the
tables. 'So much of what happens in life is unnecessary,'
he said thoughtfully, his eyes on the script. 'If there is
a good reason for half of what has happened to me, I
have yet to discover it.' He came and sat beside her,
the light from the candle-sconce polishing his head to
silver.

'Poor Jack. You have had more than your share of
trouble, certainly. Do you really have war wounds to
show?'

'I have,' he admitted. 'They go with my profession,
you know. But I would not dream of showing them.'

He was so near to her that she could see the dusting
of gold on his thick eyelashes. He must have had very
fair hair before it turned grey, she thought, but it would
not have gone with his skin, for, even allowing for his
deep tan, he had a clear olive skin such as she had only
seen before on Spanish men.

That skin and his clipped hair set him apart from the
other men here at Greenwich, she also thought,
although he would have been distinctive anywhere for
his height and breadth of shoulder, the wary, cat-like
walk, and his air of being answerable to no other for
what he was.

Still believing her to be thinking of her rocky love affair, he continued, 'And don't think too much of his words on your being compromised at Tranmere—men in love say desperately unkind things when they feel at a disadvantage.'

Distracted from the contemplation of his looks, she said, 'But he didn't *believe* me, Jack. I would always believe those I loved were speaking truth to me.' She bent her head and picked at the embroidered pearls on her skirt. One was severed from its silken thread and fell away. He reached out a swift hand to prevent it from rolling to the floor. Dropping it into her hand, his fingers touched hers and a thrill ran from his fingertips throughout his body. He drew back, shocked.

'What is it?' she asked.

'Nothing.' He got up and stood looking down at her. Years—ages—ago, he and Marie Claire had had a favourite walk in southern France: an avenue of trees, so close-growing that those side by side were bark to bark, their overhead branches so intermingled that they shut out the light.

At the end of the avenue could be seen the dancing sunlight of the Mediterranean, flickering. He and Marie Claire had, many times, walked slowly towards that light, to the circle of gold. Now he felt himself again in some dark tunnel, at the end of which there was a bright light. He wished to remain in the shadows, but the light drew him on. It drew him on.

Anne rose too. 'You look so strange, Jack. Have I said something to offend?'

'No, no, of course not.' But he was afraid. Wounded animals, he thought, were better left alone in their dark lairs with their pain. Without even knowing it, Anne Latimar was dragging him out of that hiding place and forcing him to know that, though he might feel as dead as the woman he had loved so much and lost, close within him stirred vibrant life.

With another thrill, this time of disgust, he knew that he could—in this dim room—have taken Anne in his arms and kissed her and enjoyed it. It was very disturbing knowledge.

'We should return now to the assembly,' he said stiffly.

'Yes, yes, of course,' she agreed, still puzzled by his tenseness.

'And it may be that if you approach Lord Ralph again, with due caution, you might be able to patch the matter up.' Let her be some other man's concern, he thought. For what he had felt in the last few moments was nothing short of *more* betrayal.

'Maybe,' Anne said. 'Although I would rather smack his face for his intransigence!'

Her childish words broke the spell for him. He laughed as he opened the door and they stepped out into the passageway. 'A very healthy reaction, I am sure. But don't do that—you have decided, and your family are in agreement, so be a little forgiving, Anne.'

'My family,' Anne said thoughtfully as they re-entered the noisy hall. 'I don't really know how they feel about this. One thing I do know, however, is that George doesn't like him. George doesn't like Ralph.'

'Oh?' Jack paused, looking over the lively, colourful scene before them. He had not known George as an adult for long, but he had already formed a great respect for his opinion. Young Latimar was ten years younger than himself—or more—yet he had dealt with the explosive situation in the hall earlier with considerable grace.

'Tis not my problem, he thought; Anne Latimar and
her family, Ralph Monterey, *et al.*, are not my problem.

With something approaching relief he gave Anne up
to one of the hovering gallants and left the hall. But as
he wandered up and down the cold stone passages of
Greenwich, waiting for the opportunity to retire, he
was uneasy. Anne, he realised, was no longer simply
the daughter of a good friend, but a person in her own
right. . .a living, breathing and supremely attractive
woman who disturbed his dreams and confused his
daylight hours.

CHAPTER ELEVEN

YULETIDE came to Greenwich Palace—the fun, the pageantry, the gifts, the outrageous displays of a society spoiled and rich, the endless masques and plays and entertainments, the underlying decadence of those in court life bent on enjoying themselves.

At the gates crowds of beggars cried for alms for families grey and starved and frozen in this, the Lord's season. Those tattered scarecrows were sent away with very little, but then they did not expect anything else. The dividing line between rich and poor was never so marked as at this time.

Caught up in the exhausting round of gaiety, Anne had little time to brood. Ralph was affectionate and attentive and the best of company, and that was all she asked. He was undoubtedly becoming one of the stars of the Tudor court and others, recognising this, promptly cultivated both him and his lady. Anne suddenly found that everything she had ever been ambitious for was miraculously possible and she rebuked herself for not being totally grateful and happy.

For she was neither. She was growing more thoughtful these days, more observant. Someone who had known her for the whole of her life might have remarked now, Well, Anne has grown up at last! Her brother George had always said to her, 'Look at all, listen to all—then pick and choose what and whom is of value.'

She was now doing this. Always smiling and ready to enjoy any situation, Anne yet held back and coolly assessed the merit of what was happening, and those who were taking part. For the first time in her life, sociable creature that she was, she discovered a need within her for solitude to think on her reactions.

And each day the longing to be home grew greater. But that was impossible for the weather had decreed that no sensible person would travel—by providing first snow, then a hard freeze, then a sudden thaw with its consequent slush, then more snow, and so on, in an endless cycle of perversity. The Queen, who liked to keep the Christmas season at Hampton, resigned herself to remaining in the capital.

Jack Hamilton was another member of the court who was not relishing these glittering sociable times, but for a more puzzling reason. He, who had always held himself aloof from such things, now found himself joining the gatherings for only one reason: a chance to see Anne Latimar.

Not a particularly introspective man, he constantly asked himself *why*. Why should this young girl have so invaded his senses that he must take every opportunity to be near her? Why, when she was the very opposite of his former love, should she be the one to bring him so painfully back to life? For it was painful.

She was so young. She fitted into this company so well, always the centre of attention, with her amusing tongue, dressed in her beautiful gowns and bedecked with glittering jewellery. And she had chosen the perfect mate, Ralph Monterey, who was her equal—an elegant, ambitious courtier.

Yet Jack lived for the few moments he was allowed to touch Anne in the dance, brush shoulders with her as they sat watching another interminable play or exhibition of juggling, or tumbling or acrobatics. Most of all, he both enjoyed and feared their frequent private conversations together.

For Anne had now slotted him into a convenient pigeon-hole—that of trusted friend. As such she often poured out her troubles to him, confided in him where she would not have dreamed of doing so with another lady in her dorter, or even her own brother.

Jack listened to it all, his unreadable face protecting his own thoughts. For, having admitted to himself that she meant more to him than his enduring affection for her father, he was also prepared to admit that she was growing more important every day, and this he dared not show, for obviously there was no future in it. The last ten years had been, for him, a constant nursing of a bruise. What he felt for Anne now was a blow upon that bruise.

When Yuletide was done and the new year moved on, Anne's thoughts turned again to Maiden Court. Months ago Elizabeth had said that she might grant permission for her least favourite lady-in-waiting to go home for a visit.

On a mild February day, Anne went to the stables and surveyed the landcape beyond. Snow had not fallen for weeks; sleet and freezing rain had taken its place. Surely she could escape for a day now. Whilst she was deliberating she saw Jack Hamilton's great grey horse being walked into a stall. A few seconds later she saw Jack crossing the yard and disappearing into the stall. She followed.

He was carefully examining the animal's legs and said sharply, 'Stay back, Anne! He is nervous.'

From the cover of the hay box Anne asked, 'Is there something wrong with him?'

'No, no, except he is not at home here. You cannot persuade a war horse to become a well-mannered saddle horse by putting him into the same stable.'

Anne smiled. The same could be said of Valiant's master, she thought, for Jack was no more at home at Greenwich than his horse. No other courtier had ventured out this day; they were all safely in the warmth of the palace, playing games or dozing or bickering amongst themselves. She said, 'I suppose you will not take him out today, then?'

Jack looked up. 'I intend to. Both he and I will be gaol-crazy if I don't.'

'Oh, good, because I want to visit Maiden Court briefly—'

'Don't be foolish, Anne,' he interrupted irritably. 'I shall ride Valiant around within a mile of the palace. To go across country would be madness.'

'So you won't take me?' she asked.

Jack re-corked the bottle of linament he had been massaging into his horse's legs. 'I won't take you,' he agreed, 'and you are not going.'

'But you cannot stop me! Ages ago I asked Her Majesty's permission to go, and she gave it.'

'Ages ago? Well, go and ask her now and see what she says.'

Anne said sulkily, 'Well, of course she won't give it *today*. But I know I can get there, with your help.'

Jack began to saddle up. 'The last time I. . .helped you it was not auspiciously successful.'

'Oh, but it was! You save my life, after all, and I shall always be grateful to you.'

'Thank you, but that gesture resulted in my being

called out.' Jack buckled the girth and straightened up.
'If you are so set on this, why don't you ask Monterey
to take you?'

Anne rolled her eyes heavenwards. 'Now *you* are
being foolish! Ralph is the last person—I mean—' she
caught herself up '—he has other duties at this time.'

'Oh?' Jack looked around for his hat which he had
removed on entering the stall. 'What might they be, I
wonder?'

Anne pushed her bare hands into the sleeves of her
gown. Ralph was engaged in another of his interminable card games. It had been going on now for a night,
a day and a night, and, although she had sat in on the
early stages, it had soon palled. The airless room, the
soft-speaking, gorgeously clad men and women, the
unhealthy atmosphere of well-bred spite as the cards
went round and coins clinked and markers whispered
across the polished table did not appeal to her at all.

She tried to imagine Ralph's face if she broke in to
enquire if he wanted to ride out with her, and smiled
again. She had no quarrel with his obsession with
gambling; indeed, it seemed quite natural to her—he
was that sort of man—but for what she intended to do
this day she needed another kind.

'Please, Jack,' she said, keeping a wary eye on
Valiant and moving forward to lay a hand on his arm.
'Please take me. It will not be like...Tranmere. If we
should find ourselves in difficulties again, why, I know
so many people in the villages we must pass through
and they would all give us the help and shelter we
needed.'

Jack moved away from the touch of her hand. He
could not trust himself, now, to be in this public place
with her, with the grooms and stable-lads whistling and

going to and fro about their work beyond the stall door, let alone on miles of deserted countryside.

She felt his withdrawal. 'I thought you were my friend!'

'No friend would encourage you in this. In fact, I absolutely forbid it. If you must get a little air, get your mount and come with me.'

'I want to go to Maiden Court!' She was suddenly alight. 'I *need* to go!'

He looked at her. Their friendship had developed so much in the last week that he could hardly remember that he had once thought her a light and weightless woman. The desperation in her voice touched a sensitivity in him that he would have denied existed. 'Why? Why, sweetheart?'

The quality in his voice, and the endearment, passed unnoticed by her, but she answered his question. 'I must talk with my father and mother. I *must* see them, and ask—I need their advice.'

'George is here at Greenwich,' he pointed out. 'No better man could give you advice.'

'Oh, George,' she said impatiently. 'George thinks of nothing but Judith! They do not come down in the evenings to the dance or entertainments any more. If I go looking for him he is pleased, but his mind is always on *Judith*.'

'Well, of course,' Jack said. 'Love is like that, you know.'

'And I am happy it should be so for them,' she said quickly. 'But my father—my father will talk to me, listen to me.'

Jack drew on his riding gloves. Carefully stretching the fingers, he considered that it was the way of the Latimars to love hard. Harry Latimar had given up an heiress for Bess, and George had given away a potentially glittering career to marry his love. Anne must love Ralph Monterey in the same, all-consuming way.

Jack writhed inwardly at this revelation. Here at Greenwich, those old enough to remember Anne's father smiled into their beards and said that his daughter had apparently chosen another just like him. Jack knew that this was not so. Harry Latimar, in spite of his reputation, had a steel core of intregity, his son the same.

Ralph resembled neither, Jack though angrily, and had only the same veneer of charm and white-skinned grace. He was also as active as a stable tom; Jack knew of at least three women he had been intimate with since returning from Ravensglass.

But Anne loved him and was in despair over some aspect of their relationship, and Jack wanted to help her. 'I thought you were my friend!' she had declared.

He said, 'Very well. But you must do something first: go and tell your brother what you intend while I see to your horse.'

Anne grimaced. George would put all sorts of obstacles in her way. But one glance into Jack's face told her that there was no option. 'And change into warmer clothes,' he called after her.

She went first to her chamber and obeyed his last instructions. Clad in wool and fur, she then climbed more stairs to her brother's small apartment which he shared with his wife. They were both there and greeted her fondly.

'Why are you dressed so?' George enquired.

'I am going riding,' she replied ambiguously. 'For a short time only.' It will be, she assured herself.

'Who goes with you?'

'Jack Hamilton.'

'Ah.' George found no fault with this. He had got to know Jack recently and still found him very difficult indeed to understand, but they had established a mutual respect for each other. George dropped into a chair beside Anne and looked her over. Something was brewing, he thought, and wondered if she had come to discuss it, but his eyes soon returned to his wife.

They are even more wrapped up in each other than usual, Anne thought enviously as Judith pottered about the room and her brother's eyes followed her. When George stepped out to request that food be brought, Judith stopped her aimless wandering and caught Anne's arm.

'Anne,' she said, her eyes shining, 'I would like you to be the first to know! George and I expect a very happy event in the future. I am to bear his child! I am sure this very week!'

A child! Anne experienced conflicting emotions— firstly envy again, for this would set the seal of absolute contentment on her brother's marriage. Then she felt dismay, for women were terribly at risk in childbirth in these times, and she suddenly could not bear to think of anything happening to Judith.

Finally, a very strange thought occurred to her: Judith would grow plain and ungainly; she would never again be the slender beauty who had stood in the Maiden Court chapel and pledged eternal love to George.

But George would not mind, thought Anne in her new maturity. Indeed, he would adore his wife whatever shape she was. What would be Ralph's reaction to her in the same state? Anne wondered inevitably. They had talked of it once.

'Naturally you will bear my sons,' Ralph had said. 'And will be safe at Abbey Hall when you do so.' Tucked away on his estate, Anne had thought then. Safely out of the way, growing fat and placid.

'What are you thinking of?' Judith asked now. 'You look so sad.'

'Oh, nothing.' Anne tore her mind away from useless speculation. 'I do congratulate you most sincerely. I suppose you are planning to go as soon as possible to Maiden Court?'

'Why, no,' Judith said. 'Actually, George has just accepted a temporary post within the Queen's government and intends being with her court for at least a year.'

'Then you will have your child here?'

'Oh, here or at some other palace. It all depends on where Her Majesty is.' Judith smiled. 'Dear Anne, I know what you are thinking. You love Maiden Court and so do I; I would dearly love my baby to be born there, but George—George will just not let me be away from him.'

No, thought Anne, and that is how it should be. She got up. 'I must go, Judith. The weather is fair at present, but may change at any moment.'

Judith followed her to the door. Something in the other girl's face concerned her. 'Anne, is all well with you? Your liaison with Ralph Monterey progresses well?' Closer inspection of Anne's betrothed had not pleased Judith. He was charming, he was gifted in all ways, but Judith did not think him worthy of George's sister.

'Ralph and I? Oh, yes, of course all is well. . . Now, Judith, promise me you will take the greatest care of yourself.'

'I will.' Judith touched Anne's hand. 'Come and talk with me tonight.'

'Tonight? Yes—yes, I will.' Anne looked up the empty passage then bent impulsively to kiss Judith's cheek. 'Goodbye for now.'

Judith watched her sister-in-law disappearing in a swirl of tawny wool and fur. George was at her elbow.

'I have ordered sweet bacon and fresh bread, and—'

'George,' Judith said urgently, 'go after Anne and see what ails her. Something is troubling her and I think she may need your help.'

George wasted no time in arguing with his wife. With unhurried grace he arrived in the stable-yard in time to see Anne ride through the main arch to the grassy lawns before the palace. He paused a moment in the brisk wind, then shrugged. Well, at least, he thought, having recognised a certain grey horse, and the set of the shoulders of the man riding him, she is quite safe with Hamilton.

Halfway to Maiden Court Anne was prepared to admit that Jack had been right: it had been madness to take the open road at this time. They progressed in miserable discomfort.

'I am very sorry,' she said as they took shelter against the trunk of a giant oak during a storm of hail.

'That certainly is of comfort,' Jack said ironically, taking off his hat to shake off the icy stones. He had not suggested that they pause so far in their journey, although several times he had known it to be practical. A thaw had come to the capital, and fairer weather, but elsewhere the snow was still in evidence in rock-hard clots on the roads, and the cold was severe in unprotected open country.

Fortunately Anne had dressed warmly, and, besides, would not have complained for anything. Indeed, she made light of it all for fear that he would insist on turning back. As Maiden Court drew ever nearer and there was no question of that, she even found a certain pleasure in the expedition.

Naturally, they had to travel slowly, and thus could talk; Anne compared this journey with the one taken the previous year, and was proud that their friendship had come so far. They touched on this subject and that, but no word crossed her lips of the thing which was making her heart sore.

Oddly enough, she could have told Jack exactly what was in that heart, and welcomed his response, but something held her back. She thought that, however highly she might regard him, he still thought of her as a silly young girl, and always measured her against his late wife and judged her wanting. Lately, she had sensed an even deeper reserve in his attitude, and thought he was probably growing bored by her.

Still, he was bringing her home this day and she tried to show her gratitude by cheerfully ignoring the conditions, and entertaining him with her conversation. Now she looked at the frozen rain bouncing off the rutted roads and cast about for some new topic. 'Why did you become a soldier?' she asked.

'When I was seven my tutor advised my father that I was unlikely to be a scholar. As such I could not look for a career in the church as my father had wished and so he sent me to serve my pageship with a northern lord on the understanding that he was to push me in the direction of a soldier knight. Fortunately—' a wry smile crossed his face '—I was sturdy enough to endure what a life like that demanded.'

'Yet you were squire to my father? He is the least aggressive man I know!'

'In those days Henry—the old King—still admired the arts I excelled in. He was one of your father's greatest friends. He used to come to the practice yard and watch us boys perform and he inflicted me on Lord Harry because he always wanted the best for his special friends.

'Not that I was the best, of course, at least not in the ways of taking care of a gentleman like your father. However, Harry was always kind and ignored my sloppy service and encouraged me in all I did.'

She smiled. 'I can imagine you were chalk and cheese together—you being so physical and he being not at all that way.' She shrank further back against the broad trunk as the storm gathered ferocity. 'You know, Ralph told me that Father once fought a duel! I knew *that* could not be true, but he insisted 'twas so.'

'It was so,' Jack said. 'But after my time with him, although I was still a member of the court then.' She was wrong about her father; Jack knew that Harry could be extremely physical when roused.

'Oh, tell me all about it!' she exclaimed. 'What was it about, and who was the man he fought?'

Jack hesitated, and yet the story did no discredit to his former master. 'It was over your mother, as I understand it, and against a young man who had fallen in love with her and thought he could take her. He pushed your father too far one day, there was a violent disagreement, and Harry was called out.'

Anne's eyes were like saucers. 'My father did that? Oh, it is hard to believe.'

'Indeed. However, when they met Harry let the other

man off with a little blood-letting and that was the end of it.'

'But what happened to him? The other man?'

'I have no idea,' Jack said shortly. 'It was all a long time ago.'

'But so romantic,' Anne sighed. 'Ralph has fought five duels, you know, and killed each time.'

And they were mere boys! thought Jack angrily. Scarcely breeched and forced to challenge Monterey after a whipping from his sharp tongue. As the man challenged, Ralph had had the right to choose weapons and had always chosen the pistol—not yet an instrument favoured in such affairs.

That was long-range killing, Jack mused grimly. He liked to see his adversary's eyes when despatching him to another realm. The guns Monterey had used were from his own cherished collection, frequently handled and practised with. Did Anne consider that romantic?

The storm had passed now, and the sky had turned a bright, hard blue. 'Let us ride on,' he said brusquely. He lifted her onto Jenny's back, leaped astride his own horse and darted out from their shelter.

Anne followed without further comment, but, far from admiring Ralph for the events she had just mentioned, in her heart she rebuked him. One of his victim's sisters was her good friend at Greenwich, and, though the lady's code of behaviour prevented her from blaming a gentleman for anything done in the name of honour, she had spoken of the tragedy to Anne with tears in her eyes for her young brother and Anne's sense of justice had been outraged.

Bess Latimar was abed when they arrived at Maiden Court. She had still not fully recovered from the illness which had struck her down the previous autumn, and enjoyed early nights to try to regain her strength. Harry Latimar was still in the hall, however, when the two unexpected guests arrived and Walter showed them in.

'Father!' Anne shed her cloak and hastened into her father's arms.

'Anne!' Harry could not believe his eyes. 'Why are you here? What has happened?'

'Oh, nothing; everything is absolutely all right. But I had this sudden fancy to see you, and so I came.'

'And so you came,' Harry repeated. He turned to shake Jack's hand. 'Jack, I am pleased to welcome you.'

'Thank you, sir.' Jack sent an eloquent glance into Harry's eyes. ''Twas a sudden fancy indeed.'

'And we are starving!' Anne declared, looking around her beloved home. 'Have you *anything* we might eat?'

'I am sure we have,' Harry said. 'Walter?'

'I will arrange it immediately,' old Walter said, bowing. What a sight for sore eyes Lady Anne was, he thought, treading carefully into the kitchen. How much this house had missed her!

Harry seated his visitors before the brightly blazing fire. He added more fuel and took his own chair. 'Now, tell me all. How did you both get leave to come?'

Anne turned her cold hands in her lap. 'Her Majesty said to me, "If at any time you wish to visit your family, Lady Anne, feel free to do so." Today, I felt I must, so I came, although I did not actually apply for permission.'

'I see. And you, Jack?'

'I am a free agent within the court, sir,' Jack said

gravely. 'When the Lady Anne declared her intention of coming to Maiden Court, naturally I attended her.'

Naturally? wondered Harry. What was natural about it? If Anne had decided so precipitately to come home, then surely Ralph Monterey should have brought her. Also, if she thought that such a casual attitude would do for her position at court, she was badly wrong there. Though disorganisation might appear to reign in the over-crowded palaces, in fact, comings and goings were very strictly monitored.

Harry thought it likely that the Queen would dismiss her forthwith for such disregard for the proper conventions. But what was the point of saying that now? The night was closing in and it would be another bitter one—even if the moon remained as brilliant, the trip back tonight would be impossible. He began to ask her about her time in Northumberland.

Thawed out, so happy to be home, Anne became animated, describing the royal visit in an infectiously amusing way. Soon all three were laughing. She also described Ravensglass in glowing terms and Jack was inwardly astonished. He had often heard his home—which occupied a large space in his heart—spoken of as a bleak place, yet Anne had noticed its stark beauty and, having a way with words, brought the castle and its surrounding country to life.

Harry was also surprised. He had been to Ravensglass twice, and, like most people more at home in crowded palaces or rural manors closely guarded by trees, had found the emptiness of that part of the world intimidating. He had thought Anne the same; now she revealed an unexpected side of herself.

After an hour Jack rose, pleading fatigue, and Walter's last duty of the night was to show him to his room. Harry and Anne made no move to leave the fire. Anne had changed a great deal in the past few months, but one thing that had not changed was the way she behaved when she wanted to get something off her mind.

When the house fell silent, Harry filled his glass again, saying easily, 'Now, Anne, what is it that you wish to discuss? Or is it your mother you came to see?'

Anne let out her breath. 'No, Father, it is you. Well, Mother too, of course, but first you.'

'So begin.'

It was not so easy, Anne thought, getting up and wandering about the hall. She straightened the ornaments, rearranged a bowl of shiny-berried sprays on the table before the windows, gazed out at the moonlight silvering the lawns.

'Come along,' Harry said encouragingly. 'There is nothing you cannot say to me.'

Anne turned. The candlelight flickered over her face, ignoring the pretty flesh and highlighting the bones. Like all the Latimars, she would be beautiful when youth had fled. Harry realised afresh how very special she was to him. 'It is Monterey? Something has gone wrong there?'

Anne came and sat down. 'Not exactly wrong, Father. At least, not with him, but rather with *me*.' She paused, and he let her feel for the words she was seeking. 'He is so *right* for me, and yet I cannot seem to. . .feel I am right for him.' Gathering confidence, she went on, 'He never talks to me—at least, he talks and is very amusing and clever and complimentary and all those things, but—'

'But?'

'Well, he talks but never says anything. And when

we are together I know how much I love him but all
the time now I am thinking, Where is the rest? What
else is there? Oh, it is a sad way to be when you are
with the man you love, the man you intend loving for
the rest of your life.

'Also, when we are together I am constantly remind-
ing myself how like *you* he is, and how I always, always
wanted someone just like you, and. . .I am distressed
because. . .it does not make me happy.'

Harry looked into his glass. Poor child, he thought,
she is just now learning the first lesson of love: that the
object of one's love cannot always measure up to
expectations. He chose the last part of her discourse to
comment upon. 'Did you choose him for that reason?
Because you fancied he was like me?'

'Oh, yes, of course I did! You know it has long been
my desire to marry a man like you, Father, and no one,
until now, has ever compared!'

'But nor, by your account, has this man,' Harry
pointed out gently.

'Well, no. . .' Anne's white forehead crinkled. 'But
that is why I have come home to you, Father—to seek
your advice upon how I am going wrong in this.'

Harry finished his wine. It was a mystery to him why
his lovely, talented daughter, who had been courted by
so many fine men, should wish to link her fortunes with
a man such as himself. In his youth, Harry had been
less than exemplary; fortunately, his lovely Bess had
come along to bring out the best in him—her words.
But, obviously, that best had lain in his heart waiting
for her to find it; Harry wondered very much if
Monterey possessed such spiritual gold.

He said, 'I am not sure how to advise you in this; I
can only offer some suggestions. Perhaps you are too

critical? Ralph is a young man, finding his way in the world. The Queen has shown him great favour—even in rural Kew we hear the gossip, you know—and he has an addiction to pleasure. He passes his days in idle pursuits, he gambles too much, and turns away from any serious conversation. The same could probably be said of most of Elizabeth's gentlemen courtiers.

'But he came to me quite humbly to ask for your hand—that is to his credit. He also comes from a great and honourable family. Have you disagreed over something in particular?'

'We did have an argument,' Anne admitted. 'What happened is this. . .' She recounted the events at Tranmere, and after, with candour. 'Ralph was greatly annoyed by it all,' she ended.

Harry raised an eyebrow. 'And no wonder! What can you—or Jack—have been thinking of?'

Anne shook back her hair impatiently. 'We were thinking of nothing but staying alive!' she assured him. 'But Ralph did not listen to what I said properly and tried to persuade Jack to fight a duel over my honour! Of course I could not allow that, and I was angry in my turn that he thought there was anything to fight *about*. However—'

'What happened when they met?' Harry enquired.

'Oh, they didn't. Jack told me he would speak to Ralph about it, and I presume he did.'

'Well, thank God for that,' Harry half laughed. 'Otherwise you would not have a betrothed to be worried about.'

Anne was silent for a moment, then said, 'We seem to have drifted from the point. What I have just told you happened some time ago—'tis since then that I have had all these doubts. So I came home that you might reassure me.'

She gave him the same look she had given him so many times. Make it right, Father! A sore finger, a bruised knee, a favourite sick animal, a grandmother who dared to die when I loved her so!

Not so simple, thought Harry wryly, for he was hampered by a dislike of Ralph Monterey which made him unable to plead the man's case any more success-fully than he had already done. What Anne had just told him did not enhance him in her father's eyes either. He considered Ralph damned insolent to disbe-lieve what Anne had declared, and also doubt the word of Hamilton.

Smiling inwardly, Harry thought, I would have liked to be present when Jack spoke— On this thought came another, even more disturbing. 'There is no other man who has caught your eye?' he asked.

'Oh, no!' exclaimed Anne. 'Of course not! At court—at Greenwich—Ralph and I are already con-sidered to be a pair. No other man has approached me in that way seriously, and I have not even noticed anyone else.'

'Not. . . Jack Hamilton?'

Anne looked genuinely amazed. '*No*, Father. Why, he thinks of no one in that way except for his dead wife. Do you know there is a shrine at Ravensglass in her memory? I did not mention it earlier out of respect for his feelings, but it is there and even when he is away from it she is never out of his mind.

'No, no, we are friends, he and I, of a sort, but he is not interested in me. Nor,' she added with less convic-tion, 'am I in him.' There was a silence while she reviewed this lack of conviction.

Harry watched her, thinking of the way Jack had looked at Anne that evening, of the way he had so tenderly removed her wet cloak and put her into the chair by the fire, sternly asking if her feet were wet, if she should not have a warm and comforting drink rather than the buttermilk she loved.

Harry had seen a great many unlikely lovers in the past forty years and believed he recognised the signs of attraction, and in this case it simply would not do. Better Monterey with all his faults than Jack with his curious handicap.

'Well, well, let us sleep on it all now, darling. On the morrow we will speak of it again with your mother, who is so very clever at giving the sort of advice you need.'

He rose to pinch out the candles and place a guard before the fire. Changing the subject, he then said, 'I doubt if you will escape lightly for leaving without permission. Elizabeth is very particular over such things.'

Anne reluctantly got up from her chair; she felt she could have fallen asleep before the fire quite happily. 'I am sure she will understand. I will explain it to her.'

Harry hid a smile. Anne was acute in many ways, clever and witty, swift to understand any point under discussion, but she was not clever about people. Not if she thought the Queen would understand, and not if she thought Jack Hamilton was a friend, 'of a sort'. However. . .

He ruffled the black silk of his daughter's hair and gave her his arm on the stairs.

CHAPTER TWELVE

JACK, who always rose early, came quietly down the stairs the next day just before dawn, and was surprised to find Harry already in his hall. He rose and invited Jack into the parlour for a mug of ale before he broke his fast. He had noticed that his guest had taken no wine with his meal the previous night and, when they were seated, said easily, 'You still don't drink much, Jack?'

'I do not. No one can say that once Hamilton has learned a lesson he forgets it. Once bitten, as they say...'

Harry stretched his long legs before the fire which had been hastily lit by Walter when he had heard his master on the stairs. 'And are you avoiding all occasions for being...bitten by that which might harm you?'

'Which particular area are you referring to?'

'Come, Jack, don't play with words; it doesn't suit between old friends. You have something to say to me, have you not? About Anne?'

Jack got up and stood looking at the view from the window. It was a view worth looking at even on this unprepossessing day. Bess's genius as a gardener provided colour all the year round at Maiden Court and the gay banners of spring were two months early here. He did not wonder how Harry had divined what he felt for his daughter—Harry had always had an odd facility for such things.

He said, 'I love her. I am in love with her. The miracle you spoke of all those years ago at Ravensglass has come about.'

Harry refilled his mug, although he could have fancied something stronger now. 'Well, don't beat about the bush, my boy, just tell me straight,' he said mildly.

Jack turned from the window. 'Please don't mock me, Harry.'

'I would never do that, and you should know it... but, Jack, how do you see the outcome of this?'

'I do not see it,' Jack said flatly. 'I cannot see what can come of it. But I do know this: Anne has chosen a man who is worthless. A man you would not trust with your horse, Harry.'

It was an old joke between them, an expression which Latimar used to use at court in the old days, and which was still in circulation now. Twenty years later, when discussing a new acquaintance, a gallant would say to another, Is he a good man? Would you trust your mount to him?

Harry did not smile. 'He comes from an old and revered family,' he said repressively, 'and has suddenly found favour and acknowledgment from the Queen— 'tis a heady brew for so young a man. Perhaps he needs time to adjust.'

'He was always like that,' Jack said harshly. 'At seventeen years of age he could not be counted on— with a woman, or with the small duties he was called upon to carry out at Ravensglass— But maybe you don't know I had him for a year there?'

Harry's eyebrows went up. 'No, I did not know that... but, you know, your northern fortress might frighten even the best of lads—'

'I know that! I have had a thousand boys through my hands in the past ten years. Some relish the challenge there, some do not—neither case argues a man's character to my mind. But, Ralph, he was not frightened, as you put it, he was contemptuous. Contemptuous of values which we all—oh, yes, even you, Harry—hold dear and would give our lives for.'

He stopped and glanced at the closed door. 'Naturally, I should not be speaking thus. It ill becomes a man in my position to so criticise his subordinates.'

Harry now felt that he must have some stronger liquor to enable him to cope with the emotion present in this room. He found wine and poured it liberally.

Jack Hamilton, he thought, had always been a very unusual youngster. As squire to himself, at fifteen, he had been more trouble than any other gentleman in Harry's position, then, would have tolerated. But Latimar had tolerated him; more than that, he had admired him. And still did.

He said, 'But we are speaking of Anne. How serious are your intentions towards her?'

Jack hesitated, then said, 'The most serious, Harry. I know my mind, I know myself. But I think I also know her. She loves the life at court. She is ideally equipped in every way to make her mark there. Ralph is her complement; he is handsome and talented—all the things necessary for a courtier bound for the so-called inner circle.

'But Anne is *more* than that. She is, beneath her so very attractive. . .exterior, kind and generous and thoughtful. She is far, far too good for him—' He broke off.

Harry looked at him compassionately. He knew all these things about his precious daughter, knew that what Anne thought she wanted was not necessarily what would make her happy. The next moment, Jack put this into words. 'She sells herself short constantly, you know.'

Silence fell. In the nursery above, Harry could hear his youngest son yelling for attention; in the kitchens, the cook had begun to make the first meal of the day— its savoury perfume could be enjoyed even in the parlour with its tightly closed door. Outside in the yard his servants called to each other as they exercised the horses. The day had begun.

'I don't know how I may help you in this, Jack,' he said helplessly.

'And probably would not, even if you could,' Jack said wryly. 'Is that not so?'

''Tis this way,' Harry sighed. 'Ralph Monterey is not what a fond father would choose, perhaps, if he could hand-pick the man his beloved daughter should marry. But I have to say I understand him, and know his breed. You are not so easy to categorise.'

He, too, rose and moved around the room, his glass held loosely in his hand. 'See, Jack, it is a question of experience. I am well aware that Ralph has a certain reputation already, with his regard for the gaming tables and in other ways. But I also know, from my experience, that a gentleman married to the woman he loves can overcome such. . .faults. I am a living example of that, surely.'

'But he is not like you,' Jack said violently. 'Anne feels her choice resembles you, and he does in super-ficial ways—but, my friend, I do not exaggerate when I say that were you to be domiciled at Ravensglass during the hottest of fighting I would trust you with my life and the lives of the young men under my command. In other words, 'tis acceptable in my eyes to be all the things Monterey is, so long as the heart is right. His is not.'

When he spoke again, it was with unaccustomed hesitancy. 'But you cannot understand what I am saying: naturally you would approve Monterey. He is a good match for Anne. But. . .' he looked of a sudden very young and vulnerable '. . .is he so much better than I?'

'Better? Indeed not—in fact, the reverse. It is, I think, more a question of your. . .history.'

'Which is what? I was married young, to a wife I *adored*. I lost her and could not seem to get over it in the way other men do. Did not *wish* to get over it. But now. . .now I feel differently. It is a very new thing, you understand, and I cannot yet speak of it properly, can only say. . .now I feel differently.' He added, as if he was admitting it for the first time to himself, 'Anne has wrought this difference.'

'Hmm.' Harry moved uneasily. A difference indeed in the man before him. Harry had made a career from reading others' faces in order to relieve them of their gold, and, although Jack was an easy mark when gambling, his thoughts on his private affairs were usually impossible to know. But they were plain this day.

Harry had very much liked Marie Claire Hamilton, and had thought her not unlike his own Bess, but without his wife's flashing, shrewd intelligence or, of course, her beauty. He had been delighted with his friend's happy marriage, and desolate at its tragic end. But Jack's feeling towards Marie Claire had been a gentle, polite emotion and, he fancied, quite different from what he was experiencing now.

He took a mouthful of wine, wishing he had not to take part in this difficult scene—and before the sun was even risen!

'I would welcome your candour,' Jack said. 'Although,' he added with his regained sense of humour again evident, 'probably candour and the wish not to hurt an old friend do not go hand in hand.'

Harry turned the diamond in his left ear. 'I can only say again, Jack, that Ralph may not be the ideal, but he and Anne will at least begin on equal terms. I do not speak of age in this—you will probably outlive most of the easy-living young nobles at court now. But comparisons, after all, are inevitable in any relationship and I would not wish my poor girl to have to compete with—with a lady who is so enshrined in your heart.

'Besides,' he went on when Jack did not deny this, 'Monterey is her choice. At least I have not heard to the contrary from her. Nor, I believe, has she any notion that you are interested in her—other than as a friend, of course.'

'No. Of course that is so,' Jack agreed. 'But, as I have asked for your honest reaction to all I have just said, please give it.'

Asked a direct question—especially from a friend— Harry found it hard to be less than truthful. He countered it with one of his own. 'If I say I am. . .not happy with the thought of your pursuing your suit with Anne, would it make any difference?'

Jack laughed. It was a dim echo of the joyous sound Harry remembered, for Hamilton had been a joyous boy, but how it brought the merry past back! 'Very well,' he said gravely, 'you will not be put to the test. So *I* will say frankly, No, Harry, if a second miracle should occur, and Anne should look kindly on me, then what you think and what you say, and even what you *do*, will not deter me.'

Harry put down his empty glass. From the hall he heard the unmistakable sound of the food being brought to the board. He opened the door, saying, 'So now I know, but—' he turned back and spoke softly '—if you do take up this cause—and with your usual tenacity—look first into your heart. You are an experienced man, and Anne an attractive but very innocent girl. How much of what you feel for her is a rebirth of your physical life?

'In simpler terms, if you cannot say honestly that what you feel has at least a portion of spiritual love, then in furthering it you will do her a great injustice, and that I will not forgive. Now let us break our fast.'

There was restraint at the table, both before and after Bess and Anne came down. Fortunately, none of the adults had an opportunity to speak even had they wanted to, for little Hal Latimar—who had only recently discovered the joy of verbal communication— held the floor. From being almost inarticulate before his sister went away, he apparently now could not stop talking and, like all the Latimars, made up his mind within moments of meeting a new acquaintance if he liked them or not. He now decided that Jack Hamilton was to be a firm favourite.

Jack bore the attentions of the little boy, including having to hold him on his lap for most of the meal, with apparent good grace, but Anne wondered if he remembered what he had said to her regarding his unborn child.

She was a little chastened this morning, having had an unaccustomed lecture from her mother for her desertion of the court at Greenwich. Anne had protested her need to come home, and been confronted with implacable references to duty and honour, and the shame for her family if she did not comply with the rules.

Even so, as she looked about the hall Anne felt that she would be willing to flout all these conventions and just stay here for ever. She said little, however, only watched Jack and Hal getting to know each other.

Bess, who had come down with the firm intention of reprimanding Jack for his part in the affair, said nothing either. During the conversation with her daughter, she knew she had said all the things a dutiful mother should say, but all the time had been thinking, How changed she is, my daughter!

Anne had been mad to go to court, to be a part of a life she admired, and now appeared to think nothing of it. She had changed so much in a few short months, grown so mature that Bess had been intimidated by her. The light-hearted girl who had ridden off to Greenwich was no more; instead a stranger had come back to Maiden Court, a beautiful lady with all the trappings of the society which Bess remembered, but with an inner strength she could not account for.

Harry, too, was silent during the prolonged meal. He was greatly worried by his interview with Hamilton. He knew Jack so well, knew his poetic heart which was so badly at odds with his facility for being first in any race. If Jack decided he wanted Anne for his, for whatever reason, then he would chase her to the bitter end. And during the race Ralph Monterey, with his highly desirable suit, would be swept aside—along with Anne's ambitions to serve her sovereign—perhaps for all the wrong reasons.

Jack, too, as he was smilingly dealing with the youngest Latimar, knew moments of doubt. Harry had put his finger on the crux of the matter: how much of what he felt for Anne was a genuine regard for the woman she was fast becoming, how much an extension of the now persistent dreams he had of possessing her? He had no answer for that.

'They are angry with me,' Anne sighed as they turned out of the Maiden Court drive and contemplated the winding road to the capital.

'Of course they are,' Jack said. 'They understand the way it is in court society, and 'tis a shame to disappoint them.'

'I know.' Anne lowered the hood of her cloak. The air was cold, but not unpleasant, and the going sloppy on the ground but no hazard to her surefooted mare. 'I really wanted to stay, though.'

Jack cast an experienced eye over her mount. Jenny had recovered well from her injury at Tranmere, as had her mistress, but he had a care for them both. He said, 'So I thought, but you must go back and face the music.'

'Ugh. I have always hated that expression, and even more so since I have been exposed to so many of the palace courtiers who think they have a talent for playing and singing but don't!'

Jack laughed. Really, it was becoming a habit with him lately, he who had not done so for so long. He realised, disturbingly, that he too would have liked to stay at Maiden Court. Yet surely all his thoughts should be straining towards Ravensglass? In the last ten years he had never set foot off the place without calculating exactly how soon he could return.

For want of something to say, he asked, 'Are you worried about Ralph's reaction to your little escapade?'

'Oh, no,' Anne replied airily, 'for he will not have noticed my absence.'

'Not have noticed—' Jack caught himself up before he could say the damning words: If you were mine I would *notice* everything you did from morning till night! I would be acutely aware of all your actions, however trivial. And if you set out in inclement weather on a journey of some miles without me, I would be distraught until you returned safely.

He raised his grey eyes to the sky. Dear Lord, he thought, is this love? If so, it was not the emotion he remembered, not the suitable reverent love he had felt for Marie Claire. But nor was it what Harry had inferred: an affair solely of the flesh.

It is, he thought, the hardest thing to accept that I have not been led astray by a carnal lust, but by a deeper emotion. It was a greater treason to the faith he had kept in Marie Claire's name for so long.

'That is good,' he returned lightly. 'For I would not wish to be in the same position I was in before Yuletide.'

Anne spurred her horse to run alongside his. Valiant was tetchy on this difficult ground and inclined to roll his eyes and kick up his back legs at any provocation.

From a safe distance Anne said into the wind, 'I did not hear the outcome of that, Jack. What happened? How did you extricate yourself?'

By stating the facts, Jack could have told her. By going to Monterey and telling him plainly, I am no beardless boy, and will not be despatched so easily. Choose any weapon you like and I will best you, and you must know that. I have defended myself against better men than you—so what choose you, Sir Ralph? An amicable agreement right now where we agree to disagree? Or the hard light of dawn in some deserted place, and the likelihood you may not leave that place—alive!'

Ralph had naturally seen sense. He had no real quarrel with Hamilton over Tranmere—what Ralph felt for Jack was far older in years. Moreover, the Queen, whom he had found such favour with recently, was strongly opposed to the idea of duels for honour, and he had no wish to incur her wrath, he was very sure of Anne, and—this he admitted to himself—Hamilton was not a man he would wish to tangle with. Accordingly, Ralph had retired from the situation with as much grace as was possible.

Now Jack sought some acceptable explanation of events for Anne, and said finally, 'I think Ralph was reluctant to engage. Not only for fear of upsetting you, Anne, but because I am a well-known admirer and long-term friend of your father, and it would have been. . .awkward to pursue the quarrel.'

'I'm glad,' Anne said simply. 'Ralph is quite right—my father would not have liked it if you two had seriously fallen out. So, everything is just as it was.'

Hardly, thought Jack wryly, turning his problems over in his mind for the rest of the time they were on the road.

Foremost in these deliberations was a reluctance to be in the vicinity of Ralph Monterey once more. Although he disliked the man intensely, as a brother knight—with its code attendant—he had been disloyal to Ralph, if only in his mind. No betrothal between Anne and her cavalier had been formalised yet, but it was understood and therefore any other man trespassing on this ground was guilty of unbecoming conduct.

It also went badly against the grain not to declare himself to Anne in an honest and straightforward way, but, given her apparent love for Ralph, Harry's words on the subject and his own confusion, perhaps it was just as well that he could think of no words for such a declaration.

Anne was acutely aware of his preoccupation, but obviously not the cause, and his withdrawal hurt her. It seemed to her that for every step forward she took in their relationship he forced her two steps back.

The dim pearly sun, which had never really gained ascendancy over the clouds which had lowered over them all day, was disappearing into the horizon as Greenwich loomed head.

In the stable-yard, Anne held on to Jack when he would have immediately released her after helping her to dismount. 'Jack,' she said, looking up into his face, 'whatever happens to me now—and I suppose I will be in trouble once more—I want to thank you for taking me home. It was the act of a true friend, and if I can return the favour in any way, at any time, you need only ask.'

He examined her upturned face, its delicate complexion as untouched by the rough weather they had recently encountered as if she had spent the day relaxing in her chamber, her movements still full of graceful energy despite the uncomfortable ride. 'Comparisons. . .are inevitable', Harry had said, and this was true, for Jack now compared Anne to Marie Claire, but not to Anne's disadvantage.

Marie Claire had been a poor horsewoman, and disliked the activity, always choosing to walk or take advantage of a carriage, and he had always admired this in her, considering it an example of her extreme femininity. Yet no woman could have been more feminine than Anne in the saddle, despite her brilliant handling of any animal, her unfailing cheerfulness in the face of adversity.

'What is it?' she asked, trying to decipher his unreadable face. 'Are you thinking you may be blamed for my misdeed? Don't be, for I shall tell that I made you take me, and you could do not more as a gentleman than to go with me, to save me from disaster.'

'I am not afraid on that account. But you must be nervous.'

'Well, not for the outcome, for I care nothing if I am sent away. But for the immediate—I do hate to be shouted at and reviled.'

'I am glad you are not nervous—as you have told me you never are. And—' he touched her bright hair with a gloved hand '—your hair is still beautifully in curl.'

His light tone repulsed her as usual—she had heard him use it with no other woman save herself—and she let him go. 'Then I will bid you good night, Jack. No doubt I shall see you on the morrow.'

Owing to a certain set of circumstances, Anne's absence from Greenwich had passed unnoticed, except by her brother, who had not mentioned it to anyone. At midday the previous day, the Queen had left the meal, complaining of feeling unwell, and promptly taken to her bed. An hour later she was in a state of high fever, her physicians summoned, her ladies thrown into panic.

Although subject at times to a strange aching malady which overtook her body, causing acute pain in muscles and joints, but was usually short-lived, she had not been seriously ill since contracting the deadly pox a few years before. That terrible time she had been only steps away from the grave and it, too, had begun with a fever. . .

When Anne entered her dorter, she found her fellows in various states of exhaustion, having kept vigil around the great bedchamber all through the night. Others of the ladies had been delegated to various tasks, and none knew exactly how another had passed the hours Anne had been gone.

She therefore slipped back into her place without comment and was changing her clothes when the joyful news arrived that Her Majesty was on the road to recovery, her fever abated, and even able to take some light sustenance. She was, however, wakeful and wished to be read to.

Anne instantly volunteered and made her way to the royal chambers. Going home to speak with her father had given her no relief, except that she *had* spoken of her fears and so reduced them.

In the evening, when Ralph, having concluded his marathon game to his satisfaction, came looking for her, she found him as fascinating as ever. As the Queen had commanded her courtiers to make merry to celebrate her swift return to health, there was dancing as usual in the hall and they went there.

Ralph had risen from the card tables in Lord Astwick's apartments with a heavy purse and also as the possessor of a considerable amount of valuable jewellery. This was quite usual—those gentlemen, having bet their cash, frequently offered their gems to continue in the game.

Most of it, along with the cash, Ralph had decided

must go to pay his debts, but he had kept a glowing ruby ring which he now presented to Anne. 'To replace the poor bauble I gave you last year when we plighted our troth,' he said, fixing her with his deceptively frank gaze.

Not knowing that this particular item had been wrenched from the finger of a gentleman in whose family it had been retained since taken as booty from one of Saladin's men in crusading days, and flung across the table before the young man had retired, bankrupt and almost in tears, Anne was delighted with it.

'I *love* it, Ralph; how could you possibly know that rubies are my very favourite jewels?'

'I have guessed it, darling. With those dark eyes and red lips, it has to be your gem,' Ralph answered smoothly.

It was all very gratifying and romantic and Anne wore her new jewel with pride—much as she did her relationship with Monterey, who continued in his meteoric rise as a bright star in the Tudor court. But it did not mean quite as much to her as it might have done on the night before she went to Ravensglass...

CHAPTER THIRTEEN

THREE days later, Elizabeth, very much stronger but still abed, decided to command her closest circle to attend her and share her evening. She had been given a book containing some new and unusual Italian poetry and wished it read to her; Ralph Monterey, an able scholar in the language, was invited to do this and Anne came to watch his effort.

His was a long recital and Anne, who had no Italian, as enervated by the heat in the room and the unfamiliar verse as the rest of the company, was sitting in the shadows with Robert Dudley.

Had Ralph been born to another station in life, she mused idly, he could well have been an actor. With his handsome looks, beautiful voice and grace of movement, he would have excelled in this craft. Also, he was so adept at giving any audience exactly what they wanted—

Now, where had that cynical thought come from? she wondered, appalled. Disagreeable and disloyal! Anne folded her hands in her lap and tried to listen more attentively.

Robert glanced sideways at her. She was growing more beautiful, the little Latimar girl, he thought, and, lately, something else in her drew the eye. Something hard to define, but very significant. He said, 'How like you the sight of your love parading his wares for the Queen, Anne?'

A provocative remark! Anne tightened her lips. But

the comment was justified, her common sense told her. Really, this night, Ralph might be mistaken for a fond lover romancing his lady!

'He rises fast,' Robert said softly. 'And those in his train must adjust, one would agree, and be prepared to take second place to the object of his ambition.'

Anne checked the retort forming on her lips. What was the point? What Dudley said was fact: Ralph made it plain enough that he was determined on a career as sycophant to his sovereign. But she greatly disliked the implication that she was a part of the parade! She was absolutely loyal to Elizabeth; she admired her and thought her clever and well fitted to rule all England. But there her allegiance stopped. She could never be part of the cringing, toadying circle that the Queen surrounded herself in.

The stuffy, over-perfumed room suddenly seemed insupportable to her. She longed to be out in the wild wind swirling around Greenwich, to be with people who were not a part of this stifling coterie.

Jack Hamilton. Anne snatched at his name as it came to her mind. I need to see Jack! She put down the bottle of oil she had earlier soothed the Queen's brow with and rose. 'I think I will withdraw now, my lord,' she said quietly.

Robert watched her cross the room and laughed to himself. He thought, She will never hang on the coat-tails of any man! Whoever gets Latimar's girl—and I would take any wager now that it will not be Monterey—will gain a woman determined on equal terms in the marriage. God send her a man worthy of her.

* * *

Anne looked first in the stables for Jack and was told that he had already bedded down his horse for the night. Then she looked in the hall, the antechambers and even the little writing room they had visited together. But no one had seen Hamilton that night and, short of pursuing him up in the gentlemen's quarters, she could do no more.

All the time she was searching she did not think about why she was doing so. But finally, coming to a halt in the passage at the foot of the main stairs, she did. She had not seen him for three days; he had not come to her, but obviously he knew the Queen was ill and probably assumed that her duties were consuming her time.

Anne stood, one hand on the enormous carved stairpost, lost in thought. Why did she so desperately need to see Jack? He was her friend, but then she had so many friends now. The ladies of her acquaintance—high and low—made it clear that they welcomed her company, and Ralph's peers quite frankly courted her—of course, within the conventions.

But she wanted to see Jack right now, and could not tell why. It was a puzzle, and as she stood deliberating a lady came down the staircase and Anne moved aside to allow her to pass by. The woman stopped.

'Anne? Wool-gathering?' It was Allison Monterey.

'Oh, Allison. . .yes, I am daydreaming. Am I wanted again in the sick room?'

'You are not,' Allison replied decisively. 'None of us is, for Her Majesty is feeling so much better that she now wishes to sleep the rest of the night. I am going to enjoy a little to eat and drink, for—Lord—what a long four days it has been! Will you join me, or have you a pressing engagement?'

'No. . .at least, I have been looking for Jack Hamilton, without success.'

'Hamilton? Why, I can help you there; he is in the library. Unlikely, is it not? I believe he went in there to sleep!' Allison passed on and Anne climbed the stairs to the next floor and ran down the passage to the library.

The door was open. Inside, candles were burning and she could see a tall figure in one of the chairs facing the door, distinctive for its helmet of silver hair. She tiptoed in and looked down upon Jack. He was holding a book loosely in his hands, and was indeed fast asleep.

All men looked vulnerable whilst asleep, and Jack was no exception. With his bold eyes lidded, mobile mouth unguarded, and muscled body at ease, he appeared much younger than his years.

Anne looked at him for a long time, wondering why just being in the same room with him gave her such comfort. She knew that if he should wake, sit up and speak, this illusion would vanish, but, meanwhile, she took an odd delight in it.

She leaned closer at last to examine the title of the book he held; it was one of Wyatt the younger's collection of romantic poetry. How incongruous! Reaching down, she extracted the volume and as she did so Jack woke up and, with the veteran soldier's ability to be instantly aware, straightened in his chair.

'Anne? What do you here?'

'What do *you*?' she asked, laughing. 'Pretending to extend your learning, but in reality catching up on your sleep! Did you actually read any of this before you dropped off?' She held up the book.

'Certainly I did,' Jack said sternly. 'Your brother, George, recommended it to me and I came here tonight to discover its attraction.' Feeling at a disadvantage, he uncoiled his long body and stood up to look down upon her. 'If you wish, I can quote you some passages.'

'Oh, no, I won't strain you that far! Let us sit by the fire and exchange our latest news.'

The library at Greenwich was not the most intimate place to be, but it felt so to Anne as she sat by the dull blaze and eased her tight slippers. Jack did not speak much, but then she usually did most of the talking when they were together. At length she said thoughtfully, 'I was afraid, when I couldn't find you tonight, that you might already have left for Ravensglass.'

'Without bidding you goodbye? I would not do that.'

'I'm glad of that. But surely you must have to go soon? The roads will be clear enough now to the north.'

'I am sure I know my duty,' he said stiffly. Her coming upon him so abruptly whilst he was asleep and, of course, dreaming of her, was difficult enough for him to deal with without her frivolous remarks.

'Now don't be tetchy, Jack. I am only asking—as a friend—when I can expect to be without you.' She knew now why she had looked so frantically for him that night. She had had at the back of her mind the fear that he was already gone. Gone back to an inaccessible place— But knowing this worried her afresh. Why should she feel so? It was surely inappropriate.

'That is a strange thing to say—"without you",' he said. Strange, because that was why he had tarried so long in this alien place—because he had had exactly the same thought: When I leave here, I will be without Anne.

They looked at each other, half-disbelievingly, half-warily, then she said quietly, 'I should not have said that. . . It must be embarrassing for you. . .and it is a disloyalty for me.'

The ball in this game is always returned to me to play, Jack thought. How does she feel, really? The only way to find out is to ask her, and I cannot do that in the present circumstances.

Silence, punctuated by the falling ashes in the red fire, enveloped them both.

'Jack,' Anne said, at last, 'I think there may be a lot unspoken between us.' The words were not said without thought. But Anne, assembling her thoughts, needed some explanation. In this room, with its trailing shadows, she sensed something she could not understand, and looked to Jack—her friend, her comrade—to explain it to her.

Jack rose. He was never easy remaining in one place for long, never easy in any place with four walls. Fresh air and freedom were as necessary as food and drink to him.

He went to one of the small windows and unlatched it. Leaning his weight against it, it yet resisted him, warped from the constant damp air rising from the river.

Anne got up and came to his side. She too lent her strength and the window opened with a protesting creak. 'You do not answer me,' she said, standing with one elbow relaxed against the sill, looking into his face.

Jack was looking out over the dark woods; between the bare trees could be seen the glitter of water.

'How can I? To do so might be both intrusive and inappropriate. . .in the circumstances.'

'*My* circumstances?' she asked, tilting her head so that she could see his eyes. 'My circumstances are as I so decide them. I ask you again—what is there between us, Jack?'

'Anne!' He turned away from the sharp wind flowing into the room. 'I never know what you are about! Are you flirting with me, as is so fashionable in this place? Are you asking me to declare myself in romantic terms, as the ladies who are your friends here demand of their admirers? I cannot play these games!'

'I do not speak of games,' she said slowly. 'I speak of what there is between you and me, which neither of us chooses to acknowledge.'

There, she had said what was in her mind. Something she had not known was even there. She did not know how it would be received, but his answer, she did know, was of critical importance to her. As to flirting—a blind woman could see that Jack Hamilton was not a man to flirt with; he was far too real.

A cross-draught in the room disturbed them. The door to the library had opened and Ralph Monterey entered. 'Anne?' he said enquiringly. 'I have been looking high and low for you! You left Her Majesty's chamber without waiting for dismissal.'

'The Lady Allison has told me I am no longer needed.'

'That is so. Her Grace is now sleeping, praise God. But you and I are awaited in Thornton's apartments. He invited us to a private supper this night, if you will recall.'

'I'm sorry, Ralph. I forgot all about it.'

'You forgot...' Ralph crossed the room to the window. He inclined his head to Jack, a pucker of annoyance marring his handsome face. 'It is hard to believe that someone as important as Lord Thornton can be *forgot*.' Edward Thornton, deadly enemy to

Robert Dudley, had taken up Monterey and promoted him with the Queen at every opportunity

'Oh, well,' said Anne lightly. 'I apologise for that, and will join you there as soon as I finish my conversation with Jack.'

'You will come now!' Ralph said.

'As soon as I have finished my conversation with Lord Jack,' Anne repeated.

Ralph took her arm. 'Now, I said.' Jack noted the hand on Anne's arm, but made no move.

Anne pulled away, her eyes darkening. 'Please, Ralph, do not take that tone with me.'

Ralph, his opinion of himself always inflated and swelled now by the Queen's marked preference for him in these days, said arrogantly, 'I will take any tone I choose with you, lady. As my future wife, you will not object to it. Now come.' He renewed his grip on her arm. Jack let out an impatient breath.

'Come, man, take your hand from the lady and cease bullying her.'

'I beg your pardon?' Ralph stood back a pace. 'May I enquire what business my hand on, or my words to, this lady are to you?'

Anne's annoyed expression turned to one of dismay. Was she about to provoke another confrontation between these two? She said, 'I am ready now, Ralph. Let us make haste for Lord Thornton's apartments.'

'We are not yet finished with our talk,' Jack said mildly. 'Perhaps Ralph will allow us to do that.'

'I have said,' Ralph replied with exaggerated patience, 'that we are expected to a private supper of some importance. As a gentleman you will know what a discourtesy it would be to be tardy.' He tried to stare

Jack down, but Jack was too secure in his dignity to allow him to do so.

'If you go and explain politely that the Lady Anne will be there directly, I am sure that will satisfy courtesy.'

Ralph said angrily, 'This is not the first time you have attempted to come between Anne and myself! I would ask you by what right?'

No right at all, Jack had to admit to himself. Ralph had every right to be annoyed by all this and, if he had known all of what passed through Jack's mind now when he was with Anne, he would have had every right to an even stronger emotion. He looked at Anne, who was staring at Ralph with a curious expression in her eyes.

I love this man, she was thinking doubtfully, but am not altogether sure that I *like* him.

Perhaps it was seeing the two men together—Ralph dressed immaculately in satin and velvet, his hair oiled and curled, a strong perfume about him, Jack so plainly dressed, with nothing but his all-weather dousing each morning in well water between him and a masculine scent.

But Ralph is the kind of man I always *wanted*, she thought, frustrated with her comparison. He is part of the life here in the place I always wanted to be.

'Anne?' Ralph was growing impatient. This scene was aggravating, but meant nothing serious to him. He did not consider Hamilton in any way a rival for Anne's affections. Why should he? The man was a primitive soldier knight, one of that odd, but necessary, body of men who kept the borders safe, who went in the vast transport ships from Tilbury and shed their blood on foreign soil when England defended her rights in other lands.

Elizabeth treated such men with respect, naturally, for England had not become a mighty power without them, but when they came to her court—as Jack had done—they were seen for what they were: as inappropriate in the assembly as oxen in a blood stable. What could Anne Latimar possibly have in common with one of them?

No, this tête-à-tête Jack was having with Anne in the ill-lit library this evening did not worry or annoy Ralph, but Jack himself did, as he always did on the occasions they met.

Jack's very way of standing, as if he was expecting attack at any time, his plain dress and obvious scorn of male adornment, his expression when the gentlemen of the court told their risqué, but amusing, anecdotes set Ralph's teeth on edge. The man's simplicity and sincerity, and obvious untarnished integrity, provoked dark memories for Ralph of a youth spent trying to please his father, and always failing. . .

However it was, he always felt that he must make a stand when in conflict with Hamilton, and did so now. 'Anne, I demand that you come with me now. Not to do so will encourage me to think that our relationship— our betrothal—might be in jeopardy.'

'So be it, Ralph,' Anne replied with composure.

Both men looked at her in amazement.

'I don't think you can have understood what I just said,' Ralph said slowly. Whenever he was with these two, events slipped out of his control, he realised.

'I understood perfectly,' Anne said gravely. 'You have just said that if I do not accompany you to Lord

Thornton's supper party right now you will think again about our betrothal.'

One advantage that a persistent gambler had was the ability to know when he held a losing hand. Ralph believed he held one now and promptly threw it in. 'Very well,' he said, bowing gracefully. 'I will leave you now, and hope you may be in a more. . .sensible mood on the morrow.' He left them, and closed the door with some force behind him.

'Well,' said Anne. 'That is that.'

Jack passed a hand over his cropped hair. 'What are you about, demoiselle? To speak of breaking a betrothal is a serious matter! It is not to be conducted upon a whim!'

'I know that,' Anne said. She was shaken by what had gone before, but also thoughtful. This is the rest of my life I am deciding upon now, she thought, and I want it to be absolutely right. 'I will not be dictated to, Jack. By any man.'

His eyes on her face, he said, 'All men dictate to women.'

'My father does not,' she said decisively. 'Nor, I think, would you.'

This last was a new thought for her, for Jack could be as forceful with her as any man she knew. But always for my own good, she realised; however much I might resent it at the time, he has always had my welfare at heart.

He made a dismissive gesture with one hand. 'Two men in two million— You should go now to Monterey and make all right. You cannot so treat a man of whom your family approve, who is undoubtedly set to be one of the favoured in this place—in the life you have chosen. In the life you are both so well fitted for.'

'Yes,' she agreed. 'Ralph and I are well suited to court life. But first, I am determined, we must be suited to each other. Before I commit myself to him for the rest of my days. Would you condemn me to those days in the company of someone who was not absolutely right, Jack?'

She was, in this moment, all that he disliked in a woman—speaking in that light and teasing voice, laughing behind her brilliant eyes, looking up at him with a dizzying charm. He moved away and stood tracing the bold pattern of the colourful rug with one toe of his slipper.

'Was it something which happened at home, Maiden Court, which has caused you to reappraise your situation?' he asked.

'In a way. Perhaps I went there to discover exactly how I did feel.'

'It was nothing your father said, that I do know,' Jack said unguardedly.

'*Do* you? How?' She had wanted to continue the conversation they had been having before Ralph arrived, but, as usual, Jack had retreated away from her, back into the role of trusted confidant.

Jack looked up. 'Because he spoke in favour of your match. I feel he would be very disappointed if it should fail to come about.'

'Oh.' Anne considered this. Yes, she agreed, but, after all, it was her life, was it not? She then had a strange thought—that this was the first time she had ever regarded her beloved father's views as being anything less than of vital importance.

She said, 'Well, naturally, my father's opinion means a great deal to me. But what is yours, Jack? You have

never told me what you think of my projected marriage
with Ralph?'

His face closed. He could give neither his opinion of
her contract with Ralph nor his opinion of the man
himself. Not being able to produced a backdraught of
anger directed towards her. Why should she press him
in this way? It was more, surely, than any man in his
position should have to bear?

He said harshly, 'Perhaps you think to use me in
your attempt to bring Monterey into line? To convince
him that you may not be. . .dictated to?'

For a moment she did not understand what he was
saying, then she was dismayed. 'Why, no, Jack! I never
thought of such a thing. Why should you accuse me of
it?'

'You seek my company often enough, in full view of
all the court,' he said roughly. 'You pretend an interest
in what I say when it must be obvious to all that I
cannot compete with your more worldly friends. You
even engineered this little drama tonight for the benefit
of your paramour. You must know that nothing brings
a gentleman more swiftly to heel than his lady dallying
with another man. Perhaps if we really work on the
situation, you and I, we can make Ralph truly jealous!'

His words were very unfair to her, he *knew* that. But
in his confusion he was struggling to gain a hand-hold
on a steep precipice he was not even sure he wanted to
climb.

How could he think that of me? she wondered,
shocked. She chose to be with him, in all the ways he
had described, because she believed him to be her
friend. It was a horrible notion he had produced, and
in such a frozen voice, with such a terrible look on his
face, and it made a painful mockery of her instinct that
he was a safe harbour to steer into whenever the

emotional craft of her life was afraid and uncertain. She stared at him, speechless.

'You pretend not to understand what I mean? Then allow me to demonstrate the next step in this particular comedy—' He took the short steps to her side and drew her into his arms. ''Tis this, lady—'

He bent his silver head and kissed her. It was not the polite salute of a friend, nor the fumbling, amorous overture she had grown so adept at repelling since coming to court. It was a passionate assault, which contained within it a number of elements she had never had to face before, even from Ralph, who occasionally asserted his rights over her in a physical way.

When he released her at last, she pressed her fingers to her mouth and fought bravely against the desire to burst into tears.

Jack was fighting his own demons. He had known as soon as his mouth closed upon hers that what he had been so afraid of in the last weeks was now the truth. He had fallen in love again, and with a dedicated passion.

No wraiths from his past had attended him as he had caressed Anne Latimar, for this was something entirely new and vital in its own right. Yet, even with this knowledge in the forefront of his intelligent mind, he had treated her with an unforgivable harshness.

He was ashamed. He looked at her dumbly. 'Anne Latimar shamed me this night,' Mark Bolbey had said at Ravensglass, 'with her dignity and innocence.' Jack was ashamed for different reasons, for he loved her, and knew her to be all the things that Mark had only discovered too late. In his rage, because he now felt for Anne what he believed rightfully belonged to his dead wife, he had behaved in a way which made him not fit to be the man he had always prided himself on being.

Still battling against her tears, Anne knew none of this. She tried to summon her temper, but she could not feel anger, only a tremendous sadness and another emotion she could not yet identify. Jack had very rarely touched her, except whilst dancing, or assisting her onto her horse, had never abused their seclusion together on a great many occasions by any move at all. And now this!

But he is not really like that, she thought, and knew that what she was feeling, as well as other conflicting responses, was a deep compassion. He was a hard man—the weeks at Ravensglass had made her aware of that—and he was a merciless enemy to any threat to the land he guarded for the English throne. He could be, and was, a tough commander with his men.

But in the area they had just strayed into it would be in his nature to be tender. He would be a gentle lover, she knew instinctively, with the right woman. But she was not the right woman, and the realisation gave her a sense of grief.

Before the threatened tears could fall she turned and ran from the room. He made no attempt to stop her, but turned back to the window to watch the drapes swaying in the freezing wind.

Elizabeth was surprised the following morning by the first request of the day. Jack Hamilton had stayed in her court longer than he ever had before since assuming command of his northern fortress, but had made little effort to ingratiate himself with her. Indeed, she had scarcely seen him.

Now, with the weather abominable once more, after

a brief respite, he had respectfully asked her permission
to leave Greenwich and resume his duties.

She had no objection to this, of course—presumably
the ever-present threat from the Scots demanded his
personal vigilance—but she did wonder why he had not
chosen to go the previous week. Just in case he had
heard whisper of something unusual brewing beyond
the border she did not simply send him verbal leave to
go, but asked that he attend upon her forthwith.

She was now fully recovered from her recent sickness, but still chose to remain in her vast bedchamber
for most of the morning, so Jack was received in that
room, which appeared to him to be as crowded and
busy as any of her audience chambers.

'Ah, Hamilton.' Elizabeth beckoned him to the bed.
'I have received your request, and naturally have no
objection to your going, but would wish some words
with you before then. Pray be seated.'

'Thank you, madam, I will stand.' The room, with its
heaped and blazing fire, thick velvet obscuring the
windows, half-dozen ladies scurrying to and fro, their
silk skirts rustling, felt like a cage to Jack. He also
thought that if he sat down in this overheated room he
might very well fall asleep, for he had not slept at all
the previous night.

The lack of sleep was, to him, almost frightening.
God knew he had always managed to obtain rest in
some of the most uncomfortable places in the past, yet
last night it had eluded him. His mind had simply not
allowed it. When he had closed his eyes, ignoring the
grunts and snores of his bedfellows, he had not been
able to rid himself of the image of Anne Latimar, her
white fingers pressed to her bruised mouth, her eyes so
dark and tragic and accusing.

Well might she accuse me, he had thought grimly, turning first this way then that, trying to induce sleep; I accuse myself. I betrayed both her friendship and her trust, and in the worst possible way.

Anne had been right in her instinctive assessment of Jack: he was not the kind of man to mistreat any woman, whatever her status. There had been a great many women in his life—before Marie Claire the seasoned ladies of a great court, and after his wife's death the more dubious women who came a soldier's way. Neither had ever had cause to fear Hamilton's attention.

But Anne Latimar, who was now so dear to him, had received despicable treatment and he could neither explain that nor forgive himself for it. She had given her friendship, long before he could appreciate it or return it; she had so many times shown kindness to him—

'Hamilton!' The Queen, under her pile of fur-lined covers, spoke sharply above the gentle thrumming of her lute-player. 'I have asked you: is there some special reason why you wish to return so suddenly to Ravensglass?'

'No, Majesty.'

'No—no rumour that the Scottish queen is causing dissent?'

What might have passed for a smile altered the stern contours of Jack's face. Mary Stuart was Elizabeth Tudor's particular demon, he thought, and inspired by a purely feminine unreason. He had met the Scottish queen many times in France years ago and, whilst acknowledging her magical qualities, for she was both attractive and charming, had thought her quite the silliest woman he had ever met.

Yet her English counterpart, incomparably talented in every way, was beset by the fear of her very existence. 'No,' he said flatly. 'I have heard no such rumour.'

'Ah, well, then.' Elizabeth lay back on the soft pillows and smiled. 'There is little more to say to you than Godspeed and God bless you, Lord Jack.' She raised one thin arm and he dutifully touched his lips to her fingertips. She glanced at the closed windows where the rain, slashing spitefully against the palace walls, could be heard, if not seen, and remarked, 'It is poor weather for travelling. Do you get the midday meal inside you before you leave. It will give you time to bid farewell to your friends here.'

He was dismissed, but before turning away a very disagreeable thought struck him. He had told Anne that he would not leave here without bidding her goodbye. Had he to honour that declaration? Had he to seek her out and say goodbye? With the disillusionment of last night's scene between them?

Robert Dudley, who had been lolling by the great bed while this conversation took place, looked up curiously. What was amiss with the man? he wondered. He looked poleaxed by a few simple words. When Jack left the room, Robert rose and excused himself. He followed Jack down the stairs and caught his arm as he entered the great hall.

'Hamilton—Jack—is there aught wrong?'

'No. As I told Her Grace, there is no rumour of—'

'I mean with you,' Robert said. 'Why are you really leaving us so sudden?'

'Is that your concern?' In his present state of mind, Jack was inclined to forget the rest of this company's regard for the most favoured man in the Queen's life.

Robert laughed. He hardly knew why he had hurried from the bedchamber; certainly this man was not a friend of his past or of his present. But he admired Hamilton.

Robert Dudley, the Earl of Leicester, was no tame animal tied to Elizabeth's skirts; he was intelligent and as masculine as many were not in this assembly. Physically, he was a formidable competitor in the knightly skills, but Jack was the best, and one sportsman always appreciated another.

'My concern? Why, no. At least, if your warlike duties do not recall you to Ravensglass, then I would guess at a more personal reason for wishing to quit this place. That being so, I might offer my advice, if you were in the mood to listen.'

Jack paused. He had a talent for choosing men who would be excellent in battle. He had noticed Leicester in the practice yard, of course, and registered him as a likely combatant. Obviously this would never be, but he decided to listen.

'It is the little Latimar, is it not?' Robert asked softly.

'Why should you say that?' Was there gossip about? Jack, who had never cared much for what others said of him, now found himself worried on Anne's behalf.

'I have eyes, have I not? At Ravensglass I thought I detected a mutual attraction—sternly repressed by yourself, of course,' he added teasingly.

Jack turned away. Why was he discussing something so near to his heart with this man?

Robert followed him into the hall. 'Oh, come! I beg your pardon for my light comment, but one gets into the habit of such in this place.'

He was so disarming that Jack found himself confiding, 'I would not say mutual; it is all on my part now. There is only friendship on hers—or was.'

Robert let the first part go. 'Why "was"? Something occurred last night? I was in Lord Thornton's apartments—oh, very much on sufferance, of course—when Monterey arrived, *sans* his beloved, looking like thunder. Later, I observed little Anne apparently on the point of tears in the passage of the ladies' quarters. What did you do to him—and her?'

'To him? Nothing, except remind him of his manners. To her...' The habit of exchanging personal confidences had been little known to Jack over the last ten years, but now he found himself unable to stop. 'I embraced her clumsily— Actually, 'twas little short of an attack.'

Robert smoothed his fine beard thoughtfully. How very unlikely! If he had not heard it from the man's own lips he would not have believed it. He said, 'Yes, these Latimars... I can recall many an occasion when I have wished to strangle her brother George. They can be most provocative.'

Jack was not comforted. Anne had not provoked him. 'Howsoever it was, I feel I must now leave to save—to save—'

'Embarrassment?' Robert supplied helpfully.

'I think you have not understood what I am saying, Leicester. I all but assaulted the girl.'

'Well, yes, but...surely you will have the next thirty years to make up for that.'

Jack stared at him.

'I mean,' Robert continued, 'you are in love with each other, and no maid will hold a little extra insistence on her future husband's part in such a matter—' He broke off as Jack gave him an astounded glance.

'Lord, man, don't look like that! I am sorry if you thought you had gained another hopeless cause to replace the old, but, believe me, the wench is as smitten with you as you are with her!'

'But what makes you say that? What possible indication has there been for what you are saying?'

Robert led the way to the refreshment table. He picked up the wine jug, and when Jack shook his head said, 'Oh, no, of course you don't. . .but I will.

'Now, what was I saying? Oh, yes, so—what indication? My dear friend, use your good mind for other than planning a battle strategy! Love is not merely a physical attraction, it is also affection and need and many another quality.

'Anne came to court only a short while ago and has been an instant success. She is linked now with a certain gentleman, but 'tis not to him she turns whenever she needs help or comfort. Perhaps at Ravensglass it was an extreme case, an unusual situation, but it was obvious when you came in that day that some kind of partnership had been formed.

'Here at Greenwich, Lord Ralph is all very well for having fun with, but it is *you* she seeks when unsure or uncertain. Draw conclusion from that, man, and draw the right conclusion.'

The hall was noisy, and the endless clatter and chatter might well have distracted another, but Jack stood quite still, considering Robert's words. Was it so? Did Anne love him without even knowing it? Had he been so concerned with his own personal conflict that he had not noticed hers? All Leicester said was true in the facts. Should he look behind them to discover something less easy to lay hold of, but infinitely more valuable?

As he paused, the light at the end of the tunnel which had featured in his imagination became quite blinding and the pieces of the puzzle fell rapidly into place. Who did Anne turn to when she wished to express her most private thoughts? Himself. Who did she instinctively turn to when in trouble or doubt? Himself. There was basis there for everything else which mattered.

Watching the light dawn, Robert was almost jealous. He had, with his idle observance, detected a great love affair. Two people, a girl and a man without much importance to the world, had caught his attention and he was doing his best to help them. And how he envied them!

When Jack turned purposefully towards the door he caught his arm. 'Gently now, Jack. Do not approach her with that ferocious expression, as if you had sighted a wild Scottish chieftain encroaching upon your territory! Go subtly, for she is still a little under the spell of Monterey, you know.'

Ralph Monterey! Jack had forgotten his part in the drama. He said slowly, 'He has most honourably asked for her hand. . .he thinks to marry her, and I would not treat a brother in this way.'

Robert laughed callously. 'He'll get over it. Besides, would you really condemn her to life with Ralph?'

Anne had said much the same, in similar words, Jack thought, bemused. He did not understand these people; he was out of his depth in the waters they swam so confidently in. But he knew his own mind: he loved Anne Latimar, and could now believe that she loved him. 'What should I do, then, Robert? How to approach this?'

Robert was sensitive to the other man's confusion.

'Well, not as some military exercise! Just find her now and quietly tell her your thoughts, your realisations. Urge her to consider her own. Then let Mistress Nature—and Lady Love—take her course. And. . .I wish you well.'

Watching Jack stride away, Robert thought again how much he envied such simple enterprise.

CHAPTER FOURTEEN

JACK had no idea where to look for Anne. He had no knowledge of what the ladies of Greenwich did each day, or where they performed their duties. A glance out of the palace windows told him that Anne would probably not be riding her horse in this wild weather. The breakfast hour was over and none of her comrades had yet assembled for the midday meal in the hall. Where would she be now?

In the main passage leading to the hall he saw a lady skimming lightly down the stairs. It was Lady Dacre, and she dipped a polite curtsy as she recognised him.

'Lady Dacre.' Jack stood resolutely in her path.

She dropped another curtsy. 'Yes, my lord? May I help you?'

'I am looking for the Lady Anne Latimar. Do you know where she is?'

His forbidding expression impressed itself upon the woman. What can Anne have done now, she wondered, to so anger Lord Jack? Of course, he was a family friend and might have something personal in that way to convey to Anne... 'She is in the palace still-room, sir.'

'I do not know where that is. Can you direct me, lady?'

'I can take you there,' she said graciously.

The still-room at Greenwich was attached to the main living quarters, an airy, fragrant place where herbs and dried flowers were mixed to make the cosmetics used by the ladies of the court, and the pot-pourri piled into great bowls to sweeten the great apartments. At the door, Lady Dacre peeped through the crack and said, 'Yes, Lady Anne is in there, but also the Dame.'

Lady Katharine Crawley, always called the Dame, for that was what she was to the young girls who underwent their training to serve the great ladies of the palaces, was a formidable woman. Her reputation was known through England, but not to Jack Hamilton, who neither knew nor cared about it. He entered the room with his quick, light step.

The room, glazed in the new way, overlooked a section of the palace gardens devoted to the cultivation of herbs and which was relatively wild, such plants doing better under less strict attention. Anne, her hands idly turning a bowl of dried rose petals, turned with startled eyes as Jack came to her side.

Mistaking her surprise for fear, he thought, Oh, let me never make her fear me again. Give me the chance to show her I can care for her so gently in the future that she will never again know what fear is. 'Anne, I have come—'

Lady Katharine trod heavily across to them. 'Sir, what is your business here?' she demanded.

Jack turned. 'My business is my own, madam, except that which I wish to share with this lady.'

Lady Katharine was outraged. No man or woman had dared to use such a peremptory tone to her in thirty years. 'Any business in this place is mine, sir.'

'Dame Katharine,' Anne said placatingly, 'Lord Jack is an old family friend, and I think wishes to bid me farewell before returning to the north on the Queen's commission.'

'Well...' Mention of Elizabeth cooled Lady Katharine a little. 'I do have an errand to perform now. I will return in a short time.' She moved away in a stately manner.

'Really, Jack,' Anne said. 'This place is Lady Katharine's domain.'

'What are you doing here? Have you been put to work like a scullery maid?'

'All the Queen's ladies take a turn here—it is a necessary part of our education to know how what is produced comes about. It is a pleasurable duty, too. Don't you find it a pleasant place?'

Jack looked around disparagingly. The sight of so many dead flowers and brittle, faded herbs depressed him. 'No, not really. The roses you have in your bowl should not be picked and hung to dry, but allowed to fall naturally onto the earth. Dead things should return to the clay, or so I believe.'

This was the last sentiment she had expected from him, but she said nothing and returned her attention to her task. He said, 'Would you walk outside with me for a little? I find it very warm in here.'

He could not breathe in this atmosphere, could not think clearly, and all the words he had rehearsed since leaving Dudley had disappeared from his mind. Anne looked surprised, but ceased her mindless sifting of the mixture and brushed her hands together.

'Very well, Jack. There is the door to the garden, but I am afraid it will be cold outside.' He was wearing a short cloak of velvet lined with coney fur. He removed it and, very carefully, laid it over her shoulders.

Outside, Anne looked up at the misty sky. It was not so much cold today as damp, and in the sharp wind was the promise of an end to bleak winter. 'You have come to say goodbye to me, Jack? All the palace knows you have requested leave to go, and I will therefore wish you Godspeed as I do all my friends when they set off on a journey.'

'Do you still regard me as such? A friend? After last night?' The words came out awkwardly.

'Certainly,' she replied with composure. 'It was not your fault but mine.'

'No!' he said explosively. 'It was not your fault! And I cannot ask your forgiveness humbly enough.'

Anne blinked. She could not imagine Jack humble. 'Well,' she said uncertainly, 'I do not hold it against you and will, as I have said, wish you Godspeed and mean it. When are you going?'

'When I have received from you a promise of marriage.'

He had not planned to say it so baldly. He had prepared a speech of great romantic fervour. Jack wrote beautiful poetry; as a young squire he had always had great success with the girls he had directed it to. But those words had been written, not spoken, and also a long time ago. No wonder the poor girl looked so astonished.

Anne was indeed astonished. If one of the stone gargoyles perched upon the roof of Greenwich had suddenly been granted a human tongue and spoken she could not have been more astounded. Her swift mind grappled immediately with the situation and reached an acceptable conclusion: Jack, one of the few knights given the name who lived by the ideal as well, felt compelled to make this gesture after his conduct of the previous night.

How ridiculous, she thought, and yet how typical of him. She also thought, How sad. Could he not trust her and their strong friendship enough to know that she would never feel that he must make this gesture? Never think the less of him for a momentary lapse? Far from being affronted or angry by his actions, she had never felt closer to him than in those moments. Or so alive.

But that did not make sense; so she had sternly told herself the night following, when she had been unable to sleep.

She seized at the first available reason for tactfully turning him away, and said, 'I thank you, Jack, for your proposal, but as you know I am already promised.'

Ralph Monterey! Why did he keep forgetting the man? 'I beg your pardon once again, Anne. Of course I know that and should have approached Ralph with my intentions before you. I will do that now.'

'No!' Anne said, horrified by the thought that she would cause more trouble for him. 'Well,' she continued lightly, 'I mean, this is all rather unorthodox, is it not? My father should have been the first approached.'

'I have done so,' Jack said stiffly.

'You have?' Another surprise! 'What did he say?' she asked, before she could stop herself.

'He looked with extreme disfavour on the matter,' Jack replied with a grim smile.

'Oh.' Anne hugged the cloak around her; the wind was gentle but persistent and she wore only a thin house gown.

'You cannot answer to what I have asked?' Jack said.

For a talkative woman, Anne gave little away of her thoughts. Only her great eyes ever expressed what was going on in her mind if she did not choose to convey it verbally, and those were lowered now as she turned a great ruby ring on her forefinger.

I would if I knew what to say, Anne thought. Embarrasment was an emotion she had seldom experienced—now she did. She wanted to say—but couldn't—When you took me in your arms last night you lit a fire I have failed to extinguish during a cold night and a half-day. Had you spoken last night the words you have just done, perhaps—perhaps I would have been unable to prevent myself from—

Madness! She must continue to remind herself that Jack was only making this extraordinary offer for all the wrong reasons.

'No,' she said eventually, 'I cannot answer.'

Black disappointment settled upon him like a fog. But what had he expected? A few chance words had illuminated his own feelings more truly than hers. Had he really thought they would be returned?

'I see. Then I must beg your pardon once more for behaving in such a knavish fashion. Of course you cannot answer; you have already given the answer I desire to another.'

Anne's mind revolved with sudden clarity. If I agree with him, she thought, he will walk away and I shall never see him again. For whatever reason he has asked me this day—for whatever, I will discount it and consider my own feelings. If only I could discover what they are.

'No,' she said firmly. 'I am not thinking of Ralph but of myself. What I mean is that I cannot answer now. I must think and we must talk again of the matter.'

If she was clever at concealing her thoughts, so—and more so—was he, for he revealed nothing of the upsurge of pure joy he felt on hearing her words.

'Then think now,' he said. 'Let us talk now.'

'No. If you—if we are serious in this, then I suggest

you go back to Ravensglass and give me leave to arrange my thoughts.'

Go...back? Go back to Ravensglass, to a half-forgotten life? Without—Anne? Without knowing one way or the other? Impossible! 'How long,' he asked cautiously, 'would your thinking require?'

Anne looked at him, nonplussed. Must she put a time on thinking? A fluttering of royal blue at the door of the still-room informed her that Lady Katharine had returned from her errand, and now wished her hand-maiden back inside and about her duties. 'The Dame awaits me, Jack. Do you get on your way. We will write, and when you return to Greenwich—'

'A letter from the north takes weeks to reach its destination,' he interrupted sternly. 'And I do not intend to return to the capital in the foreseeable future. I will stay here until you have thought.'

In Anne's hearing one of the gentlemen at Greenwich had once said laughingly, 'Hamilton never forgets a kindness or fails to repay an insult. Any inch of ground he is set to guard he will defend with his life. His tenacity is legend!' He was obviously prepared to apply that creed to her, and how she wished it were for the right reasons. 'Very well, Jack. Let it be so.'

They turned up the path and re-entered the still-room.

Life went on at Greenwich. March, usually a wet and windy month, walked towards April in brilliant sunshine, apparently determined to disprove the country lore which proclaimed that no English spring could arrive without its storms.

Anne, who could see from her bedchamber window, and observe from her walks in the gardens, the eternal return of new life, idled her time away and was no forrader in her thinking.

Jack Hamilton kept his distance in these days; Ralph did not. Ralph kept her constantly occupied with his attention, making it clear that he thought himself to have been in error on the night of Thornton's supper party, begging her forgiveness for his high-handed treatment of her.

March went out, not like a lion, but as meekly as a lamb, ushering in days of soft drizzle and frequent sunshine. The Queen, always reluctant to remain in the capital, which she considered unhealthy in warmer weather, prepared to reside briefly at Hampton before commencing her annual Royal Tour, and Anne's spirits soared at the thought of being within easy reach of Maiden Court.

She hoped she could defer her personal dilemma until she could gain support and confidence from going home, and investigate the mysterious remark that her father had apparently made. But one evening, as she was dressing for the last masque to be held at Greenwich before the court left, she received a message that Hamilton would wish words with her.

'Well, you can't go now,' Allison Monterey objected. 'You have promised to dress my hair and none is so clever with it as you are. Tell the page to tell Jack you'll see him later tonight.'

Happy to gain even a few extra hours' grace, Anne told the boy to advise my lord that her duties prevented her from attending upon him immediately, but that she would see him later in the evening. She then commenced battle with Allison's unruly curls.

* * *

When the supper and amusements in the hall were done with and Jack still did not appear, Anne was apprehensive. Ralph, who had been in his usual place near the Queen during the entertainment, would claim her, she knew, for the dancing.

She looked around the crowded hall, looking for a distinctive silver head but not finding it. She did see her brother George dining with his wife, and she caught his eye and he rose and came to her. She had not spoken alone with him since the day she had absconded to Maiden Court, and he kissed her fondly before climbing onto the bench beside her.

'Little sister, how beautiful you look, and what a fine dress.' Anne had put on another of her new gowns, pale green and very becoming.

'Thank you.' Seeing his eyes on her untouched plate, she added, 'It is rather snug-fitting; I simply did not dare eat this night.'

He laughed. 'I thought you may have lost your appetite. I know I would if I had Jack Hamilton breathing down my neck.'

'You know about that?'

'Of course. As your nearest male relative within easy reach, as it were, Jack felt compelled to advise me of events.'

'And what do you think of it all?'

'I think two fiancés at once a little peculiar.'

'He is not a fiancé,' Anne said tartly. 'He asked me and I am. . .thinking about it. I am still betrothed only to Ralph.'

'Then why did you not tell Jack so at once?' George asked, with his straight blue look. 'He is not a man to be played with, you know.'

'I know that! Oh, dear, George, I have got myself

into a muddle. I don't know why I didn't send Jack immediately about his business.'

'Don't you? And you are usually so perceptive!'

'Stop teasing me and tell me what to do.'

'I can't tell you what to do, Anne, but I will tell you what I think. I think if you are even giving a passing thought to Jack's offer then Ralph is not the man for you, and if he is not then you should tell him forthwith. I'm ashamed of you playing such games.'

'I'm ashamed of myself,' Anne said miserably. 'But 'tis no game to me, brother. I am unable to think, to sleep, to eat, or to concentrate on anything at all at present.'

'Well, you look very well on it,' George remarked mildly. 'Is Jack waiting on your answer before leaving us for the wilds of Northumberland?'

'Yes. But I wish he would go. Maybe if he were not here I could be more objective.'

Oh, dear, Anne, thought George ruefully; that sentiment alone should tell you which way the wind is blowing.

He considered his sister as she pushed her spoon around her plate, her eyes dark with puzzlement. She was so different from the Anne who had talked blithely about attaining her rightful place at court that he could almost have believed her a stranger. And yet that delicately modelled face was as familiar as his own. It was the personality within which had changed.

'Have you no sensible words for me?' she asked, looking up. 'I feel so alone here. I cannot discuss it with any of my friends, or—obviously—with Ralph, or with—'

'With Jack?'

'If he were not most concerned, well, yes, I could tell him everything.'

Another revealing statement! if the woman talking had been any other than his sister and the man any other but Hamilton, George would have said, If you feel like that, then reach out with both hands, lady, for fear the paragon slips away.

As it was, he said, 'Tell me how you feel for Jack.' Their nearest neighbours had all risen now to follow the Queen to the dancing chamber; George and Anne were isolated amongst the debris of the meal.

Anne had not eaten at all during the meal, but had sampled the wine liberally, and it enabled her to be completely frank.

'He is like a warm cloak on a cold day—not made of some splendid material, but of good sturdy wool to keep the wind out. He is like the first slice of bread when morning brings you hurrying down to the hall to break your fast. He makes me feel that nothing bad could never happen to me when I am in his care—' She broke off. She had not known that she felt all this—the words had sprung fully formed to her lips.

George turned her words over in his mind, then said thoughtfully, 'A proper loving family member could make you feel this.'

'Of course. But, dear George, if you were to take me into your arms now and kiss me, I would not expect my heart to turn cartwheels!' Another admission of something she had not know she felt! But it was true—that fateful night Jack had, for whatever curious reason of his own, chosen to take their relationship into another sphere and, in spite of her consternation at the time, she had been unable to forget it since.

George raised an eyebrow. 'I see. Then I must

confess, feeling as you obviously do, I cannot see the let. What are you waiting for, sister?'

'The let? The let is Marie Claire, George. Whatever I am, or could be, to Jack, I will *always* be second-best, and you know how I could never bear to be an also-ran!'

'Marie Claire,' George repeated slowly. 'Yes, his first wife.'

'And his first love! His only love, so everyone— including he—insists. Do you know there is a *shrine* at Ravensglass dedicated to her? An intrusive pink marble edifice in honour of the pesky woman, upon which he lays flowers all the year round!'

'Anne,' George said anxiously, 'how much wine have you taken this night?'

'Oh, a great deal! How else can I possibly get through all this?'

How will the rest of us? George wondered. Anne could not drink in any quantity. A glass, yes, but more and she was quite abruptly drunk. She had the weakest head in Christendom, their father always declared.

He cast an eye around the hall. Someone had taken Judith away—to dance, he supposed—otherwise she could have been relied upon to take Anne to her bed without a further mishap.

Judith had disappeared, but Ralph Monterey had not. He now descended the dais and made his way to them. As he did so one of the doors swung open and Jack Hamilton also paced his way towards them and the two men came face to face in the narrow aisle between the trestle-tables before Anne and George. They both bowed.

'Hamilton,' Ralph said. 'Not away yet to your eyrie in the north?'

'As you see,' Jack said. He turned to Anne. 'Lady Anne, will you honour me at the dance?'

Anne looked at them both across the narrow, littered space. Liquor, which loosened her tongue—often with disastrous results—also gave her acute powers of observation.

Now, she mused, if I were not personally involved with either of these two men, what would I adjudge on looks alone?

Ralph was undoubtedly the more handsome. Such patrician features, such glossy hair and fine eyes would entrance any maid. Jack? He was compelling in a quite different way. His plain black costume failed to disguise the broad shoulders, the shapely long limbs; the unkindly cropped hair could not hide the aristocratic shape of his arrogant head, and who would not notice the setting and depth of his thickly lashed grey eyes?

She got to her feet.

'I am promised to Jack for this dance, Ralph,' she said lightly. 'We have certain matters to discuss.' She willed herself to take the steps to the end of the table without mishap, then Jack took her arm and they proceeded to the door of the hall.

Ralph watched them go, then said to George, 'Your sister does not appear to know her place, Latimar.'

'If I—and she—knew where that might be, I could comment on that.'

'It is with me,' Ralph said. 'It is all arranged, and I cannot imagine what matters she could have to discuss with Hamilton.'

'Ah, well, they are friends.' George left the statement in the air. 'Now, Monterey, did you see who Judith left the hall with?'

'I did. My Lady Claremont begged leave of the
Queen to take your wife to your apartments to rest.'

Very well; Judith was quite safe. 'Good. So I am free
to take up Lord Borley's invitation to join him at cards.
I know you are invited too, Ralph—shall we go up?'

One advantage of being the son of a notorious
gambler was that others assumed one had inherited the
taint. Ralph's eyes brightened. George Latimar did not
often join the gaming tables, but when he did he was a
worthy player, and he also had a heavy purse.

George followed Ralph out of the hall. He had
misgivings about the conversation he had had with
Anne, and the manoeuvre he had made to facilitate
her tryst with Hamilton, but he knew a compelling
force when he saw it, and that was what was undoubtedly between those two now.

Anne and Jack did not do well on the dance-floor. With
a more practised partner Anne could have disguised
her unsteady steps, but with Jack she could not; several
times they almost came to grief, and after a while Jack
said, 'Perhaps we should sit out, Anne. Neither of us
seems sure in our movements tonight.'

He led her to the edge of the floor. There were chairs
there but she preferred to stand looking at her reflection in one of the beaten-silver mirrors.

'We are to talk,' Jack said, standing awkwardly while
she swayed in silk and lace beside him.

'Oh, certainly. Perhaps we should get some of the air
you are always so enthusiastic about.'

In the gardens, Anne found a seat and abruptly sat
down. Jack looked down at her disapprovingly. 'That
seat will be damp, Anne. You are not yourself tonight.'

'Am I not? What you probably mean is I am tipsy. Why not just say it?'

'I would not so cast aspersion,' he said repressively, thinking that even in this condition she was charming and graceful. He had an abhorrence for ladies who grew shrill and boisterous having taken a few too many glasses. 'But if you say so what has brought it about? I have never known you to drink to any excess.'

Anne spread her skirts; they were a beautiful shifting colour, like sea water in the moonlight. The cold light also enhanced her black and shining hair and made deep pools of her dark eyes.

She was beauitful, thought Jack, enchanted, but also unstable in her present state, and he was wary. Of her, and also of himself. In a distant tree a nightingale sang with fervent zeal, the notes rising like silver from its throat. Anne said nothing.

'Well, have you considered my suit?' Jack demanded at length.

'I have,' Anne said equably, 'and very difficult it has been.'

'Why so? A straightforward proposal of marriage— you must have received many before.'

'Oh, I have,' agreed Anne cheerfully. 'But none of them has given me such cause for heartache.'

'Not Monterey's?'

'Oh, no,' Anne replied. 'For with Ralph and myself 'twas love at first sight.'

Jack was outraged. What was wrong with the girl? She sat there under the moon talking nonsense and provoking him, when she knew he was not able to play these games.

'But at second sight,' Anne continued, 'if there be such a thing, I did not feel quite the same about him.'

She got up. 'Do you know, Jack,' she said confidingly, 'there is an aviary here at Greenwich—a little enclosure filled with wild exotic birds from far-away lands?'

'No, I did not know that.' Jack thought, Surely I have fallen out of the real world, and now find myself in some fantastic place?

'In the summer months the birds are free to fly within the confines of a very large area, but in winter they are caught and taken to another, smaller place which is kept heated by an arrangement of pottery pipes— Well, I disremember the exact way it works, but I would like to go there now.'

'Now? 'Tis close on midnight, lady. I think your name might suffer should we go there alone together.'

'Again? After Tranmere, I fear my good name is no more.'

'No one knows of that,' Jack said curtly. 'At least, only my own trusted command. In this palace the world and his brother know everything that another does.'

She looked up at him. Beneath his light hair his tanned face appeared very dark and forbidding, but she was not afraid. 'Well, I am going there now. Accompany me or not, as you choose.'

Exasperated, he said, 'Naturally I will go with you. Where is this place?' Her directions were sketchy, but Jack's innate sense of direction brought them safely to the aviary and he opened the door for her.

The closely netted high-domed area appeared empty as they entered, although two horn lanterns were burning brightly on a stone table within. But their entry disturbed the birds and the air was suddenly filled with whirring and twittering sounds. The lush plants which the inhabitants needed for support were kept well watered and the atmosphere was steamy and over-warm.

Anne tipped back her head to watch the tiny creatures overhead. 'Why, they are like jewels! Did you ever see such colours on birds before?'

'Never. They are no English species, I would swear.'

'Of course not. These delightful birds are shipped from countries you and I have never heard of. It must be sad for them to be transported away from warmth and sunshine to such a grey land. Most of them die on the journey, I have heard,' she added, with distress in her voice. 'Does that seem right to you, Jack?'

'No, it does not seem right.' His mind slipped a cog and he was transported back twelve years onto the deck of the boat which had brought him and Marie Claire to England during a freezing dawn. When introducing his new wife to her new home, she had said, 'But, *mon cher*, it is *cold*, and *grey*.' Marie Claire had been uprooted from her home—a land of golden sunshine and turquoise skies.

He is thinking of her now, thought Anne. I have grown to recognise the special look upon his face when he does so. She said abruptly, 'You sent me a message tonight that you wished to speak with me. Pray do so.'

He was brought back to the present. 'Yes. . .that is so. As I said earlier, I wish to enquire if you have considered my proposal. You said you had done so, and it had brought you. . .heartache. Pray go on.'

'I have so considered it,' Anne said quickly, 'and find it not feasible.'

'Because of Monterey?'

'No. Because of *you*, Jack.'

The extreme heat in the aviary was having an unfortunate effect on her state. She was struggling with the physical effects of her consumption of wine, and was unsteady as she got to her feet to make her point and came to his side. But her mind was sharply clear.

'You do not want a wife, Jack,' she said passionately. 'In your mind, and in your heart, you already have one.'

'You are tipsy,' he said coldly. 'Perhaps you should sit again.' He walked her back to the rustic seat.

'I will sit down,' she said with dignity, doing so, 'but I know perfectly well what I am saying, and I mean it.' She added pettishly, 'Sit down too, for pity's sake! You are always looking down on everyone!'

'It is the penalty of being taller,' he said gravely. 'Now, Anne, I think it better to postpone this discussion until such time as you are not so plainly under the influence of the bottle.'

She laughed. 'Which accusation could never be levelled at yourself! It seems curious to me that a gentleman does not enjoy wine; can you explain it?'

'I can indeed,' he said, provoked into being as aggressive as she. 'When I lost my wife I looked for solace in the wine flask. I was drunk from cockcrow until cockshut and happy to be so. It appeared to be a way of dealing with my inability to face life without Marie Claire. But, of course, it was not. So I gave up the stuff and have never trusted myself with it since.'

His quiet words were more shocking than if he had shouted them. Yet again I have trespassed upon his grief, she mourned.

'I see. I am sorry that...again...I have reminded you of...her.' She hung her head so that her thick black hair obscured her face.

Jack made a tremendous effort. He was not an articulate man, but he fumbled for the words now which might bring him what he desired. 'You do not remind me of her, Anne. There is nothing about you which reminds me of her.'

'I know,' she said, her eyes filling with tears. 'I can compare in no way with Marie Claire.'

If only she would not keep using the *name*. That beloved name which he found so hard to bring to his own lips and hated to hear on another's. 'Why should you? You are Anne, a different person altogether, about whom I feel differently.'

He reached for her hand. 'I know I have no talent for the spoken word, but I did most sincerely mean my proposal to you, and most sincerely promise you that I will be an exemplary husband, should you decide to try me.'

'Why? Why do you want to marry me? What have we in common, Jack? We are so different.'

'Yes, different.' He seized upon the word. 'We are very different, Anne, but need that deter us? You have engaged yourself to a man who is your male like in every way, whose ways you understand, but does he please you? No, he does not.

'My father always said to me, "'Tis well when like marries like, for then there is always common ground." But, Anne, anyone who was *my* like would not make me see life in the way you do. Any woman who was my like would not be aware of the things you have made me notice. Even about my own home, which I love so passionately. If you were mine I would gladly agree to differ, and be happy whilst doing so.'

No talent for the spoken word? Such eloquence would not have shamed a romantic poet, Anne thought. If only he were saying it for the right reason. But could a man speak such words without meaning them? Surely not Jack Hamilton who scorned to lie? Perhaps it might help if her head were not reeling with the influence of liquor, but she did not think so. Even stone-cold sober she would have been finding this whole interview impossible to understand.

Jack said sternly, 'Well, at least my flow of words has dried your tears. Do you feel able now to tell me what you think of the matter?'

'I hardly know what to think. In fact, I cannot think at all.'

'You were supposed to have been thinking for the past weeks. If my case is hopeless, then tell me now and let us be done with it.'

'What if I did? What if I said tonight, Your suit is hopeless, Jack? What would you do then?'

What indeed? Jack considered. Anne was definitely drunk, but she was like no drunk he had ever encountered before. She was as lucid and deserving of an honest answer as when she was entirely sober. So he said, 'I would argue against your words, in the strongest possible terms! I love you, Anne. You will find that hard to believe, but 'tis true nonetheless.'

Anne was looking upwards gain at the myriad coloured birds still fluttering above them. 'It is not enough,' she said casually.

'Not enough! What can weigh greater in the balance than love?' Jack looked at her lovely upturned face and sought for a footing in the shifting sands of a personality he could not comprehend. 'I have stated my case honestly. Can you not give me a straightforward answer?'

Anne stopped looking at the distracting birds and looked at him. She looked carefully for several moments, then said, 'I don't know—can I? Are you so. . .straightforward? You ask me to marry you. You claim total honesty, but 'tis not really so, is it?

'To accept you I must give up a great deal, Jack. I must give up a man who is set to become a significant force in the life I have thought I could excel in. To accept you I must go against my father whom I have loved above all other men. To accept you I must commit myself to a place where women are as nothing. Is all this not true?'

'It is all true,' he admitted, admiring her clear thought.

'So I must ask myself, What have you to offer in exchange for all these things?' Anne scarcely knew herself. She was not by nature someone who thought all around a subject and arranged her feelings. At least, she had not been so far in her life, but then she was discovering new parts of herself every day now. 'Unfortunately,' she added, 'I do not have the answer.'

'I have,' he answered gravely, 'my ancient name, my protection, my loyalty to offer in exchange. My home I do not make excuse for—'tis as you know one of Her Majesty's garrisons. I am confident that you will be nothing less than a great asset to it.'

'No mention of love?'

'I have already stated that I love you. I imagine—as I said—that you may find that hard to believe. But there are all kinds of love, Anne.'

'Mmm. Actually, I know that. Perhaps we will come back to that later. . . Now we must discuss why you have made me this offer. It is because of what happened in the library, is it not?'

For a moment he looked blank, then the colour came and went beneath the smooth olive skin of his face and his eyes darkened. 'Why, no, that is not so—I mean—

Obviously, that was disgraceful behaviour on my part. I accept full responsibility and understand full well how shocked and distressed you must have been by it—'

'Not so,' she interrupted him calmly. 'I was neither of those things. On the contrary, in retrospect, I have discovered I liked it. I liked your arms around me, and your lips upon mine, Jack.' The little feathered inmates of the aviary were silent now, returned to sleep. There was a hushed pause.

'You—?'

'Yes. Am I too bold? However, now I have admitted that, you can return the compliment and be honest as to why, after several months of being nothing more than a friend, you suddenly proposed. I am right, am I not, when I say 'twas for the reason I have just given?'

Jack could think of nothing but the words she had spoken about their passage in the library. When Robert Dudley had spoken his momentous words, Jack had only taken in the fact that Anne turned to him when in need. Now, from her own mouth, he had the evidence of another crucial factor in the relationship between a man and a woman. He allowed himself to assimilate this knowledge with the utmost joy.

'No,' he then said deliberately. 'That is not so. Forgive me if I am too frank, but whatever had happened between us then, however I felt for your family and consequently for you, I would not have been prepared to give up the rest of my life for it.

'I have made this offer for you yourself, Anne, not for any reasons of. . .chivalry or honour. . .' His words tailed off, but they expressed what Anne wanted to hear. Now she had no idea what to say. He had just demolished her argument for refusing him.

'There is still Ralph. . .' she said faintly.

CHAPTER FIFTEEN

As IF summoned by her speaking his name, at that moment Ralph opened the door and stepped inside. Once more the birds were disturbed and rose in resentful confusion from their nesting places. Amid this kaleidoscope of colour Ralph looked first at Anne, then at Jack.

'This is too much!' he said. A sly comment passed at the card table had brought him here, in spite of George Latimar's efforts to prevent him. Anne's marked preference for Hamilton in public places Ralph had been willing to swallow, because he did not consider the man a threat to his relationship with her, and also because Jack's ties with the Latimar family made it acceptable.

But to seek a secluded, secret place at this hour of the night to pursue their damned *friendship* — This would make proud Monterey a laughing stock amongst his new society, and that Ralph could not permit.

Jack said quietly, 'Your arrival is most opportune, Monterey. I have considered speaking with you in the past days, and now can put it off no longer.'

'You have my full attention,' Ralph said ironically. His blue eyes looked the other man over, and he felt the usual antagonism in his presence.

'I have asked the Lady Anne to be my wife. We came here tonight to discuss it.'

'Good *God*!' Ralph was outraged. 'I cannot believe I am hearing this. And from a fellow knight. Where in this matter are your much vaunted ethics, Hamilton?

Those ethics you were at such pains to beat into me a decade ago?' In spite of his aggressive response, Ralph did not think that Anne was involved; he only considered it an insult to himself.

'Sadly awry,' Jack said ruefully. 'I must apologise for not coming to you first.'

'If not to me, then my lord earl, the lady's father—'

'I did speak to him,' Jack put in.

Ralph stared at him. 'And what had Harry Latimar to say to you?'

'He disliked the idea instantly.'

'So I should think!' Ralph turned to Anne and offered his hand. 'Come, Anne, let me take you away from here and away from this. . .gentleman.'

Anne folded her hands in her lap. She lifted her dark eyes to his face. 'You have a talent, Ralph,' she said gently, 'for breaking in on the very private conversations I have with Jack. He came to me most correctly and asked for my hand. I have yet to give him my answer.'

'Then do so!' Ralph said impatiently.

Anne transferred her vibrant gaze to Jack. There were two gamblers in this odd little self-contained world tonight: she and Ralph both liked to challenge the odds. But Jack Hamilton did not. He had decided he wanted her for wife without apparently considering any of the obvious disadvantages, and he was a man whose opinions she valued. She was not a safe bet for him, nor he for her. They were both—for each other— the outside chance.

'Consider your stake and the ultimate prize,' she had so often heard her father advise any gambler, and she had done this in the few short seconds after Ralph had extended his hand to her. Her stake was herself and the ambition she had thought so essential to her happiness: a life within the excitement of the Tudor court. The prize was Jack, an unknown quantity who may or may not provide a very different happiness. But she had heard her brother declare of his love, Judith, 'I am alive when I am with her,' and Anne could now understand those words.

She said, 'Having thought carefully on the matter, Jack, I have decided I will accept your offer. I will be your wife.'

The two men, equally astounded, moved closer to her. 'You are crazed!' exclaimed Ralph. 'Or drunk, or— You would marry *Hamilton*, whose commitment to his first wife was legend even when I was a boy? Dear Anne, what can you ever be to him?'

'I don't know,' Anne said simply.

'She will be everything to me,' Jack said very deliberately. The dream had suddenly taken shape for him. Anne sat there, as lovely and composed as any statue, yet she spoke words which changed him. Having awakened him from his stupor, now she continued to lead him a little further into the world each time they were together.

'Everything!' Ralph said scornfully, unaware of the swift currents moving between the two others. 'You say that in the presence of a man who has seen you prostrate before the tomb of your divine Marie Claire!'

Marie Claire. . . Jack had always hated to hear her name on another's lips, and certainly a year ago he would have knocked any man down for using it in such a way, but now the pain was unaccountably blunted. Ignoring Ralph, he said, 'You are serious, Anne? It will not be an easy life, you know.'

'I know that,' she said quietly.

'It will be no life at all!' Ralph exclaimed. 'How can you, Anne? How can you so disappoint myself—your father—?'

'Were it my father's life I was considering, I would perhaps pause longer, but 'tis *mine*, Ralph, and I intend to live it the way I wish.'

Ralph had a flair for the dramatic. He was an accomplished actor, both in public and private life. 'You cannot compete with what is known throughout the whole of England, Anne! Hamilton has made a fetish of his grief; whatever his motives for asking you to be his wife, trust me, you will spend the rest of your days arguing against a wraith!'

'Is that so, Jack?' Anne gave Jack the straight blue Latimar look. She did not wish to have this particular conversation before a third person, but it had to be faced, and she was afraid that, if she let slip the opportunity now, Jack would be too elusive for her another time.

Jack was experiencing conflicting emotions. He wished himself a mile away, but, like Anne, was afraid that if he avoided this skirmish it might never be refought, and suddenly he knew it must be. Indeed, wanted it to be.

The past, which had consumed him for so long, was growing more deeply buried within him and that was not healthy, any more than when clean flesh healed over an errant piece of musket ball. Sooner or later the resultant festering was forced to the surface. He was determined that his marriage to Anne—if the marriage took place, and he still could not quite believe that it would—would begin with no hidden wounds.

He said haltingly, 'It is not so, Anne—'

'I beg your pardon for intruding once more,' Ralph

broke in with deadly sarcasm, 'but I believe I have some say in this.'

Jack turned to him. Once again he had discounted and half forgotten Monterey. He said gravely, 'Ralph, I think you must know now that what has happened here was not intended as an insult or embarrassment to yourself. Rather it is something not easily explained, but very sincere.

'In your place I am sure I would feel compelled to take some positive action, but need it be so? You are established now in a place both exalted and insecure. Might it not be that you can be graceful on this occasion and let Anne free from her promise? Might it not be that the lady you have shown even greater a regard for may well welcome and appreciate such action?'

Not eloquent? thought Anne again. Jack's words were clever. Elizabeth did not care for her chosen cavaliers to be wed, to place any woman above their queen. If they did so, she wished to formulate the liaison herself, to prove that she was more significant in the arrangement than the female concerned.

Ralph let a long silence develop. Beside him was positioned some rare and exotic plant, its vivid green leaves bursting with succulence, its single flower of a colour and size never seen on any English plant.

In his mind Ralph drew a parallel between this specimen and the girl he was betrothed to. He understood neither, and feared that neither would flourish in the environment he occupied. Nevertheless, he unexpectedly showed a care for the girl whom he did not love but admired very much.

'And if I don't choose to withdraw. . .gracefully from this? What will you do, Hamilton?'

'I'll kill you,' Jack said softly. 'If you now try to hold

her—to come between us—we will eventually meet on the field you have in the past called that of honour, and I'll kill you.'

Ralph fingered his jewelled belt. It had been a present from Elizabeth and was rich with emeralds and diamonds. My God, he thought, he does love her... There could be no other explanation for Hamilton's turning on its head the strictest rule he had always upheld towards duelling. And that tone of voice... Ralph had never heard that odd mixture of diffidence and passion in Hamilton's clipped tones.

He glanced at Anne. He had claimed to his brother, Tom, that he knew women, and he did. She loves him too, he thought, with a pang of jealousy.

As he bent over her and lifted her hand to kiss, Ralph waved goodbye to the fine dowry her father had promised, dismissed the opportunity to acquire a wife he both desired and knew would be a singular asset in his ambitions.

And such a favoured child, he thought regretfully, remembering Henry Tudor's will. But how weigh these against the conviction of Jack Hamilton's threat?

He said, 'If you have decided, Anne, and I believe you have, then I will not dispute it. The greatest luck in your venture, sweetheart.' Leaving the aviary for the cool, rainy night, he thought that they would both need it.

Anne and Jack were left alone. She spoke first. 'So, Jack, you have vanquished the opposition; now 'tis your more difficult task to overcome me.'

When Ralph had gone out, Jack had fingered his uncomfortable ruff and breathed in the cold draught of air which had flowed into the aviary. Now he came and sat beside her. 'I must overcome you? Why so? From your own mouth I have the assurance I was listening for. Do you wish to withdraw it?'

She did not look at him. 'No. Qualify it, perhaps. For, Jack, there are various things to discuss. For instance, I will not be mistress of Ravensglass and look from my window and see you traversing my own courtyard to pay homage to a long-dead wife.'

'You would wish for me to deny she ever existed? I cannot do that!'

'Not deny she existed,' Anne said thoughtfully, 'but admit that she is *dead*. The past is past, and all men must bury their dead and. . .not forget them, but put them in their rightful place.'

Jack took her hands, rubbing his calloused thumb over her smooth fingers. ''Tis not so easy, darling.'

She turned her head at last to look at him. 'You call me darling? Yet you are not a man who dispenses endearments without thought. I want to be your— darling. I want to be the most important person in your life. I will be your new wife, I will care for you and love you and bear your children, but I will not be second-best! Never that, for 'tis a role I am unfitted for.'

'Do you think I would ask you to be?' He raised her hand to his lips. It was the first time he had shown her this courtesy which came so easily to other men and had in the past, even from Ralph, meant little to her.

When she could concentrate again, she said, 'I don't want to replace Marie Claire in your heart, Jack, but neither will I share you with her. Also, I know you can express what you want to say well enough, for you did so just now with Ralph. Why,' she asked thoughtfully, 'do you think he gave in so easily? 'Tis not entirely flattering to me.'

He half smiled. 'Probably he decided he would rather be a live courtier than a dead suitor.'

'Would you really have met him?'

Jack's eyes darkened. 'Yes, I would. And done what I told him I would. But I am content that it did not come to that.'

She released her hand abruptly and stood up. One of the minute birds had, in its restless fluttering, become entangled in a stretch of netting over the door-opening. When she struggled to free it, it gave her a spiteful peck on one hand before flying to freedom. She examined the bright bead of blood.

'Not all creatures—wild creatures—are grateful to the one which sets them free,' she said quietly.

The analogy was not lost upon him.

'But I am grateful to you, Anne. Can you not accept that? What more would you wish me to say?' He too had risen as he spoke, and for a time paused, irresolute, then went on, 'I know you are doubtful still, and can appreciate why. But we would not be having this conversation were I not completely sure that I could fulfil my part of the bargain we will make if we wed.'

He came to an abrupt halt, seeking the correct words, his eyes fixed on her face. One false move, he had found in his career, could result in a loss greater than ever dreamed of. He could not, *would* not make that false move in this.

Anne gave him no help. She remained standing, facing him, only her great dark eyes giving away the fact that she knew this was the place they had been travelling towards for a long time, possibly from the moment they had met. He began to speak, and she had to strain to hear.

'As to speaking of...Marie Claire, I can only say

that that was then and this is now. She was the one woman I loved—adored, *then*, as the man I was then. But you are another. I *swear* I do not compare you. How could I? For I am no longer a boy in my twenties but a mature man who has since moved on in the game of life.

'With no possible disrespect to her memory, I will say to you that I love you in a completely different way. And if you ask me,' he added desperately, 'I will demolish her statue at Ravensglass, but. . .if you are the woman I think you are you will not ask that. You will not feel so threatened by a pile of cold marble as to insist upon it.'

It was a strange victory, but Anne understood it. She held out her hand, all barriers down.

He came to her. 'Will we now speak of love? You laid the subject aside earlier, but tell me now. How much do you love me?'

She considered him carefully. Yes, love. . . She believed that she only now fully recognised the emotion. Along with all the rest of her unworthy ambitions, she had had entirely the wrong view of that too.

She hesitated so long that he put his arms about her in a painful grip. 'Can you not say it? Please, sweetheart, I know I am not the right man for you—'

'But you are!' She lifted her head to look up at him and now he relished the battery of charm she let loose, for it was all directed at him, for him. 'I love you, Jack. Perhaps I have done from the start, when you so annoyed me for being so determined not to fit in with my ideal of the. . .right man.'

LEGACY *of* LOVE

Coming next month

THE STANDISH INHERITANCE
Louisa Gray
Regency

To Max, Earl of Rivington, coming home battle-weary
from the Wars, Lucinda Standish was an oasis of calm.
Her loving, easy handling of her two fatherless boys gave
him hope that he might win his own small daughter's
love—and Luciana's. But as the idyllic days passed he
became aware that to protect the boys' inheritance he *must*
wed Luciana—and risk losing her love when his secrets
were known…

THE LOST PRINCESS
Paula Marshall
Tuscany 1460

Never having met her future husband, Marina Bordoni,
lady of Novera, reluctantly set off to her wedding—only to
be kidnapped and held to ransom! Rescued by Niccolo a
Stresa, Marina began with him a madcap trail across Italy,
seeking safety in the Dukedom of Montefiore.

Flung closer to a man than ever in her life before, taking on
disguises to confuse their pursuers, Marina shocked herself
by relishing every danger…and Niccolo! How could she
part from him at the journey's end to wed a stranger—
Leonardo di Montefiore?

Flower Power

How would you like to win a year's supply of simply irresistible romances? Well, you can and they're free! Simply unscramble the words below and send the completed puzzle to us by 31st August 1996. The first 5 correct entries picked after the closing date will win a years supply of Temptation novels (four books every month—worth over £100).

1	LTIUP	TULIP
2	FIDLADFO	
3	ERSO	
4	AHTNYHCI	
5	GIBANOE	
6	NEAPUTI	
7	YDSIA	
8	SIIR	
9	NNAIATCRO	
10	LDIAAH	
11	RRSEOIMP	
12	LEGXFOOV	
13	OYPPP	
14	LZEAAA	
15	COIRDH	

Please turn over for details of how to enter 🖙

H🌸w t🌸 enter

Listed overleaf are 15 jumbled-up names of flowers. All you have to do is unscramble the names and write your answer in the space provided. We've done the first one for you!

When you have found all the words, don't forget to fill in your name and address in the space provided below and pop this page into an envelope (you don't need a stamp) and post it today. Hurry—competition ends 31st August 1996.

Mills & Boon Flower Puzzle
FREEPOST
Croydon
Surrey
CR9 3WZ

Are you a Reader Service Subscriber?   Yes ❑   No ❑

Ms/Mrs/Miss/Mr _____

Address _____

_____

_____ Postcode _____

One application per household.

You may be mailed with other offers from other reputable companies as a result of this application. If you would prefer not to receive such offers, please tick box. ❑

COMP396
B